Hit By His Pitch

A Columbia Gems Baseball Romance

MJ Compton

Comptonplations Publishing

Note from Author

Hit By His Pitch was originally published as Stealing Home by Loose-Id LLC in 2016.

Major League Baseball, like most other sports, periodically updates its rules. Some practices in Triple A baseball have changes since I first wrote the story. Any errors are my own.

WARNING

This book contains sexually explicit scenes and adult language and may be considered offensive so some readers. This book is for sale to adults ONLY, as defined by the laws of the country in which you made your purchase. Please store your files wisely, where they cannot be accessed by under-aged readers.

Contents

Chapter One

When my name was Chelsea Lyndon, I was a romantic fantasy slut.

But I was not a cliché. I didn't break off the heel of my shoe as I rushed to be somewhere. I was already where I wanted to be when I stumbled and twisted my ankle, which snapped the straps of my platform espadrilles and sent me face-first into a patch of mud.

This wouldn't have been so bad, except I was on my fantasy date. The date about which I'd dreamed since I was a little girl.

Thank goodness I wasn't with anyone who mattered.

My Grandma Judy loved watching movies, and one of her favorites was *Moonstruck* with Nicholas Cage and Cher. There was a scene where Cage invites Cher to the Met. For some reason—probably because I was only about eight years old the first time I saw the movie—I decided that an opera date meant true love. So when Baird McKechnie, a casual business acquaintance, invited me to the opera, I accepted.

Like generations of women in my family, I was looking for a happy ending.

Oh, I was careful. World-class summer opera sounded a bit sketchy. Besides, I didn't know Baird all that well. And I wasn't completely stupid. I checked the

Internet to make sure the Glimmerglass Opera was legit. The opera was for real. Based on the website, its potential for fantasy fulfillment was high, especially if the outing included one of the advertised gourmet picnics. And Cooperstown was also the hometown of the guy who wrote the book on which *The Last of the Mohicans*—the movie with Daniel Day Lewis—was based, and it was only about an hour and a half from Syracuse, where I lived at the time. Overall, the Glimmerglass possibilities outweighed *Moonstruck*.

I should have known better.

Baird purchased our meal in a restaurant in the village. I noticed immediately it was not the one listed on the Glimmerglass website. Shaneybrook's was cute on the outside: white stucco with Mediterranean-blue trim. Festive pink-and-white-striped petunias filled planters on either side of the door. I waited in the car.

We made it as far as the opera's picnic grounds high on a hill above the theater. I noted the other picnickers had bottles of wine, stemware, wicker, brightly hued tableware, fabric napkins, and tablecloths. The setting appeared so civilized, so surreal—almost like a movie set. There was no gaily-striped tablecloth to spread over our table, no napkins, and no glasses.

I tried to eat the sandwich from Shaneybrook's, while I longed for lemony grilled chicken with orzo salad or duck confit on a bed of wheat berries.

Instead, I had pink processed meat and white American cheese on bread so stiff and dry that it reminded me of the asphalt shingles on my grandmother's apartment building. Mayo, iceberg lettuce, tomato, and onion. I'm sure that was someone's dream sandwich, and another woman might find it wildly romantic, but not me.

And it was hot. Humid. My long sundress clung to my thighs. Perspiration trickled down the sides of my face, along with my makeup. The air was so thick it was like breathing yogurt.

My footing in my platform shoes was a bit wobbly as we started down the hill to the theater. Then I fell. In the mud.

So much for a romantic date. Baird didn't even help me to my feet, leaving that honor to an older gentleman who'd been eating at the picnic table next to us.

Fifteen minutes later, we were back in Cooperstown parked in front of those ragged-edged petunias. Baird didn't say a word to me but grabbed the lunch bag with our leftovers and stalked through the front door of the restaurant.

I needed a restroom, so I followed him despite being an embarrassed, muddy, barefoot mess and despite the pain shooting up my left calf and thigh like splintery, ragged spears attacking me. I gritted my teeth and limped onward. Wetting myself wasn't an option.

The dining room was nearly full. I looked for someone to ask about using the restroom. That's when I heard Baird scream, "You bitch!"

He couldn't possibly be talking to me, but the words still sliced through me like a hot knife through cold butter. I followed the sound of his vitriol and pushed through the swinging doors at the rear of the room.

Roasting garlic perfumed the air of the restaurant kitchen. Something sizzled in a pan on the stove. Baird was screaming at a man in chef whites, who brandished a knife at him. A big knife. Baird threw the bag with the leftovers, and the chef skewered it midair.

Something flew past me. An onion hit Baird on the head, halting the stream of obscenities spewing from his mouth.

I turned to see who had hurled the onion.

Daylight poured through a huge window, catching the culprit in a shaft of gold, turning his sun-kissed hair into a brilliant nimbus. Everything about him glowed, like an award statuette in a spotlight.

I'd like to win him, I thought.

"Who are you?" the knife wielder shouted, finally noticing me. "What are you doing in my kitchen? You're filthy! You're not wearing any shoes! You are a walking health-code violation!"

"I'm with him," I said, my voice cracking. I jabbed my thumb in Baird's general direction. I couldn't tear my gaze from the trophy model.

Who was staring at me.

"And you have the nerve to call *me* a bitch?" the knife man shrieked.

More insults flew, coming from both Baird and his opponent.

I blinked back tears, totally shaken by what I heard. Baird was gay. The chef was his significant other. I'd been a tool.

Trophy Man stepped out of the light. He touched my elbow. "Are you all right?" He was the second stranger in an hour to ask me that question.

Except he didn't seem like a stranger. He was familiar. And not because he looked like a movie award.

I inhaled deeply and winced. I'd landed on a rock buried in the mud when I fell. My ribs felt bruised.

"Restroom," I whispered.

Trophy Man pointed toward the dining room. "Go left," he instructed.

I lowered my face as I limped past him.

"You're hurt." His tone changed. Sharpened.

"More angry than hurt," I admitted in a low voice. People like me can't afford tender feelings.

"You're limping."

Oh. He meant my foot.

"Did McKechnie do this to you?"

I shook my head and scurried for the bathroom.

Several minutes later, my bladder was happy, and I risked a glance in the mirror. Oh. Dear. Lord. Freckles of dried mud spattered my face. My dark brown hair was matted with perspiration and clung to my cheeks. Most of my makeup had melted off. My gray eyes looked unfocused and wild. The front of my dress—especially at the knees—was a total loss. No wonder Trophy Man had stared.

I washed my face, repaired my makeup as best I could, squared my shoulders, and left the restroom. Trophy Man was waiting in the hall. I ignored him and hobbled through the still-busy dining room and out the front door, gritting my teeth against the pain in my foot with every step.

Baird's car was gone.

I squelched a surge of panic.

He'd just gone for cigarettes or something. Moved the car to a better spot.

Trophy Man joined me on the sidewalk.

"Where's Baird?" I asked, trying to project cool, calm, and control, none of which were in my repertoire at the moment.

Trophy Man watched me with caramel-colored eyes. Either I was in panic mode, or he was so handsome that looking at him and breathing at the same time took all of my concentration. "I think Penn and Baird went to the opera."

"I'm sorry?" I thought he'd said Baird had gone to the opera without me.

Trophy Man's hand hovered near my cheek and then dropped. I took a step backward, keeping my weight on the foot that didn't ache.

"No, I'm sorry. Baird is a real...jerk sometimes, and he brings out the worst in my brother."

I felt as if I'd fallen down a hill again.

"I'm Tripp Shaneybrook, by the way."

"Chelsea Lyndon," I said as I took his offered hand.

His touch was like a puncture to my lungs. Air eluded me. His palm was callused. And big. I wondered if that old wives' tale about the size of a man's hands was true. I wanted those hands on other parts of my body.

Tripp didn't let go, and that didn't bother me at all. God, he was beautiful. Sun-streaked blond hair, honey-hued eyes, and taller than me by at least a foot. Double dimples in each of his cheeks framed his mouth like parentheses that deepened with his aw-shucks grin.

"Penn deserted the restaurant on the busiest weekend of the year. I don't suppose you can cook?" He eyed the front of my dress. "Never mind."

I freed my fingers and turned to reenter the restaurant. I needed the bathroom again. If I was going to melt down—and I was on the verge—I was going to puddle in private.

The next thing I knew, Tripp swept me into his arms. Literally.

"Put me down," I squealed.

"What happened?" He didn't seem to mind the mud smearing his clothes. "Did McKechnie—"

"I fell out of my shoe and twisted my ankle," I mumbled, embarrassed to admit such a silly thing.

He carried me through the restaurant and deposited me on a stool in the kitchen. Then he knelt in front of me. He lifted my skirt an inch or two, as if I were some sort of Victorian maiden and he was about to get the erotic thrill of his lifetime. Each of his hands skimmed one of my ankles. Chills turned to sparks and skittered up my legs and went straight to a place they had no business going.

"Your left ankle is pretty swollen." He winced as he poked me.

I gripped the seat of the stool to keep from whimpering.

"You should have this x-rayed." He glanced at me. His expression was solemn. "I guess you won't be waiting on tables tonight."

I had no intention of waiting tables that night or ever again. I'd moved beyond the family vocation. I could pay my own way. I even had a savings account and health insurance.

"It's just twisted," I said.

"Sprained, at the very least," he argued.

I thought I heard a trace of the South in his voice.

His hands slid up my calves.

My first thought was gratitude I'd shaved that morning. My second thought was to wonder what he was doing and hope that he'd keep doing it. Was his breathing getting a little heavier, or was that just wishful thinking on my part?

I wanted to close my eyes and fall into this erotic massage, but I couldn't tear my gaze away from Tripp's honeyed eyes. I wanted to moan at how good his strong fingers felt as they kneaded the tense muscles, but I didn't have the strength. I wanted to...not fall into my mother's self-destructive ways.

"Let's get you over to the health center for an X-ray."

I thought his voice sounded huskier than before.

"Josh?" he called out. "Take over for a bit, will you?"

That's when I realized there were several other people bustling around the kitchen. I'd been aware of only Tripp.

"Sure." The red-haired man who answered looked harassed. "Where's Penn?"

"He took off." Reality reached Tripp's voice again. He stood, the front of his slacks not hiding his...reaction at all.

Mama would have said something bawdy, but I remained silent as heat flashed through my face.

He scooped me off the stool as if I were a drop of water he'd flicked from a leaf of lettuce.

"I can walk," I said.

"Not until that ankle is x-rayed."

He was solid. I noted muscles of granite as he carried me through the kitchen and out the back door to a black high-end sport utility vehicle. I opened the door because Tripp's hands were full of me. The SUV was a far manlier vehicle than Baird's ecologically correct hybrid.

Tripp kept his arms around me as he placed me on the leather seat. He pressed his forehead against mine. Our noses bumped. His breathing was as ragged as mine. He had the excuse of hauling me out to the car. I was just pathetic.

"I needed to get you out of there before I turned you into a cliché," he whispered.

"What?"

"You're barefoot and were in the kitchen," he explained. "All I could think about was making you pregnant."

Whoa! Talk about a dash of frigid reality. Fortunately, the lessons of my mother's life had not deserted me. Except my body was going, *What a great idea!*

"Not a good idea." My voice was more of a croak than anything else.

"You're out of the kitchen. You're safe for now."

"Maybe I'd better find the bus station," I said.

"You need to go to the health center. I'm really concerned about that ankle."

My ankle was throbbing. Of course, the throbbing was now in unison with the pulse thrumming through other parts of my body. "All right."

I knew Cooperstown wasn't very big, so the number of people clogging the streets surprised me. When I asked Tripp about it—just making conversation while he drove—he seemed surprised.

"It's induction weekend. The restaurant's biggest weekend of the year, which is why Baird's timing is so lousy. It wouldn't surprise me if Baird chose this weekend on purpose. He hates Penn being in Cooperstown. He would love nothing more than the restaurant to fail, so Penn will move someplace else. With him."

Tripp stopped to let yet another swarm of pedestrians cross the street.

"Induction weekend?" I didn't care about Baird or his boyfriend.

Tripp shot me a look as if I was crazy. "Baseball Hall of Fame induction weekend." This repetition contained a little more information.

"Oh! It's a sports thing," I said. I'd come to Cooperstown for the opera. I'd heard of the Baseball Hall of Fame but hadn't known it was in the vicinity.

"You say that as if sports is a bad thing."

"Outside of movies, I don't know much about sports except I don't like football."

"Smart girl," Tripp replied. "Someone once pointed out football combines the two worst things about America: violence and committee meetings."

I laughed. Sharp pain stabbed my ribs, and I tried not to wince.

"What about baseball?" he asked. "Do you like baseball?"

"Are you a baseball player or something?"

"Retired."

Okay, he had a reason for wanting to know. But that didn't explain the sense that I'd seen him before. I hadn't lied about my lack of athletic knowl-edge. "The best sports movies are about baseball."

"I knew I liked you." He grinned at me. "So why were you with Baird McKechnie?"

I reached for the roll bar when he took a street corner too quickly. "We were supposed to go to the opera."

"Why him?"

"Because he asked me."

Tripp shook his head and then stomped on his brakes at a stop sign. "Did he just walk up to you on the street and say, 'Beautiful lady, come to the opera with me?'"

Tripp thought I was beautiful? Even covered in mud?

"No," I said, my face growing warm. "We met at a chamber of commerce thingy. Event."

"Are you in love with him? Because he doesn't play for your team, and I'd hate to see you—"

"No!" My initial reaction was that who I dated was none of Tripp Shaneybrook's business.

Except he was cleaning up Baird's mess, so I suppose that made it his business. A little. "This was our first date. I've always wanted to go to the opera."

"You don't need McKechnie—or anyone—to go the opera."

How could I explain about Nicholas Cage and Cher? He'd think I was out of my mind. So I said the next thing that popped into my head. "Baird McKechnie has a great name."

Tripp nearly ran off the road. "What? You went out with a guy because you liked his stupid name?"

He made my logic sound like a bad thing.

"You have a great name too."

A smile spread slowly across his features. The late afternoon sun playing hide-and-seek through the trees lining the street dappled his face. "I do, don't I?"

"Yeah. I can just hear it now. The fans shouting, 'Tripp! Tripp,' as you run the bases. Great name, especially for a baseball player."

He laughed. "No one has ever dared say that to my face."

I'd never made a man laugh before, and very few men could make me laugh. I could probably count them on one hand. One finger.

I'd grown up laughing at movies. Grandma Judy had loved romantic comedies, but I knew those stories weren't about real people. Not the people I knew, anyway. Yet there I was. Covered in mud, laughing after my fantasy date self-destructed.

At least I had something salvageable from the day. I'd laughed with the best-looking man I would ever meet.

Chapter Two

My ankle was badly sprained. The nurse-practitioner ordered me to stay off it and keep it elevated. And I planned to. Once I was home. In Syracuse.

But before I could head for the bus station or the airport, I needed a pair of shoes. The blue paper booties furnished by the health center weren't going to cut it.

One little problem. I couldn't go into a store to buy a pair of shoes because of my bare feet. I asked Tripp to run into the chain drugstore I'd spied on Main Street. Surely they stocked flip-flops, and I had a twenty-dollar bill in my purse. I explained my dilemma about the shoes, the airport or bus station, and home.

Tripp didn't help me. "I would have run in if there'd been a place to park, but I don't have time now. I need to work," he said as he carried me up a dark, narrow damp-carpet-smelling staircase in the back of the restaurant.

We stepped into a patchwork quilt of light and textures. "My brother's apartment," he explained. He carried me through the kaleidoscope of colors into an enormous old-fashioned bathroom, where he deposited me on the closed lid of the toilet as if he were placing crown jewels on a velvet cushion.

"Besides, there's no commercial airport." He started to unbutton his yellow shirt, which had been pristine before he'd hauled me around but which now bore scrapes of dirt, probably transferred from my dress.

I swallowed hard and averted my gaze. "How about the bus station?"

"There isn't a bus station. A couple of buses a day stop at the auto club, but you probably missed them." He gazed at me, his golden eyes burning like twin suns in the heavens. "I'll get us some clean shirts."

"I'm not wearing one of your brother's shirts." *Ick, ick, ick.*

"You're not. You'll wear one of *mine.*" He sounded firm, as though the matter was settled.

Okay.

He wasn't gone that long. He returned wearing a long-sleeved white dress shirt hanging open off his shoulders. His very broad shoulders. He wore a white T-shirt beneath it. He handed me a watermelon-colored T-shirt.

"This should fit," he said. He hesitated. "I'll give you some privacy."

Oh, Lord. Something was arcing between us, but I didn't know what to call it, much less what to do about it. I whipped off my red-and-white daisy-patterned tank dress. Fortunately my bra and panties had been spared the mud bath. I'd just tugged the T-shirt over my hips when Tripp rapped on the bathroom door.

"Are you okay in there?"

"Yes," I said, and he opened the door.

His shirt was buttoned, open at the collar, but not tucked into his pleated front dress slacks. He smiled when he saw me in the oversize T-shirt and then knelt in front of me again, as if to examine my ankle.

He kissed me instead.

That sounds so lame, so boring, when the reality was neither of those things. His lips were soft, and the touch was tentative. More of an inquiry than a kiss, at least at first. I should have stopped it at that stage, but it was so unexpected and so gentle after the way the rest of the day had gone. And Lord if he didn't taste like—better than anything I'd ever known in all my twenty-six years.

His fingers tangled in my hair. His tongue touched my lips, as if asking a question. Of course, I opened my mouth to respond. Then I lost track of everything except kissing Tripp Shaneybrook.

I'd always considered kissing to be a prelude, a warm-up exercise, or an appetizer. I'd never considered it to be the main course. Even in grammar-school spin-the-bottle, we all knew kissing was just the beginning—a teaser to more adult things to come.

Tripp destroyed every preconceived notion I had about kissing.

When we finally stopped—why did we stop?—Tripp's face reflected my dazedness. I couldn't speak. He didn't. I blinked a couple of times, thinking maybe I was dreaming or something. My lips felt swollen. His seemed a little puffier, but it was difficult to tell. I wasn't familiar with his face yet.

We simply gazed at each other and were grateful we didn't need to think in order to breathe.

Finally, he climbed to his feet. I glanced away from the tented front of his slacks. Then his back was to me, as he stood at the sink and ran the water.

A moment later, he was again on his knees in front of me, where he carefully wiped my feet with a damp washcloth. The cool water felt good.

I'd been cleaned up a bit at the health center, but Tripp was very careful and very thorough. Maybe too thorough. My feet weren't ticklish, yet each swipe of textured terry cloth between my toes, around my cherry-polished nails, and across the stubborn calluses on my soles did very odd things to the rest of my body. It was all I could do to keep from writhing like Susan Sarandon as Kevin Costner painted her toenails in *Bull Durham*. Then Tripp kissed the top of my left foot.

I knew I should be frightened, upset, and wary. I didn't know Tripp Shaneybrook from a serial killer, a politician, or an insurance salesman. But insurance salesmen and serial killers don't have restaurants named after them, and I distinctly recalled his name on the restaurant awning.

Tripp nibbled his way around the swelling in my ankle, and I forgot to be scared or cautious. Talk about kissing something to make it better! Everything this man did melted the elements of my body—muscle, bone, and enamel. My heart didn't beat. It flowed. Air gurgled in what had been my lungs. I swear his eyelashes brushed my skin.

I never knew my ankle was an erogenous zone.

Neither did my stomach, and it grumbled. Loudly.

"Food," Tripp muttered right after he nipped my calf.

"How long have you had this foot fetish?" I asked.

He still looked dazed. Stunned. "Since you got here."

Scary.

"Look," I said, trying to gather the remnants of my sanity. "I don't know you, you don't know me, and this is crazy."

"I have forgiven Baird McKechnie for every rotten thing he's ever done to my brother."

I had absolutely no clue what he was talking about. "That's really nice of you," I said, keeping my gaze focused firmly on his.

"Oh, I owe him." Tripp shook his head. Inhaled deeply. "Okay. I'm Tripp. You're Chelsea. You need something to eat." He inhaled deeply again.

"Look," I said. "I'll be fine. Really. I just want to go home."

"Before you ask, there's no train station either. The car-rental office is also at the auto club, and they're closed on the weekends." He didn't need to sound so pleased.

As each avenue of departure vanished, my sense of impending doom increased.

"How do tourists get here?" I asked. I'd seen the people. They didn't just fall from the sky or climb out of the lake like some low-budget 1950s black-and-white creature feature.

"They drive," he said.

I sighed. I'd have to call Caitlin and ask her to feed Foggy. "Can you recommend a hotel?"

"It's induction weekend. All the hotels, motels, bed-and-breakfasts, and flop-houses have been booked solid for months." He grinned at me. "Don't worry about it. You can stay here."

As if I'd take his word as gospel. Of course, any hotel I found needed to be walking distance of Shaneybrook's, and that didn't seem likely.

"Maybe Baird will drive me home when he goes back," I said, more to myself than to Tripp.

"You're not waiting for McKechnie."

I didn't like his presumptuous attitude. As long as Tripp wasn't touching me, I could stay sane. Sanity reminded me that no man dictated my life to me. Everything about Tripp Shaneybrook screamed control freak.

It wasn't a huge gap between control freak and alpha male.

My family taught me everything I knew about avoiding alpha males.

Yet each time Tripp touched me, every ounce of self-preservation I possessed dissolved into hormones.

The key was to stay away from him.

My stomach made embarrassing noises again.

"Let's get you fed," Tripp said.

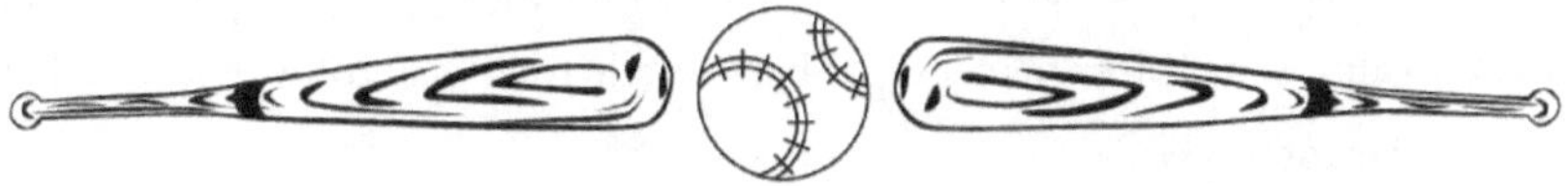

Tripp carried me down the stairs and settled me at a small round table in the corner of the kitchen. He didn't have much choice, because I'd threatened to walk down those steep stairs myself.

He signaled one of waiters, who set a small plate of hummus bordered with slices of multicolored peppers, tiny red and yellow tomatoes, and shiny green and black olives in front of me.

"Eat," Tripp ordered. "Your stomach is gurgling."

My stomach gurgled because I'd barely touched the dreadful sandwich Baird had given me. Based on that meal, I didn't trust the food at Shaneybrook's.

But I was not one of those women who can't eat when they're upset. Usually, it was quite the opposite. Those books where the heroine is slender and the least little upsetting incident steals her appetite? Fiction. I have never in my life known a woman like that. I was a normal, healthy American female, and when I was upset, I wanted chocolate. I wanted ice cream. Potato chips and French onion dip.

And I was upset. I was furious at Baird, annoyed about my broken shoe, and anxious to get home.

Another unfortunate side effect of my childhood was eating whatever was put in front of me. Too many years of not knowing if there would be food tomorrow turned me into a panic eater.

So I ate.

The hummus was great, not too garlicky and not grainy at all. The veggies were so fresh, I almost didn't recognize them.

Half an hour later, Tripp returned to my table with a clear glass bowl filled with green grapes and blueberries, as well as a glass of chilled white wine. A sauvignon blanc. Cool and crisp paired with cool and sweet. Perfect.

Next came a tiny loaf of olive bread and seasoned dipping oil. Other little snacks—almost as if I were in a tapas bar—made their way to my corner table at irregular intervals.

I hoped Tripp took credit cards, because I hadn't brought much cash, and the quality of the food hinted that Shaneybrook's was a classier place than my initial experience—that horrible opera sandwich—led me to believe. And classier usually meant pricier.

I'd never seen the inner workings of a restaurant kitchen before and was surprised by the hectic, almost frantic pace at which everyone moved. Nor could I figure out Tripp's function. He wasn't cooking. He wasn't serving. He wasn't the sommelier or the maître d'. He was just Tripp, being everywhere at once and his fingers on every pulse of the establishment, which now seemed to include me.

I didn't get it. He was a former baseball player. Two people at the health center had hit him up for autographs, so he must be famous. Why was he doing this restaurant thing?

The wine switched to a soft rosé when Tripp brought me a small plate of white beans with chopped tomato, fresh basil, and other heavenly seasonings. I tried to sip the wine slowly, but the kitchen was hot, I was thirsty, and the wine was chilled.

I kept glancing at the clock over the back door, wondering where Baird was. I couldn't believe he'd simply abandon me.

I needed to get home. I had laundry to do and a job to go to on Monday morning. I had a life, one that was going to go merrily on its way without Baird McKechnie.

Maybe I could convince Tripp to drive me back to Syracuse.

Except he looked tired. The dining room was full, and there was even a wait for tables. Not that the restaurant was all that big, but this induction weekend thing kept not only the streets but also the eateries full. Tripp's energy never flagged. But dark circles were sinking into the skin beneath his eyes. Fine lines fanned from their corners and bracketed his ever-ready smile.

I tried calling a few motels, but it seemed Tripp hadn't lied about the accommodations shortage.

The clock over the door read nine thirty when Josh burst into the kitchen. "You're not going to believe this," he said in a low, tight voice. "Willie, Frank, and Lou just came in for dinner."

Apparently these people were so famous they didn't need surnames.

Tripp squared his shoulders, his face lighting up like Christmas. You'd have thought Josh had said the Holy Trinity was waiting for a table.

"I hope everyone wants overtime," Tripp said to the kitchen staff.

The announcement seemed to imbue everyone with a fresh infusion of energy.

Tripp came over to me. "I'm sorry. This is taking longer than I'd thought. Do you want to go upstairs, grab a shower, or something?"

I shook my head. "I'm waiting for Baird."

His smile dissolved, replaced by a scowl. "He's with my brother. I doubt they'll be back tonight." He glanced at the dining room door. "Serves them right," he muttered.

"Go." I waved my hand in the direction of his gaze. "I'm fine."

He knelt in front of me and clasped my small hands in his huge ones. "You are amazing. Utterly, charmingly amazing. I'd kiss you again, but the health department frowns on sex in restaurant kitchens."

My girl parts clenched. My nipples tightened and tingled. He had no business talking to me like that, and I wished he'd keep doing it.

"Tripp." Josh sounded worried.

Oops. Witnesses.

Tripp stood, straightened his clothes and his shoulders, shot me a look of longing, and then went into the dining room to greet his latest patrons.

Josh signaled one of the waiters to refill my wineglass.

I dug through my purse for my cell phone. Two bars of power remained, but that would be enough to call my cousin, Caitlin, and ask her to feed my cat. If Foggy didn't get fed on a semiregular basis, he got cranky, and twenty pounds of cranky cat was not something I wanted to deal with when I finally got home.

I half hoped I could bribe Caitlin into driving to Cooperstown to pick me up, but that was something guaranteed to irk her obnoxious husband. He'd already be crotchety if I asked her to drive to my apartment to feed Foggy. A two-hour drive into the wilds of rural upstate New York might push him too far. Spencer was not a nice guy. I couldn't figure out why Caitlin was still with him. They didn't have kids, so that wasn't her excuse.

No answer.

I had to depend on the kindness of strangers, to channel Vivien Leigh in *A Streetcar Named Desire*. Tripp or one of his minions might be amenable to a midnight drive to Syracuse.

I yawned. The wine and the hour conspired against me. Aches invaded every bone in my body. My ankle throbbed despite random applications of ice. My skin itched from dried perspiration. I wanted a shower. I wanted my bed.

I tried calling Caitlin again. Still no answer. She didn't have a landline, only her pay-as-you go cell phone, and she was pretty good about keeping the battery charged.

So where was she?

Pain played in my ribs, and I groaned.

"Easy there," someone male murmured.

I struggled out of a deep sleep to find myself bouncing rather uncomfortably. And upside down. "What?"

"It's okay, honey," the male replied.

Then I remembered. Baird. Abandonment. Tripp. Kissing Tripp.

I was slung over someone's shoulder as he climbed narrow stairs. Tripp. The T-shirt had ridden up, exposing the backs of my thighs to the night air. He fumbled a bit when we reached the top of the stairs, and then the colorful living room flashed into view. He carefully placed me on the pale yellow leather sofa.

He plopped next to me. "How are you holding up?" he asked.

I rubbed my eyes, remembering too late I was probably smearing black mascara over my face. "Okay. What time is it?"

"Three a.m.," he replied. "It was a great night. We had so many Hall of Famers in tonight—it was fantastic."

He sounded excited. Enthusiastic. Awake.

Maybe he would drive me home.

"It's everything Penn and I thought about when we decided to open the place." His tone darkened. "And damn Baird McKechnie stole it from him."

I knew all about Baird McKechnie spoiling dreams.

I started to point out that Penn was a big boy and that no one had forced him to take off with Baird, but then, I was kind of irritated with Baird too. The jerk had ditched me. What had I ever done to him? Nothing. I did not deserve to be abandoned like a stinky sneaker. Plus he had my espadrilles in his car. I might have been able to fix the broken ankle strap, but I needed the stupid shoe in order to do it.

"God," Tripp continued. "I love hanging out with other ballplayers. And the stories! And they really seemed to like the food, even if Penn himself wasn't here to cook it."

He plucked my uninjured foot from the floor and rested it in his lap. His thumbs worked some kind of magic as he rambled on about the stories in the bar. It was that touching thing again. He touched me, and every moral I ever had dissolved along with the components of my body.

His stories were amusing, even if I didn't know the players, and some of the humor was way over my nonsporting head. I studied him, trying to pinpoint where I might have seen him before. I wished I wasn't so tired. But I was as comfortable as I could be in the circumstances. And Tripp's foot massage only added to my lethargy.

I yawned. "I'm so sorry!" I said, mortified that I'd done it practically in his face.

"It's okay, honey. You've had a long day, and here I am keeping you awake talking."

Honey? Had Tripp Shaneybrook just called me honey?

I was having a difficult time remembering that he was a professional athlete and practiced in charming fans.

"You probably want to take a shower, get some sleep—"

"Go home," I interjected.

He looked stricken, as if I'd sucker punched him or something. "It's kind of late," he pointed out. "Are you sure I can't convince you to camp out here?"

He sounded so sincere. So sweet.

"I'm kind of beat too." His smile deepened his dimples. His eyes glowed like honey-colored flames. The pressure of his thumbs on my good foot increased.

It was all I could do to keep from moaning.

"You and I can shower here. Separately if you insist," he continued. "I keep clothes in the spare bedroom in case I need them. You can borrow another one of my shirts. If you insist."

I ignored the blatant come-on. "You don't live here?"

"This is Penn's place. I have a cottage on the other end of the lake," he said. "But I stay here sometimes, when I'm too tired or otherwise incapacitated and shouldn't be driving."

Like tonight.

He didn't say it aloud, but the thought was there. It *was* late. And he'd probably had a drink or two with his baseball buddies. It wasn't his fault Baird was a jerk.

"Besides, I rented out my cottage for the weekend."

But I didn't want to be beholden to Tripp. I barely knew him.

I yawned again. It was too late to do anything. Frankly, I could have fallen asleep on the wonderfully buttery-soft leather sofa.

"Okay," I said.

Danger, Chelsea Lyndon, danger.

I pulled my foot out of his lap. "I'll take my shower now, so if you'll find me another shirt—"

"I don't think you should shower alone. Your ankle. You're supposed to stay off it." His delivery was pure innocence.

I blinked at him.

My body was going, *Fun!* while the brain kept saying, *You don't know this man. He could be a serial killer. He could be riddled with STDs, and you mean nothing to him. You're handy. That's it.*

So what? the body shrieked. *He's handy. Use him!*

"All you'd need to do is kiss me again," I admitted. Okay, I handed him a weapon. Not very bright on my part, sabotaging myself like that. My only excuse was I was tired.

"Is that all?" His smile broadened. "That could very easily be arranged."

"You said you would lend me something to sleep in."

His exaggerated sigh nearly had me giggling like a tipsy schoolgirl. "I suppose," he said. "But I'm staying in the bathroom with you."

"No." Even I had standards.

"What if you fall? Most fatal falls occur in the bathroom. Something like ninety-nine percent," he said. "With your gimpy ankle—"

"You can stand outside the closed bathroom door."

"But I won't be able to see you," he protested.

"That's the point."

"I bet you look real nice without my shirt."

"Do you sweet talk every female you meet?" I asked.

He seemed startled by the question. His teasing grin faded. "I'm not sweet talking you. I'm one hundred percent honest here."

I hadn't seen him with any other women except the nurse at the health center, so maybe I was out of line. But I didn't think so. Besides, no one ever said sweet talk had to be dishonest.

"I need my privacy," I said. I wanted to appease him, but I was not taking a community shower with a man I'd met mere hours earlier. A girl had to draw the line somewhere, and that was mine.

"All right," he conceded. "But I'm right outside the unlocked door in case you fall or something."

I could compromise with an unlocked door. I nodded.

"Let me find you a clean shirt and a towel."

Ten minutes later had me wishing I wasn't quite such a prude. My ankle hurt like crazy, and I was so tired that I felt drunk. The room didn't exactly spin. It was more like a wavering, like old movie depictions of a mirage in the desert. But I was careful. I struggled to keep my head dry, because I didn't want to sleep with wet hair. The hot water sluicing down my body felt fantastic. I'm not a big fan of manly scented cosmetics, but one of the bars of soap in the shower was pretty good. Cypress. Maybe cedar. It seemed to have some kind of exfoliating agent in it too, which was heaven after being sweaty, sticky, muddy, and awful.

I rinsed out my bra and panties, but the dress—still where I'd left it on the floor—needed something bigger than a bathroom sink. I really didn't want to drape my lingerie in the bathroom, but didn't have much of a choice. I just hoped Tripp didn't get weird about it. I was certain he'd seen plenty of women's under things.

Tripp had given me a mango-colored T-shirt to wear, and I was a little hurt. That afternoon, he'd been adamant that I wouldn't wear anything of his brother's. Only his. These fruit colors, to me, were gay guy colors. Maybe it was payback for refusing to shower with him.

I hobbled to the door, opened it, and sure enough, he was sitting on the floor in front of it.

"Honey, you look great in my shirt," he said as he scrambled to his feet.

"Yours?" I plucked the fabric away from my still-damp skin.

"Christmas gift from Penn, but yeah, mine. I told you. You're wearing my clothes, not my brother's and certainly not Baird's."

Something stilled inside me. "Baird's?"

Tripp shrugged. "He keeps stuff here. In Penn's room."

I didn't want to know about this. Really.

I must have swayed or something—that wavering-room thing again—because Tripp picked me up as if I weighed no more than his shirt and carried me across the living room into a dark room. Then I was on a bed. A big bed.

Tripp sprawled next to me.

I tensed.

"You want me to crash on the sofa?" he whispered. "I will, if you want."

How could I do that to the man? He'd been so considerate of me. We could sleep in the same bed and not... And just sleep. He was exhausted. I had seen it in the circles under his eyes and the fine lines etched around his facial features. He'd been kind. He'd taken time out of his hectic day to drive me to the health center, had tried to pay for an X-ray (I had health insurance, thank you very much), had fed me, and had pampered me as much as I had let him.

I couldn't kick him out of his own bed.

"Stay," I whispered.

"Thanks." He kissed my cheek, then rolled away from me. "I'll be back in a second."

I fell asleep listening to him moving around the apartment.

The room was dark and strange. Something much larger than Foggy stretched along my side.

I jerked awake, completely disoriented. A soft snoring told me that I was in bed with a man. *Tripp.*

But what had awakened me?

I lay very still, listening to the unfamiliar sounds of the unfamiliar building. Creaking. Like footsteps on old floorboards. Plush rugs couldn't muffle that sound.

I tensed.

Voices, low and urgent. A sliver of light glimmered between the closed door and the carpet. It was like the nightmares before I went to live with Grandma Judy.

Tripp let out a loud snuffle and then turned over, reaching for me—or for the body of whatever woman happened to be in his bed that night—and cuddled against me. He nuzzled the crook of my neck.

The voices grew louder. The door slammed open, and the overhead light flashed on.

I screamed, Tripp sat up, and Baird and Tripp's brother, Penn-the-chef, stood in the doorway.

"What is that skank still doing here?" Penn demanded.

"How should I know?" Baird retorted.

Tripp leaped from the bed and pinned his brother against the wall. "She is not a skank, and you'd better apologize to her right now."

The sight of Tripp's bare shoulders and back distracted me from the insult.

Dear Lord, the man was ripped. Muscles corded every inch of flesh I could see. And his tan. He was lightly, goldenly tanned, like a trophy. Silvery raised ridges marred the perfection of his skin on his right shoulder. He wore navy-blue boxer shorts that clung to his backside in an intriguing manner. Golden curls dusted his powerful-looking calf muscles.

"Then why is Baird's date in bed with you?" Penn sounded smug.

Tripp increased his grip on Penn, who made a gagging sound. "Because you're the skank who stole her date."

"Penn can have Baird," I said, finally finding my voice.

Looking at Tripp was much nicer than arguing about Baird McKechnie.

Baird made some kind of noise, which was probably rude, but I really didn't care. I wanted to watch Tripp. Good grief, the man was defending my honor. He didn't even know me, but he wasn't letting his brother insult me.

I got all warm and fuzzy about then.

"You want her, you can have her," Baird told Tripp. "Now let go of Penn and go back to bed." He barely spared me a glance.

"I don't need your permission." Tripp's tone was cold. He released his brother. "Get out of here."

"It's my apartment," Penn said.

"Yeah, well, it's your restaurant too, but that didn't stop you from taking off on the busiest weekend of the year." Tripp stayed close to Penn, as if he were waiting for an excuse to grab him again, maybe do some damage.

Or maybe that was just wishful thinking on my part.

"And I'm backing you because I thought you were a good investment, not because you're my brother. Today's shenanigans have me thinking maybe you're not such a sound risk after all."

Penn blanched. Like Baird, he was dressed in khaki cargo pants and a tight black T-shirt. His dark blond hair was slicked off his face with a lot of gel. It looked greasy to me. His coloring was similar to Tripp's, but he lacked Tripp's glow and golden aura. Looking at him didn't turn me molten.

"Do you have any idea what happened here tonight?" Tripp continued. "What you missed? Who you could have impressed with your culinary art?" He sneered the last two words.

"This is all your fault!" Penn turned on Baird. "And you did it on purpose. You brought your floozy with you this weekend on purpose. You want me to fail!"

Floozy?

Tripp lunged for Penn again, gripping the front of his shirt this time. "Damn it, I told you to apologize."

Penn looked at me and rolled his eyes. "I'm sorry Baird used you to get to me."

Yeah, well, that part sucked. "Me too," I said. "But that doesn't give you the right to call me names. He's the one you should be mad at."

"Hey!" Baird said.

Tripp released Penn again. "Go kiss and make up or something, before I really get mad."

"Why are you even here?" Penn asked, straightening his shirt.

"Because I rented out my cabin for the weekend. Remember? And Willie and Frank didn't want to leave."

"Willie Mays?" Penn sounded weak.

"Yeah, the Say Hey Kid himself was sitting in your dining room and eating food off your menu. Food you didn't cook."

"Shit," Penn said. He turned to Baird again. "I will never forgive you for this." He stalked out of the room without hurling another insult at me.

Baird closed the door on his way out of the room.

Tripp turned and looked at me. His chest was even better than his back. Reddish curls formed an inverted triangle in the middle of his chest, tapering down to a very narrow treasure trail that disappeared into the waistband of his boxers. His massive thighs were as solid and golden as oak.

I was still in bed with the navy-and-white pin-striped sheet pulled up to my waist. I was definitely decent. There was no way he could tell my T-shirt—his T-shirt—had ridden up, baring my backside. At least, not until he crawled between the sheets again.

He stayed where he was.

"I'm sorry you had to be exposed to that," he said. "Baird brings out the worst in Penn. I hope you're not too disappointed that things won't work out with him."

"I told you before, there was no attraction."

A slow smile slid across his face. "Yeah, you did. Well, now I'm awake, thanks to them. Not tired at all."

I never should have let my gaze drift off his face. No, he certainly wasn't tired—at least parts of him weren't. One part. One really impressive part.

I wasn't tired anymore either. My mouth was dry, because all the fluid in my body drained a lot lower. Like a guy, when all the blood left his brain to pool below his waist.

Other parts of me, like my breasts and girl stuff, tingled.

Bad idea, whispered the brain.

Go for it! shouted all the dry, wet, and tingling parts.

Tripp finally stepped to the side of the bed. "Chelsea?" His hand hovered over my right cheek, as if he were afraid touch me.

I swallowed. Hard. "Turn off the light," I whispered.

Some emotion skittered across his face, and then he nodded.

What was wrong with me? Did I think that if I couldn't see what was happening, it wasn't real?

He left me and turned off the overhead, plunging the room into absolute darkness. Even the light under the crack of door was gone. I didn't want to think about Baird and Penn sharing a room.

The mattress sank beneath Tripp's weight when he joined me. I rolled toward him.

"Hello," he said, pulling me closer.

His body was like a blast furnace. Heat poured off him in waves. If the room hadn't been air-conditioned, I doubt I would have enjoyed being as close to him as much as I did. Because I really, really liked being near him.

"You gonna get upset if I kiss you again?" he asked.

No! my body screamed.

"No," I whispered.

"Good." The word was almost a sigh, and broken off as he found my mouth with his. In the dark. One hundred percent accurate.

Lights burst behind my closed eyes. He tasted exactly the way he had that afternoon the first time he'd kissed me. When I'd fallen in love with him.

Oh. Impossible. I'd fallen in lust with him, not love. I didn't know him. How could I love him? Besides, I knew there was no such thing as love. Happily ever after didn't exist.

On the other hand, did it matter? He was holding me. He was kissing me. Again. And if he never touched me in any other way as long as I lived, as long as he kissed me, it was enough.

But he did touch me. The rigid length of his erection pressed against my belly. My breasts flattened against his marvelous chest. Both of his hands cupped my face, as if he were afraid I would somehow escape him.

"Chelsea," he said, and it sounded reverent. He'd stopped kissing me, and that irritated me.

One of his hands found one of my breasts. Sensation stabbed through me. No one else's touch was ever this perfect or would ever again be this right.

"It's okay?" he asked. "Please?"

I kissed him again. If we kissed, we couldn't talk. If we didn't talk, we couldn't say things we might regret later. Seemed like a perfect strategy to me.

His hand left my breast, leaving it lonely and forlorn. He grasped the collar of the T-shirt with both hands and pulled. The fabric tore. Seemed a little extreme to me, but then it wasn't my T-shirt. And then his hands were on my bare breasts while his tongue frolicked in my mouth.

And he wasn't the only one whose hands had purpose. My own fingers explored the contours of that magnificent chest. His nipples were as tight and drawn as my own. His breath hitched as I plucked the puckered nubs.

He pressed closer to me, rubbing that intriguing ridge against me. I brushed his belly, ever so slightly, as I made my way to the elastic waistband of his boxers. He stopped kissing me then and pressed his forehead against mine.

"I'm not strong enough to tear them off," I whispered. I was worried about this. He obviously was experienced with this sex stuff, while I'd barely left off being a newbie. I sort of knew what I was doing. Slot A, tab B, et cetera.

"It's okay. I want you to be sure. That's all."

Sure? Since when did a guy on the verge of getting laid care about the girl being sure?

I slid my hand into his boxers and had no problem finding the treasure at the end of his trail.

He was huge. Hot. Hard.

I was a molten pool, and he was like a diamond.

He inhaled sharply through his teeth. "Careful, honey. I'm about ready to explode."

I wrapped my fingers wrapped around him. The pulse in the engorged veins throbbed in my hand.

He had worked his way from my breast to ground zero. One swipe of his finger, and I was ready to climax.

He pulled out of my grasp and shucked his boxers. My eyes had adjusted to the darkness, and I could see some things in the muted glow of the alarm clock. Shapes. Like his fully erect profile. He fumbled about a bit. I heard the slide of wood on wood as he opened the night table drawer and the crackle of plastic as he tore open a condom packet. I helped him roll the thin latex over his length. There was a lot of him. I was a little worried that there might be too much.

But he knew what he was doing. He tipped me onto my back and buried his hand between my legs, fingers stroking, probing, and prepping me.

Suddenly I didn't feel so good about what we were doing. I didn't want to be a faceless woman he'd plucked from a crowd and then seduced-by-the-number.

Partly my own doing, especially the facelessness, because I'd insisted he turn out the light.

"What's wrong?" he asked, his fingers still active between my legs. "You just went all tense. Am I hurting you?"

He hadn't gone mindless either.

"Nothing," I lied. It felt good. Physically, I was right there. Unfortunately, I was a romantic, especially then. I wanted...romance.

I tried to focus on how he'd defended me against his brother's insults and how he'd come to my rescue all day. He was a good guy. A walking seduction. Maybe if he kissed me again—

Oh. I didn't mean kiss me *there*. On the other hand, who was I to argue with that magic tongue of his? An orgasm ambushed me, leaving me weak, disoriented, and not altogether coherent. Which a great orgasm should do.

Tripp shifted position, kissing his way up my body and pausing for several minutes at my breasts, which liked his attention just fine. I finally understood what they meant when they said the brain was the most important sex organ of all.

Tripp splayed my legs. His erection pulsed against my inner thigh. His mouth found mine, and once again all rational thought—all conscious thought—fled. He pressed his penis at the opening of my vagina. I was slick and ready for him, but he was...more than anything I'd ever encountered.

"Chelsea," he said. And I was grateful he'd remembered my name.

He thrust, and suddenly I couldn't breathe. He filled all the empty places inside me, compressed my organs, and drove the air from my lungs, and oh, what had I been missing and never known?

I must have whimpered, because he shushed against my ear. It didn't hurt. Not at all. It was so incredibly good that I didn't care that professional athletes were notoriously promiscuous. I was the woman in his bed right then, and that was all that mattered.

For a very long time.

CHAPTER THREE

I was never going to have sex again.

Tripp Shaneybrook had completely ruined me for any other man. I sprawled across his chest, sucking in as much air as I could. My arms and legs still trembled. Even sweaty, Tripp smelled better than any man I'd ever known. I buried my nose in his chest hair.

"Chelsea?"

"Hmm," I replied, bracing myself for a stupid question. He was a guy, and guys asked really stupid questions after sex, like, *Was it good for you?*

No, I thought, *I always scream, claw at my partner's back, and lose consciousness during mediocre sex.*

Okay, slight exaggeration. I hadn't screamed, but I'd moaned a lot. And I'd probably defaced if not further scarred those fabulous shoulders of his.

"Why did you say that?" His voice was quiet. His heart thudded against my breast, his breathing as ragged as my own.

"Say what?" I didn't remember saying anything. At least, anything coherent.

"About professional athletes being notoriously promiscuous."

Uh-oh.

"I didn't say that." I hoped.

"I heard you."

Good grief. If Tripp Shaneybrook could read my mind, I was in huge trouble.

He stroked my hair the way I petted Foggy. I'd never been more comfortable in my life. His voice was a deep rumble in his chest beneath my ear. He smelled fantastic. Perfect. Sexy.

Why did he have to ruin the moment with a question about something I'd thought?

"Chelsea? Why?"

Okay, he wasn't going to let go of this.

"I didn't realize I'd said it aloud," I confessed, hoping that would appease him.

He rolled over, carrying me with him until I was on my back again. I gazed up at him and wished for enough light so I could read the expression on his face.

"Oh, that makes a big difference."

I'm the first to admit I was really good at lying to myself about stuff, trying to romanticize it. I certainly wouldn't be in Tripp Shaneybrook's bed if I hadn't lied to myself about Baird McKechnie's potential. It ran in my family. My cousin Caitlin was a perfect example. But I rarely lied to other people.

"Look, it was a reality check, okay?" I said. "I'm always reading about this one's love child, that one's mistress breaking up the marriage, or the other one's wife beating out the car windows with a golf club. That golfer guy made tabloid headlines for months. There was a week or two when a new woman popped out of the woodwork every day."

Tripp went very still, like a tombstone pressing me into the mattress.

"I'm just trying to protect myself," I continued, keeping my voice low. He didn't need me shrieking all of my insecurities at him. "I mean, here you are, a gorgeous guy and a fantastic lover in bed with a muddy waif who happened to wash up on the doorstep of your restaurant. I know I'm not the dream girl of somebody like you."

Oh, God. Even I didn't like where I was going with this.

"You thought that was a pity fuck?"

"Well, no. Not exactly. But I usually don't indulge in sex for the sake of sex. I just need to keep perspective."

He nudged my legs apart with his penis poised. "Well, let me explain something to you," he said. "Something you seem to have forgotten, or maybe I never made it real clear in the first place."

He kissed me. Hard.

"This notoriously promiscuous professional athlete...is retired."

He pushed into me as far as he could go.

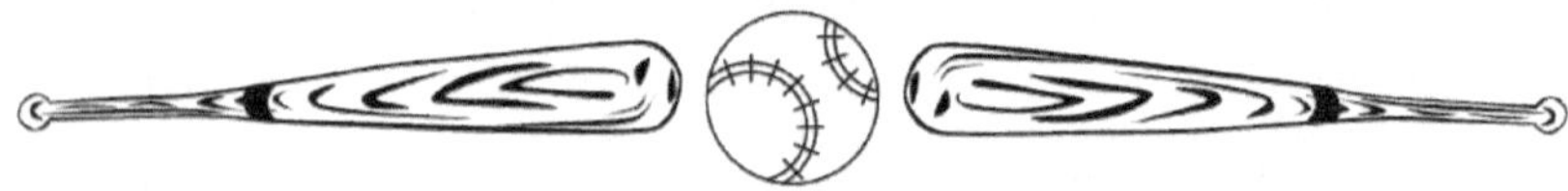

The sun poured through the half-opened miniblinds like apricot nectar, spilling across my face and the empty pillow next to me. I could see the imprint of Tripp's head, feel lingering warmth on the sheet, and smell traces of hot sex.

I was sore in places I'd forgotten I had. My sprained ankle throbbed. My ribs ached. My thigh muscles burned. And my vagina sealed itself in protest.

Pieces of the mango T-shirt littered the floor. Couldn't wear that. My muddy dress was still in the bathroom along with my lingerie. The possibility there were three men in the apartment, one of whom I'd tried to date and another with whom I'd had sex—great sex, ruin-me-for-anyone-else-ever-again sex—kept me in the bedroom.

Tripp had mentioned he was staying at Penn's for the weekend because he'd rented his cottage to some tourists. That meant he should have more clothes stashed here. Maybe not a lot, but my only other option was to fashion a toga from the sheets and hope for the best.

I inched toward the edge of the mattress, every muscle and ligament in my body shrieking at the action. *Suck it up,* I told myself. The room wasn't large. The bureau wasn't far from the bed, but I was like a Taser victim and had no control.

The door opened, and Tripp entered.

"You're awake." He sounded surprised.

The yellow towel knotted at his waist absorbing droplets of water fleeing his chest indicated he was fresh from the shower. He smelled like cypress. The sun kissed his body with blessings. I could have stared at him all day.

Then I realized my red bra and panties dangled from his fingers. My face heated. I reached for the sheet to cover my inadequate nudity.

"These were hanging on our doorknob."

Our doorknob?

His lazy smile flashed. "I guess Penn and Baird were offended by the presence of female in their bathroom."

Their bathroom?

"So Baird lives here with your brother?"

His smile faded. The sun must have slipped behind a cloud, because all that warm, sticky light turned chilly and gray. "You care?"

I shook my head, clutching the sheet tighter to my chest. "Any sign of my dress?"

I needed to get dressed, buy some shoes, find my cell phone, and call Caitlin again. Foggy had to be fed.

Tripp dropped my lingerie onto the bed. The red was a brilliant splash against the navy-and-white stripes. Then he dropped his towel.

How could I not look? He was beautiful. And now I got to see everything in the full light of day. Every incredible, impressive inch.

He strolled toward the bed. "You could stay for the weekend."

Didn't he know guys were supposed to avoid the morning after, not invite the woman to stay?

"I need to get home. I have responsibilities," I explained.

He arched one perfect, golden eyebrow. McDonald's could have sued for trademark infringement.

"Maybe Baird—"

"No!" His tone was sharp. "You don't need to have anything more to do with Baird McKechnie. I'll drive you. I'll work it out somehow."

The mattress dipped as he sat next to me. His erection jutted out like a baseball bat.

No bat-and-ball jokes. He's probably heard them all.

"Thank you," I whispered.

His finger brushed the tops of my breasts. "Last night when you wanted me to turn out the lights, and when you wouldn't let me shower with you, I thought you might be scarred or something."

The heat in my face increased until I thought my cheeks would spontaneously combust. I shook my head. "I wasn't ready for...you know."

"Making love?"

Oh, why did he have to call it that?

I nodded, even though I didn't agree with the description. I had a feeling I wouldn't be calling Caitlin, taking a shower, or buying shoes for a while.

He loosened the tuck in the sheet that held it in place as it protected my modesty. The fabric fell away, revealing my less than spectacular breasts.

Tripp's breath hitched. "Nice," he murmured. He leaned close and ran his tongue over my left nipple. The areola puckered, as if standing up to greet him. "At least I found a way to keep you off that ankle."

My mouth opened, and my breathing faltered.

He pulled the nipple into his mouth gently at first and gradually increased his suction. Abruptly, he released the flesh and me. He pulled the sheet away from my body.

"Lie down," he whispered. "I want to see you."

The sun appeared in the window again, dappling across my fish-belly pale flesh like a summer meadow.

"What's this?" He frowned and traced a fist-size bruise on the left side of my rib cage.

"I landed on a rock when I fell yesterday."

His scowl deepened. "You should have had it x-rayed."

"It's okay," I said. I didn't want to admit to my clumsiness, which often resulted in bruises I couldn't remember getting.

Like a blind man, Tripp had used his hands and mouth the previous evening. Today, he used his gaze, and the molten honey of his eyes warmed me all over. I resisted the urge to cross my arms over by breasts or to hide the thick thatch of hair at the juncture of my thighs.

"You're so beautiful," he said.

He was confused. He, not I, was the beautiful one.

The tips of his fingers started at the part in my hair and then slowly traced the lines of my eyes, my cheeks, my nose, and my lips. Lightly. I shivered even though humid July heat puddled in the room. Overhead, a paddle fan wafted the air around us, its faint hum providing a harmonic line to the chorus of our breath. He kissed me lightly on the mouth again.

Amazing how lust rearranged both of our priorities.

I wanted to touch him, but he shook his head. His fingers continued their journey around my ears, my chin, and across my collarbone.

I couldn't tell you how long it took for him to explore my entire body right down to the tips of my toes, but it seemed as if it was forever. I never wanted him to stop looking at me with reverence or touching me with holy intent.

"Sexy," he murmured, taking the big toe of my left foot into his mouth and sucking.

I nearly leaped from the mattress. Who knew toes were erogenous zones?

He licked his way between each of my toes, giving the individual digits very personalized attention.

He slipped my legs over his shoulders, completely exposing my most private parts. He took his time, separating each flap of flesh and smoothing every fold. I was half-surprised he didn't pull out a magnifying glass to take a closer look as he blew, licked, sucked, and nipped.

"You're sore," he said. His voice vibrated pleasantly against me. He could probably see where he'd chafed my most sensitive flesh. He inserted two fingers inside me as he bore down on my clitoris, and bingo. Instant orgasm.

"God, you're even more beautiful when you come," he said.

I was too busy inhaling oxygen for my brain to answer.

He crawled up my body.

"What?" I panted. "What makes you think I climaxed?"

A smile twisted his lips. "I have proof. You contract so hard around my cock and even my fingers. It's the most amazing feeling. Wet, hot, and tight." He kissed me.

I didn't want him to stop, but he did.

"I want to see your face when I slide inside you," he said. His voice was hoarse, husky, and strained. "I want to watch you while I fuck you, while you come, and when I come."

Oh, man. He was arousing more with his words than he had with his touch. I'd never thought I'd like a man to use the *f*-word when he talked to me. I mean, I hated when Kim Basinger kept saying it in *LA Confidential*. *"He taught me to fuck."* Overdone.

But the way the word fell from Tripp's mouth was really erotic. When he said it, I wanted him to suit action to word. I just didn't know if I could handle him again and so soon. His endowment was way beyond generous. He could have been a porn star.

I reached for him.

He flinched as I explored. "Chelsea, honey." His breath whistled between clenched teeth. "I won't last. I want you too much."

He tore open a condom package, quickly covered himself, and then positioned himself between my legs.

He wasn't the only one who wanted. I reached between us to guide him. His mouth opened, and his eyes went unfocused for a moment. Slowly and carefully, he started to rock his way inside me. My sore flesh didn't want to admit him. His gaze never left mine as he entered me millimeter by millimeter.

"Oh, God you feel so good," he whispered.

"So do you," I told him. "Really, really good."

He withdrew just a little. I winced. Last night had been the first time in a really long time that I'd had sex, and Tripp belonged in a category by himself.

He pushed in all the way again. "Am I hurting you?"

I shook my head. There was discomfort, but he wasn't actively hurting me. My eyes drifted closed.

"Look at me," he said. "Please. I need you to look at me."

Confused, I opened my eyes again and was caught in the caramel of his gaze.

"It's just you and me," he whispered. He increased the pace of his rocking, gradually working his way to thrusting. My body responded, answering each of his movements. The discomfort faded and was replaced by comfort, which in turn morphed to pleasure. The bedsprings squawked beneath us, and I hoped the restaurant below was empty.

He reached between us to touch me, and once again my eyes drifted shut of their own accord. The sensations threatened to overwhelm.

"Look at me." Tripp groaned.

I didn't want to climax with him watching. If I kept my eyes closed, I could hide from him. Kind of ostrichesque, but my brain wasn't exactly hitting on all cylinders at that point.

"Please."

My lids fluttered up, but I had no control over anything. I was on the verge of completely coming apart. The colors in the room radiated like a Janet Fish painting. Everything shimmered. Light saturated, penetrated, reflected. Each object in the room had its own aura. The hues and the luminosity hurt my eyes.

Then everything went white, except for Tripp's face. White light, as if I'd died and the light beckoned me.

"Yes, yes," Tripp chanted, encouraging me. He sounded proud. "I'm right behind you."

I gathered enough of my wits to reach between us. I had to stretch quite a bit to reach his testicles, but I very gently and very carefully cupped the soft, fragile sac.

Tripp caught his breath. His eyes crossed. Then he groaned and started driving into me. I nearly lost my clasp on him but managed a tender squeeze. A drop of sweat dripped from his forehead onto mine. One final thrust, and he held himself still, buried deeply in my body. His body shuddered, shook, and trembled. His gaze never left mine.

Finally, he relaxed. I closed my eyes, and he didn't argue. The steel of his muscles softened and became more pliable. He kissed me. Softly and tenderly. Completely opposite of the way he'd climaxed. The only sounds in the room were the hum of the fan over the bed and the harsh rasp of our breathing.

"As soon as your ankle heals, you can be on top," he muttered.

"Okay," I said, not believing I'd still be around when said ankle healed.

I was coming back to myself from my Tripp trip. *Find phone. Call Caitlin. Shower and shoes. Syracuse.*

I wasn't the kind of person who lost sight of what she needed to do, even when fantastic sex was involved. I might have been temporarily distracted, but in the end, I knew my priorities.

"It's going to be a long day," Tripp said. "I have things I need to do. I won't be able to drive you home until late, if at all."

"I'll take a bus," I said. "Just drop me off somewhere to buy shoes. Flip-flops even."

"No buses on the weekend," he reminded me. He rolled off me, dealt with the condom, stood, and walked to the bureau. He had gorgeous buns. Tight. Smooth. Muscular. All that baseball playing kept him in fantastic shape. I felt a surge of pride that I'd been intimate with that ass.

I searched for my cell phone. It was on the nightstand right where I'd left it.

"I need to feed my cat," I said. I picked up the phone and dialed Caitlin again.

"Can't you call someone to do that?" he asked.

"I'm trying," I said as I listened to Caitlin's phone ring. Unanswered. This was not good. I hoped nothing had happened to my cousin. With Spencer around, anything was possible.

Chapter Four

Tripp, claiming he was worried about my bum ankle, insisted on getting in the shower with me. He was very businesslike, shampooing and rinsing my hair before soaping my breasts and between my legs and then propping me against the shower wall and having his way. I didn't know a man could perform that often in such a short period of time without chemical assistance.

I might never be able to walk again.

When I looked in the bathroom mirror, I couldn't miss the whisker burn on the side of my neck, around my breasts, or between my thighs.

A little while later, I sat on a bench outside of a cutely named boutique on the main drag in the middle of Cooperstown's downtown. The vivid blue-and-purple bruises spreading across the top of my foot and shooting up my calf had convinced the bench's previous occupant to share.

Tripp hadn't been happy about my insistence on accompanying him, but short of tying me up and locking me in a closet, there wasn't much he could do about it. Yeah, my ankle hurt. Bad. But I wanted to pick out my shoes and my dress. I couldn't keep wearing his T-shirts.

If one didn't want to buy baseball paraphernalia, Cooperstown didn't offer a lot of shopping options. Every team in the world—past, present, and possibly future—was represented in one form or another.

I hadn't been allowed in the store without shoes. Baird and his car had disappeared before I could retrieve my espadrilles. Not that I could have worn them, even if I could have fixed the broken ankle strap. My left foot was too swollen.

I'd handed Tripp a twenty-dollar bill—the extent of the cash in my wallet—to buy me a pair of flip-flops. He could have purchased them in the drugstore. But no, he wanted me to have something from the boutique, even though I'd told him I would refuse to wear anything for which he'd paid.

So there I sat on a curbside bench, watching late morning pedestrians while Tripp pretended to use my money to buy me a pair of flip-flops. He finally came out of the store with a pair of really cute thong shoes, something I might have bought for myself, but I knew just by looking at them they'd cost more than twenty dollars. But oh, they were adorable, and they were my size. Before I'd sprained the ankle.

"I had the clerk put aside a couple of dresses," he said, kneeling like some kind of prince or fairy-tale character in front of me right on the sidewalk on the busiest Sunday of the year in Cooperstown.

The right sandal slid onto my foot no problem. The left side was more difficult. I finally forced my way into it, the red bands chewing uncomfortably into my swollen flesh. The color contrasted with the purple and blue of my sprain.

I had to admit, he had great taste in dresses—or had intuited enough about me to pick out the same dresses I would have chosen for myself. After trying them on, I settled on a gauzy turquoise tank dress. It clashed horribly with the new red shoes, but I didn't care.

I looked at the price tag and went light-headed. Not that I had a choice. I had my credit cards and my ATM card. I was not letting Tripp buy my clothes. I'd suck it up. Eat ramen for the next month.

Tripp's low whistle when I emerged from the dressing room assured me I'd chosen the right dress. The sales clerk beamed at him, and I felt of pang of... nothing. I felt nothing. At least, that's what I told myself.

Right.

I handed the clerk my credit card.

"You look great," Tripp said. "Good enough to eat."

Heat flashed through me.

"Excuse me, Ms. Lyndon," the clerk interrupted. She seemed embarrassed. "Your card's been rejected."

"What?"

"I'm sorry. I can't use this card to ring up your purchase."

"I-I don't understand." I dug through my wallet and found my other credit card. "Try this one."

I'd made my payments on time, and I always tried to double the minimum if I couldn't zero balance. There shouldn't have been a problem with the first card. I waited for the girl to slide through the second. My right foot tapped.

Color suffused the clerk's face. "I'm sorry," she said, handing both cards back to me.

I didn't understand, but I wasn't going to stand there and argue. I whipped out the debit card for my checking account. I'd been paid on Friday. Direct deposit. Plenty of cash available.

I smiled feebly at Tripp, who watched me without expression. Did he think I was going to freeload off him?

Tears floated in the clerk's eyes. She was probably as embarrassed as I was. "I'm sorry." She slid the plastic across the counter to me.

I dumped the useless cards into my bag and limped toward the dressing room. Tripp's T-shirt was in my purse, and that would have to do. My hands shook. What had happened to my money? Was I a victim of identity theft? Was that why Baird had brought me to Cooperstown?

Without my credit cards and without my debit card, I was helpless. No clothes. No way to purchase a bus ticket, even if the buses ran on Sunday.

The bank. I needed to find a branch of my bank and check my balance. See if my paycheck had been deposited.

Tripp grabbed my arm right before I reached the curtained cubicle that served as a changing room. "Don't ignore me. Don't walk away from me when I'm talking to you. I said I'd buy the dress."

I hadn't heard him through the panic static in my head. "No," I said. "I don't want anything from you."

He looked as if I'd slapped him.

"That came out wrong," I said. "I'm sorry. I can't think right now."

"You're really pale. Are you okay?" His grip on my elbow was secure.

I shook my head. "I don't understand this. My balances aren't anywhere close to my limits." Too much information. He didn't need to know my finances.

"Let me buy the dress. Then we can work on figuring it out," he said.

"I need to go to my bank. A branch. I want to check my balance at an ATM machine."

"Fine," he said. "The clerk is running my credit card through right now."

"I can't let you buy me this dress."

He looked as if he wanted to argue with me. "We'll work it out later." He sounded grim. "Come on. Lean on me, or I'm going to carry you out of here."

I didn't have the mental acuity to argue with him. His credit card went through, no problem.

"Don't sell this autograph," he teased the clerked as he scrawled his name across the bottom of the receipt.

As soon as we left the store, I yanked my arm out of Tripp's grasp and wandered away. I retrieved my cell phone from my purse. One bar of battery remaining. Not good. Caitlin's phone rang three times before she picked up.

"Where have you been?" I struggled to keep the stress from my voice. "I've been trying to call you. I need a favor. I'm stuck in Cooperstown, and Foggy needs to be fed."

"I'm not your servant!" Caitlin snapped. "You should have thought about your stupid cat before you left town."

"Look. I have more than hungry cat problems right now. I think someone has stolen my identity."

"Uh-oh," Caitlin said.

Everything in me stilled. "Uh-oh?" I echoed. I knew that tone of voice. I knew Caitlin. "You didn't let your husband use my credit cards, did you?"

For some stupid reason, I'd let Caitlin have access to my cards. Well, not stupid. She's all the family I have, and if something should happen to me, she needed to be able to deal with things. Plus sometimes she needed emergency cash for those times of crisis that always seemed to pop up in her life.

"I needed to post bail for Spencer, and our joint account was a little short," she admitted.

Short on brains. "What did he do now?"

"And I needed to guarantee payment to the hospital emergency room."

I stopped and leaned against a tree in front of a shop selling used baseballs and baseball cards. "Caitlin?"

"We had an argument. I had to spend the night in the hospital for observation."

"Oh damn it, Caitlin." I turned my back on Tripp and lowered my voice. "Tell me you didn't post his bail because he was arrested for beating you up."

She didn't answer.

"Tell me you are not that much of an idiot."

"You've never understood him," she replied and disconnected the call.

"Is everything okay?" Tripp stood right behind me and nearly scared me out of my skin when he spoke.

"No."

I was stunned. Stupefied. I couldn't think of one more thing to go wrong for me, unless a dog happening by mistook me for a tree.

"I wasn't trying to eavesdrop," Tripp said.

"It's okay," I said. I hoped he hadn't heard much. Good thing he was only a weekend fling.

"Let's get you home," he said. "We can talk there."

Home. Thank goodness. Now I wouldn't have to worry about whether or not Caitlin would feed Foggy.

"You'll drive me back? I owe you big for that, Shaneybrook," I said.

"As much as I'm intrigued by the idea of you being in my debt, I meant back to the restaurant."

"Right. Busiest weekend of the year and all that." I understood. Really. I did.

He slipped his arm around my waist as we slowly climbed the hill to Shaneybrook's. My ankle hurt. Someone was watering the petunias in front. Tripp helped me climb the stairs to Penn's apartment and then assisted me across the room to the sofa. He sat next to me, lifting my bad foot into his lap.

"Gotta keep it elevated," he reminded me. "I should have gone shopping without you." His strong, lean fingers gently massaged my swollen flesh. Sunlight pouring through the windows facing the street glinted off the golden hair scattered on the backs of his hands.

I'd never been one to go for blond guys, but Tripp was breaking a lot of my self-imposed taboos. I'd once read to beware of golden men for they love only themselves, and my limited experience had proven that true. Tripp was doing an admirable job of shattering that stereotype.

"Is everything okay?" he asked.

I didn't want to share the ugliness of Caitlin's life, but he'd probably already heard some of the recent disaster. Now he was stuck with me because of what had happened. I resolved to hit him up for a loan—just enough to rent a car.

I didn't know where to begin. The details of how Caitlin and I had ended up living with Grandma Judy were too boring to relate and not really relevant.

Neither was the story of how I'd followed Caitlin to Syracuse from Akron after she'd married Spencer. And the stuff about how we each reacted to our childhoods—well, that had bearing on both situations, but again, Tripp was just a really nice guy, one I'd probably never see again. A really great memory.

"My cousin is having problems with her husband." I couldn't look Tripp in the eye.

The pressure of his thumbs massaging my foot increased, and I winced.

He must have noticed. "Sorry," he muttered, and his touch turned tender again.

"You know, you're a decent human being, I said. He really was.

His mouth twisted into a smile. His lips were thin and tight. "Thanks. So is your cousin going to feed your cat? I know you were worried about him."

"Not sure," I admitted. I didn't want to say anything else but couldn't help adding, "This is really embarrassing. Just because we slept together doesn't give me the right to dump my personal business on you."

He looked hurt, then bewildered, and then outraged. "We slept together? That's all it was to you? Oh, that's right. I forgot. I'm one of those notoriously promiscuous professional athletes."

Heat flared in my cheeks.

My lack of sleep and all the tension swirling inside me caught up to me. I was weary of the drama. I slumped against the back of the sofa, feeling as boneless as I had after Tripp brought me to climax.

I swallowed my pride. He had no idea how difficult it was for me to ask, but I was anxious to get home. "I don't suppose you'd lend me enough money to rent a car."

After I'd insulted him? Right.

"Absolutely not." He didn't hesitate, even to inhale. "I'll drive you home tonight."

"I'll pay you back," I said. Then I realized I might be sniveling. I didn't want to sound whiny. I wanted to sound in charge. In control.

A muscle in his jaw throbbed. Now, I'd read about that in books before, but I'd never seen it up close and personal. I was fascinated.

He released my foot. "I told you I would drive you home tonight. Right now, I have a lot on my plate. This weekend comes only once a year."

He was good at laying on the guilt.

There was a knock on the door. It opened and a tall, dark-haired man stuck his head through the gap. "Hey, boss, Ricky and Pudge are here for the brunch meeting."

"Thanks, Faboo."

So he was ditching me. Fine. I didn't care. Better sooner than later.

"Chelsea, this is Vito Fabrizio, but everyone calls him Faboo. He works for me, and he's also one of those notoriously promiscuous athletes who worry you."

Okay, Tripp was doing his best to embarrass me, and maybe I deserved a little humiliation.

"Chelsea sprained her ankle yesterday. Please don't do anything that she might misconstrue as promiscuous. She might hurt you."

Wow. I really did make him mad.

"Sure," Faboo agreed. "But I'm not sure what that word means."

"I didn't think so." Tripp left the apartment without a backward glance.

I inhaled deeply and then exhaled. I stretched my mouth into a huge smile. "Can I borrow money to rent a car?"

Faboo looked startled. And stubborn. He was so big, he looked like a football player. "I don't think that's a good idea, Kelsey."

"Chelsea," I corrected.

"Tripp wants you to stay here."

"I need to go home. I have a family situation."

"I don't think the car-rental place is open on the weekend."

I could tell he wasn't lying.

"Can I pay you to drive me to Syracuse?"

He shook his head. "Tripp has a lot of meetings set up today, because all the players are in town, and that's keeping me busy. This is the best time to hit them up for donations to the camp."

"What camp?" I asked.

"Tripp's camp. You know. The baseball camp for kids from abusive homes."

Really? "I thought Tripp owned Shaneybrook's."

Faboo shrugged. "The restaurant is his brother's. Tripp just leant him the money to get started. And it's a good investment for when the Hall of Famers come to town. Gives them a private place to eat and meet."

Huh? "I thought the restaurant is open to the public."

"It is, but there are a couple of private rooms, and with Tripp's connections, he lets it be known the guys can come here with their families and not be hassled. Except by Tripp. It's a great setup." Faboo's expression was solemn.

The guy obviously admired Tripp.

"I gotta go. You gonna be okay here?" Faboo fidgeted. Looked at everything in the room except me.

The sun brushed the space with gold. An air-conditioning unit clattered in the front window but did its job. The room was cool enough to be comfortable. I could have been stranded in worse places.

"I'd be better on my way to Syracuse," I tried again.

Faboo grinned. "Yeah, but I'm better if you're here where Tripp wants you." He turned to leave. "Stop worrying, okay? Tripp takes care of everything. He'll take care of you too."

Chapter Five

My stomach growled as loudly as Foggy when he was hungry. Penn barely had a kitchen in his apartment and no food. Didn't that just figure? Right about then, I'd have been happy for one of the opera sandwiches

Sunday afternoon television offered only infomercials and golf. Penn had lousy taste in movies. There were no magazines, and the book selection was worse than the DVD library—cookbooks.

I tried calling Caitlin again, but my battery died. I looked for a landline but found nothing. The only room I didn't explore was Penn's bedroom. I couldn't bring myself to go in there.

I also searched for laundry facilities. If I could wash my red dress, then I wouldn't have to wear the one Tripp bought. He could either return it or save it for the next woman he rescued and seduced.

Maybe I was being unreasonable, but I had standards. I had boundaries. A loan I could repay was one thing. Accepting a gift of pricey clothing was something else. Tripp had violated what I considered permissible.

He was controlling. Like Spencer, only without the accompanying violence—which didn't make it any better. He wanted me to stay where he put me until he deemed otherwise. Even last night in the restaurant, he hadn't given me a menu but had decided which foods and wines to send to my table, as if I were a child instead of an adult who made major decisions all by herself, every day.

How had that happened? How had I let that happen?

Faboo returned to the apartment around one thirty. I was so bored that seeing him was a high point.

"Tripp wants you to eat, but he's tied up and can't get away to have lunch with you," Faboo said. He handed me a menu. "It's on the house."

I don't think so, I thought as I snatched the menu from him. I planned to write down the prices of the food I'd eaten last night and today and then mail Penn a check as soon as I got paid again.

The prices on the menu made me light-headed. I'd known last night that the quality of the food was good. I had deduced the opera sandwiches were anomalies. But I never expected the price of an individual entree to equal my weekly grocery bill—including cat food and litter.

I settled on citrus shrimp and black beans in mango salsa. It sounded like what I'd expected Baird to order yesterday for the opera.

Only yesterday.

I sighed as I handed the menu to Faboo.

When Faboo delivered my lunch, I asked him if he felt like a jailer.

He gave me a weird look as he placed a sweaty half carafe of white wine on the breakfast bar that separated the kitchen from the living room. "You're not a prisoner. Anytime you want to leave, the door is unlocked."

Which made me feel about an inch tall and totally bitchy. I apologized and then asked how Tripp's meetings were going.

"I think he's getting some hefty donations. The guys always feel real generous on induction weekend."

Well, that was good.

The shrimp was totally to die for, and the sauvignon blanc someone had so nicely provided with it was amazing.

But wine with lunch combined with little sleep the previous evening caught up to me. I surrendered to my exhaustion, stripped to my underwear, and crawled into Tripp's bed.

I fell asleep inhaling sex, cypress from his soap, and the aroma that was uniquely Tripp Shaneybrook.

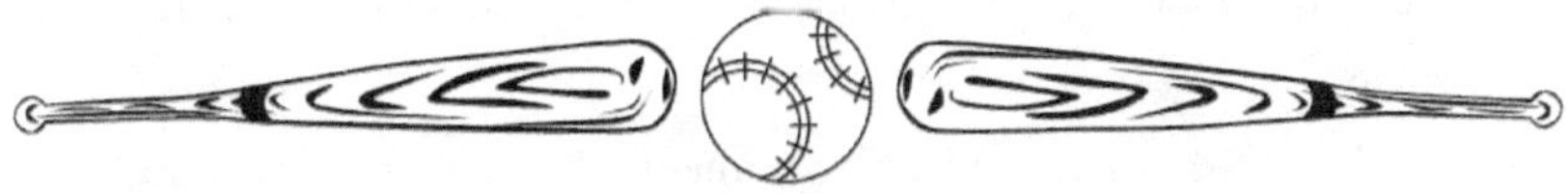

The room was dark when I awoke. I lay still for a moment, trying to orient myself. Bright green alarm clock numbers read twelve.

Midnight? Wow. I must have been more tired than I thought.

"Chelsea?"

I recognized the whisper. "I'm awake," I said.

The overhead light flashed on. Tripp leaned against the door frame. "I'm sorry."

"Faboo said you had a productive day," I replied.

He gave me a look I couldn't read. "Have you eaten?"

I thought about the shrimp, black beans, and mango salsa I'd had hours ago. "Yeah. Faboo took care of me. Thanks."

"He's a great guy," Tripp said. He didn't move from the doorway. "Dependable. Don't know what I'd do without him."

"I'm sure you'd find someone else."

"Yeah. Well, if you're ready to go, I guess I can drive you home now." He sounded tired. Exhausted. He looked ready to drop.

Driving to Syracuse took nearly two hours, and then he faced a return trip. He'd worked all day. Maybe not physical labor, but sometimes the mental stuff was more brutal.

"You look tired," I said. "Maybe we should wait until the morning."

He shook his head. "I promised you that I would drive you home tonight. I'm fine."

My heart lurched. He was trying to get rid of me. I hadn't been very nice to him at all. I had no excuse for a lot of my rudeness, except my insecurities.

"I'll wait in the living room while you get dressed," he said. The door quietly snicked behind him.

I quickly pulled on the turquoise dress and red sandals. I'd already wadded my ruined sundress in a plastic grocery bag and stuffed it into my purse. I was ready to go.

I limped to the door. Tripp didn't comment. He helped me down the stairs. The silence between us wasn't tense or awkward, but neither was it quite comfortable.

"Thank you for everything," I said as I buckled my seat belt.

He grunted a response.

The night was dark, but the sky was clear. Stars littered the heavens, and part of a moon played hide and seek with the SUV between the branches of the trees crowding the edge of the road. The highway wound uphill through the forest. Tripp turned on the radio to some sports talk station.

I thought about Caitlin, Foggy, and going back to work later that morning and didn't pay attention to Tripp or the road until we mowed down a strip of weeds and briars growing next to a deep ditch.

"Tripp!" I screamed and reached for the steering wheel, shoving it as far to the left as I could.

His head jerked up. "Whoa," he said. He took control of the wheel from me just before we hit the ditch on the opposite side of the road. "What are you doing?" he yelled.

"Keeping us out of the ditch," I yelled back.

"You were headed right for it. I suppose you'd be one of those pitchers who'd insist his curve ball was really a sinker."

"Did you fall asleep?" I kept my hand on the steering wheel. Insurance.

He pulled to the side of the road and stopped. "I might have nodded off for a second," he admitted. "Just a second."

Oh God, if we'd been on the thruway doing sixty-five or seventy miles per hour, we'd have been toast.

"We're swapping places," I announced. "Get out."

"I'm fine."

"You're going to get us both killed. You could barely keep your eyes open when you came to get me."

"You can't drive with a sprained ankle."

"It's my left foot. I can drive just fine." I unbuckled my seat belt and then reached for his. I could be very stubborn.

He took my hands off his seat belt buckle and thrust them toward my lap. "This is a stick. A manual transmission. Even if you know how to drive it, you can't use the clutch with that ankle of yours."

Well, nuts. He had me there. But only partly.

"I know how to drive a standard. My grandmother didn't raise any stupid granddaughters."

"That's debatable," he muttered. He had to be talking about Caitlin.

"I heard that," I said. "Now let me drive. I had a long nap, you've been working all day, and you probably had a drink or two with your cronies tonight. Doing business, of course, but you didn't get much sleep last night, and—"

He shut me up the only way he could. He kissed me. I mean, really kissed me. I banged my knee on the gearshift as I tried to crawl over the console so I could plant myself on his lap.

He lifted me until I straddled him. My skirt was hiked up to my waist, and my panties were damp from wanting him. I cradled the steely ridge beneath his zipper between my legs.

"Jesus, Chelsea," he said a minute or ten later.

I reached for the button at the top of his fly.

"I haven't done it in a car since I was seventeen," he said, pushing away my hand. "I don't have any protection."

I rested my forehead against his. Breathing was really difficult. I thought about telling him I was on the pill, but that was a lie. And then there were STDs. Not from me, but...

"Let me drive," I said.

"No," he said.

"Just back to Cooperstown." I was pretty sure my foot could hold up that long. I'd been off it last night and all day today. I could feel the straps of my sandals cutting into the swelling, so I knew that hadn't abated. Still, I ought to be able to drive two or three miles back to the village.

"I'm okay now," Tripp said. His voice trembled. "Especially if we're just going back to Cooperstown."

I didn't say anything.

"It's your call. But if we go back to Cooperstown, we're making love."

I needed to go work in the morning. My cat needed feeding. My cell phone was dead. I had the world's sexiest man wanting to bang my brains out.

Brain banging won. Twenty-six years of resistance to my mama's genes lost. I'd always wanted an adventure. Okay, I'd wanted a romantic adventure, and brain banging wasn't exactly romantic. But it would do. I promised myself I would not regret my decision. If nothing else, I would always have the memories of truly stupendous sex.

Tripp helped me return to the passenger seat. His three-point turn to get the SUV headed in the right direction was flawless despite the way his hands shook. Maybe he took the curves of the serpentine road a little too quickly for my liking, but I didn't blame him.

I'll be darned if he didn't carry me up the narrow stairwell again. I looped my arms around his neck and pressed my mouth against the side of his throat. He tasted salty with perspiration and wonderfully Tripp. Magnificently Tripp. If there were some way to bottle his scent and his flavor, I could be a rich woman and never have to go back to my job.

He shuddered under my ministrations. I thought about all the ways I could make him shudder. Not that I was all that good—or even experienced—at some of the lascivious thoughts running through my little old brain, but sometimes enthusiasm made up for know-how or mouth-on experience.

He tumbled me onto the bed. We bounced for a moment or two before we pressed together in need. Experience hadn't yet rendered his kisses mundane or ordinary. My breasts ached for his mouth.

He sat up, pulling me with him, and then unzipped my dress and drew it over my head. I fumbled with the buttons on the front of his shirt.

One-handed bra removal. Yep, the guy had experience. I shoved that thought aside. I was the one he wanted to be with that night. That was all that mattered.

My bra slid forward, and the straps caught on my arms. Tripp filled each of his palms, cupping the globes so that my nipples were somehow caught between his thumbs and his forefingers.

I shimmied out of the dress, a much more difficult maneuver than one would think. Tripp wasn't letting go of my breasts. In fact, he leaned forward and licked each nipple.

"Need help with the panties?" he asked between tongue strokes.

"Not yet," I replied. "But you need to lose some clothes."

He seemed to like that idea and somehow managed to twist his body so I could push his shirtsleeves down his arms until his cuffs caught on his wrists. He was going to have to let go of my breasts or keep the shirt. The maneuver felt like an aerobic workout, and the things he was doing to my lucky nipples were very distracting. I just wanted to lie back and let him do his thing, but that was lazy. He deserved so much more than a passive body.

In fact, he was tired, having put in a long day while I'd napped away the afternoon and evening. And I couldn't reach his chest to reciprocate the attention he gave to mine. I was going to have to take desperate measures. I kissed him and reached for his fly.

He was already aroused. Belt buckle. Button. Zipper—careful there. Slowly, not just to taunt but because I didn't want to hurt him. The metal teeth barely restrained his erection.

He groaned as I reached into his opened pants and cupped him through his boxers. His penis seemed to have a life of its own, pulsing and throbbing under my ministrations.

Tripp's breath whistled through his teeth. "Chelsea," he said, a warning tone in his voice.

I gently squeezed the shaft. It twitched in response.

I kicked away my dress, and using my free hand, I stripped off my panties, using a little toe action to pull them off one ankle. They wreathed the other—my sprained one—like a kinky bracelet.

"Hey," Tripp whispered. "What do you have in mind here?" Then he latched on to my right breast and sucked the nipple into his mouth. Hard. I could barely keep a groan from escaping my throat.

"Condom." At least I remembered the word.

He seemed reluctant to release my breasts, but he did, using his free hand to open the bedside drawer. "Can you do it?" he asked when he came up for air. He handed me the package and then returned his mouth to my breast.

My fingers trembled as I mutilated the foil. They outright shook as I rolled the thin latex down his length. He was so huge that I was afraid the condom wasn't big enough to accommodate him.

He wasn't any help. His mouth on one breast and his hand tweaking the opposite nipple. I felt like a circus contortionist—one who was really close to climaxing.

How could that be? He'd done nothing but make love to my breasts, yet my girl parts grew more humid. I needed him inside me.

I placed my palms in the center of his exposed chest and pushed, making sure my torso followed. He still wore his slacks, but the part I needed was exposed and ready. I leaned over him so he could continue with what he was doing, but using my free hand, I held his penis upright and positioned myself over it.

"Chelsea." Tripp seemed to choke.

"Stop talking," I whispered and jiggled my dangling breast right over his mouth.

He took the hint, while I slowly sank onto Mount Everest.

Slowly was the operative word. Have I mentioned that the angels smiled on Tripp the day his private parts were created? No matter how ready to take him that I thought I was, I still needed to do it slowly. Lowering myself for half an inch, withdrawing ever so slightly, and then forcing another half inch inside my body.

Tripp abandoned my breasts and grasped my hips, which allowed me to reposition the angle in which I took him. He didn't try to force me deeper, didn't do anything except hold my butt steady and stare up at me with an expression of pure ecstasy on his face.

"How's your ankle?" he whispered.

"I'm not using my ankle," I replied.

Actually I was, and it complained about all the weight it was being asked to bear. But what was going on at the other end of my leg felt better.

"You're killing me."

"Good."

He pinched me.

"Hey, you're cheating."

"You think what you're doing to me is fair?"

He surged upward. I fell forward, feeling limp and useless. I was stretched so tight, I swear I could feel the thick vein in his penis pulse.

After I caught my breath, I began to move slowly and teasingly. He moved with me, filling, hollowing, filling, and hollowing.

The pace gradually increased as I became more comfortable with him inside me. I sat up straight, my breasts jutting out, and rode him.

His hands left my hips. One found a breast and resumed its earlier torment. One finger from the other burrowed until it found my clitoris. Sparks shot through me. Little spikes of intensified feeling. The soles of my feet grew warm. My breathing became more labored.

I glanced at Tripp, and he was watching my face, as if looking for a sign. I couldn't focus my vision. All I knew was the incredible pleasure of having him pumping inside me and having his finger on me. I didn't want this to end. Ever. I didn't even need an orgasm, not when he was making me feel so good.

"Chels," he moaned in a hoarse whisper. "It's time."

I didn't understand.

He released my breast, withdrew his finger, and gripped my ass again. He increased the pace.

"Touch yourself."

I stared down at him, not understanding.

"Use your finger on your clit while I fuck you. Play with your tits. Touch yourself. Please. For me."

His grip held me steady, and even though I was on top, he'd taken control of the pace.

I was reluctant to do as he asked. Masturbation was a private activity. And why should I masturbate when I had a perfectly capable man buried deep inside me?

I cupped my own breasts. It didn't feel the same. It wasn't as good as Tripp's touch.

"Pinch your nipples," he instructed.

I did. My nipples stuck out like those pink eraser caps I'd used on my pencils in elementary school.

"Nice," he murmured. "Now rub your clit."

I shook my head, my hair brushing the tops of my shoulders.

"For me? Please?"

I let my hand brush the coarse curls on his belly. His penis seemed to grow even larger. The skin around the entrance to my vagina was taut.

I couldn't tear my gaze from Tripp's.

"Touch your clit," he repeated. His chest heaved with every inhalation.

The skin below his belly button felt thinner than that above it, thinner and more vulnerable. I lightly stroked, and his breathing grew more labored. "Don't you know how to touch yourself?"

I shook my head again.

I wanted to reach behind me and cup his balls, but he removed one hand from my butt and seized my fingers. "Then let me teach you."

Placing one finger atop mine, he found the right spot on the first try. "How do you like to be touched best?" he asked as his finger led mine in a minuet across slick skin.

I caught my breath at a particularly intense stroke.

"Oh, I think we've got it," he said. "Just keep doing that."

His hand returned to my ass, gripping it tightly. Then he raised me almost off him and slammed me down.

I cried out. Not in pain, but in pleasure so complete, it defied words. Again. And again. And again and again.

"Yes." The word came out of him in a hiss. He increased the pace, pumping into me while I stroked myself. Orgasm surged through me, catching me completely unawares.

I squealed like a trapped animal, but I couldn't stop. Tripp continued to whisper encouragement. I collapsed, and he surged into me one final time. His cock twitched and jerked inside me. His own cry was hoarse and loud.

And that was the last thing I remembered until I awoke almost twelve hours later.

Chapter Six

I was embarrassed to open my eyes and look at Tripp. I'd dreamed about what we'd done all night and relived it all several times—including that final mind-blowing orgasm. We'd slept twined together with his penis still inside me.

The man had a morning erection. Waste not, want not, and it seemed we both wanted. Wanted enough to ignore the obvious.

"I lost the condom," he said a few minutes later. His chest heaved as he gulped in air. His heart pounded against my breasts. "You wouldn't by any chance happen to be on the pill or anything?"

He lost the condom? Good grief, he'd lost the condom. I could just see the screaming tabloid headline in another nine months: *Tripp Shaneybrook's love child with Genevieve Hart-Darling Foundation executive assistant.*

Not the kind of publicity the foundation wanted.

Then I remembered it was Monday, and I'd been due at work hours ago. Hours. Which seemed trivial at the moment.

"What do you mean you lost it?" I squeaked. My throat still felt raw from last night. "How can you lose a condom?"

"I take that's a no," he said.

I tried really hard not to hyperventilate. "That's a no."

How could something as amazing as last night lead to such a disaster? He'd lost the condom, but I'd be blamed.

"How did you lose the condom?"

"Hey," he said. "Calm down." He reached inside me with two fingers and started searching. It was very weird. "I fell asleep before I had a chance to take it off. Remember? I nearly fell asleep at the wheel last night. And then you seduced me. Very nicely, I might add." He kissed my forehead. "And then this morning, well you felt so fantastic, all snug around me that I didn't stop to remember I wasn't suited up."

Okay. I'd fallen asleep right away too. But I wasn't the one dealing with the condom. That was his job. If I were on the pill, it would be my job to swallow them.

I tried to figure out where I was in my cycle, but I'd never been very regular, and frankly, I was upset and distracted. And Tripp wasn't helping any with all that poking and prodding as he looked for the condom.

If that was what he was doing. His thumb on my clitoris was definitely not part of the condom search.

"Hey," I said.

"Got it," he said, and then he kissed me.

The scrap of latex was empty. We stared at it as if it was something hideous and awful. I had zillions of Tripp Shaneybrook's boys swarming toward my egg. Hopefully either a far from ripe one or one way past its prime.

Tripp grabbed a handful of tissue from the box on the night table and wadded everything together. Then he turned to me and pressed his forehead against mine.

"It's okay. If you're pregnant, we'll deal."

How could he be so calm? Of course, it wouldn't be his life disrupted by an unwanted pregnancy.

Just thinking about the word nauseated me.

I had plans for my life. Plans that didn't include continuing the family tradition of single motherhood.

His honey-hued gaze never left mine. How could he not see my panic?

This Cooperstown weekend had been an interlude, like a fantasy: rescued by a gorgeous guy, indulging in world-class, never-to-be-topped sex. But in the end, only sex.

He was some kind of famous baseball player, and I was just a glorified secretary with a twenty-pound gray cat and a cousin who let her husband use her for a punching bag. Tripp owned a restaurant, ran a camp for needy children, and used designer soap, while I used the drugstore equivalent of the mall chain scented product. Which I couldn't even buy right now because I was flat broke with two maxed-out credit cards.

And I might be pregnant.

Losing the condom was a reality check. I might secretly long for incredible adventures—*Thank you, Grandma Judy and your movie addiction*—but I knew there was no such thing as happily ever after.

"Relax," he repeated. "We'll be fine."

He was being honorable, and I didn't want honorable. I wanted romance. Champagne, the prospective groom on his knees, and either a string quartet or a harpist providing live music. Candles. Flowers. Poetry.

Pregnancy wasn't romantic. It was morning sickness, bloating, roller-coaster emotions, and raging hormones for the woman and a trap for the man.

Hadn't I seen my cousin go through it all, and wasn't I constantly bailing her out of the aftermath? I wasn't willing to turn any man into another Spencer Madison.

Tripp rolled away from me. Presented his magnificent back. Broad shoulders. Bulging biceps. I closed my eyes and tried imagining waking up next to him every morning for the rest of my life.

I didn't deserve that.

I hadn't even deserved the past two nights with him.

I clutched the sheet to my chest. "Is it possible to borrow a phone to make a long-distance call or two?" I asked. "My battery died, and I didn't bring a charger."

"Sure. Help yourself. My phone is on the nightstand. I'll be right back."

He stood up and left me alone in the bedroom.

Why did I feel like crying?

I swallowed the lump in my throat and picked up his phone. First I called in to work, apologizing to my boss for not calling in sooner and explaining that I'd had an accident, had hurt my ankle, and was supposed to stay off it for a few days.

Then I called Caitlin, who, miracle of miracles, answered on the first ring.

"Yes, I fed your stupid cat," she said after I identified myself. "And I picked up your mail. In fact, I'm staying at your place, so don't worry about your cat."

She didn't even ask whose phone with its unknown number I was using.

Nor did she elaborate on why she was at my apartment, but then, she didn't need to. If Spencer was out of jail, she would do well to lie low for a while. Although my place wasn't exactly a secret. He was the kind of moron who blamed the woman he'd pummeled for getting him into trouble for beating her. Just like he'd blamed her because she'd miscarried his son after he threw her down a flight of stairs.

Thank goodness she'd never gotten pregnant again.

And still she stayed with him. Probably because she'd gotten him to marry her, a first in our family. Now she was hiding in my apartment, even though Spencer's cousin was my landlord. The two of them deserved each other.

I disconnected. Things in Syracuse were covered for another day. Now to deal with things in Cooperstown. I grabbed a clean shirt from the bureau drawer, pulled it over my head, and went in search of Tripp.

I found him in the kitchen, watching coffee drip into a carafe. "Make your calls?"

"Yes, thanks."

Awkward silence.

"What's wrong?" he asked.

If I had to tell him...

"If you're still worried about the condom, it was an accident," he said. "I didn't do it on purpose."

I never thought he had. "Maybe I goofed when I put it on you or something."

He shook his head. "I fell asleep. You felt so good. Making love to you was so good. I just got careless and fell asleep." He cupped my cheek. "I don't want you to worry. I've wanted to put a baby in you since the first time I met you. Remember? Barefoot in the kitchen? So if there's a baby, that's fine."

"You were joking." I clenched my fists to keep from reaching for him.

"No, I wasn't."

The intensity of his gaze was more than I could handle. I left the kitchen for the bathroom and a much-needed shower.

Tripp stepped into the tub as I was rinsing shampoo from my hair.

His eyes narrowed. "What happened to you?" He gripped my shoulders and turned me around. "Oh, Jesus."

"What?" I looked down. Purple splotches decorated my hips.

"Oh, honey, I'm so sorry." He slid a hand down, placing a finger over each bruise. "I held you too tightly."

Seeing his golden tanned hands on my frog-belly-pale skin was somehow erotic. It was mesmerizing.

"I guess I need to handle you with care."

I jerked my gaze from my hip to his face.

"Do they hurt?"

I shook my head. Droplets of water sprang from the ends of my hair.

"I will never intentionally hurt you," he said.

I yearned to believe him. These past couple of days had surpassed any fantasy I could conjure. I'd wanted a fairy tale my whole life. But it had to be real, not forced, and no matter how great and honorable a guy Tripp was, if I was pregnant, I'd never know if the romance was real.

Because of Caitlin and Spencer. Because of my mom, Caitlin's mom, and Grandma Judy. Generations of really good reasons.

Tripp's eyes darkened to the color of whiskey. Drops of water clung to his lashes. "Okay, maybe the shower isn't the place to discuss the future." He sounded reluctant. "But we *will* discuss the future."

He grabbed the soap and started to work it into a lather.

"Let's get you cleaned up," he murmured.

"That works two ways," I replied, taking the soap from him as he covered my breasts with sudsy hands.

Now, we'd already had shower sex, which had been tricky with my gimp ankle and all, but I'd never imagined playing with a bar of soap could be so much fun. Of course, Tripp had great hands and never forgot a thing he'd learned about my body. He lathered every inch of me, teasing, using a variety of strokes.

I tried to reciprocate, but he was so much taller than I, although his chest got quite a massage. The suds were rich and potent. I loved sculpting his chest hair, twirling it around my fingers, and tormenting his flat nipples.

I really wasn't trying to arouse him again—not that he ever seemed to need much help with that. It was playtime. He was doing deliciously naughty things to me while pretending to wash me. Payback could be fun. And when his slick hands slipped between my thighs and when those sly fingers began dancing across too-tender flesh, what else was I supposed to do except...reciprocate?

Only instead of fingers, I used palms. Different anatomy for different anatomy.

He was a big guy. Even flaccid, he was impressive. His testicles filled both of my hands. My playing revived him. I didn't do it on purpose. His penis seemed to have a mind of its own. I'd never really explored male genitalia before, so watching his cock twitch, expand, and feeling it grow heavier as I held it was fascinating.

His breath whistled between his teeth as he inhaled. "You're going to be the death of me yet—and I can't think of another way I'd rather die." No shower sex, because we hadn't brought a condom into the bathroom. Just because we'd had an accident didn't mean I wanted to tempt fate. And for all his talk about wanting to give me babies, Tripp had a generous supply of condoms that until an hour or so ago, he'd never hesitated to use.

"Rinse time," he said. He pulled the showerhead from the bracket that held it in place and quickly sprayed the lather from our bodies.

He then lifted me out of the tub and wrapped me in one of his brother's marvelous thick yellow terry bath sheets. He knotted another around his waist, the front tenting out, cracked open the bathroom door to see if anyone was about.

"The coast is clear," he announced.

We'd almost reached the safety of his bedroom when the apartment door opened and Penn came in.

I don't know who squealed louder, Penn or me.

Tripp stepped between us with his back toward his brother.

"I don't mind if you crash here," Penn said, "but could you use a little discretion?" Disgust tainted his voice.

"Aren't you supposed to be getting ready for lunch?" Tripp asked.

"Aren't you?" Penn countered. "Reservations for three at one thirty. Your name."

"I have time," Tripp said.

Oops. No, he didn't, and it was all my fault. If I hadn't waylaid him—well, not the laid part, but in the shower—he would have made his lunch on time.

Penn shook his head. "Johnny and Wade left. Got tired of waiting for you. I put their meals on your tab."

Tripp swore. "What time is it?"

"Almost three. It's a good thing the restaurant has big hot water tanks." Penn sneered the last words.

"Why didn't you come get me?"

"I sent Josh, but he said you two were in the shower, and he didn't want to interrupt."

Poor Josh. At least we hadn't been loud.

And it was my fault Tripp had missed his meeting.

"Oh," Penn continued. "Your tenants dropped off your key, so I called your cleaning lady. I think we're even now."

Tripp's jaw was doing that throbbing thing again. "What did Johnny and Wade say?"

Penn shrugged. "Nothing as far as far as I know. But then, I was in the kitchen. Working."

Tripp excused himself and lunged for the bedroom.

I followed.

He sat on the edge of the bed, speaking into his phone in a very sincere tone.

I gathered my clothes and took them to the bathroom. When I emerged, Penn was gone, and Tripp was waiting outside for me.

"Is everything okay?" I asked.

He shrugged. The afternoon sunlight glinted off the bronze of his bare shoulders and turned the scars to phosphorescence. "I don't know. I got voice mail."

"I'm sorry," I said.

"It's not your fault," he lied.

"How many more meetings do you have?"

"That was the final one, and those guys stayed in town this afternoon just to meet with me after the members-only roundtable."

Oh boy. I didn't do anything halfway, did I?

"Let me shave and get dressed. Then we'll head out."

Okay. He was ditching me. Well, I wanted to go home, go to work, and pet my cat. Resume my life.

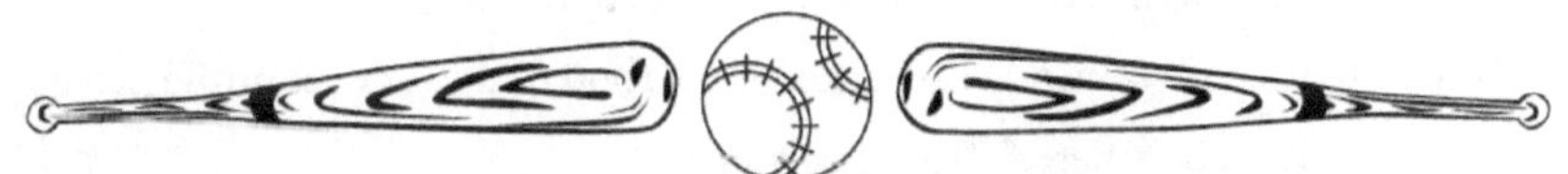

Tripp drove about fifteen minutes before pulling into a driveway next to a modern-looking house on the edge of the lake. We'd driven by a lot of waterfront shacks and rusty trailers, so this newer, well-maintained building was a bit of a surprise.

"Why are we stopping here?" I asked.

"This is my place. I wanted to show it to you."

Oh.

He carried me inside.

The house was great. It was practically a movie set or magazine layout. The entire wall facing the water was glass. Sunlight streamed in, gilding everything with summer. The first floor was open, with the kitchen on the driveway side of the structure. The opposite wall housed a huge stone fireplace.

He carried me through conversation areas, furnished in an eclectic mix of leathers and mutely toned fabrics with glass and chrome tables. The bleached wide-plank floor gleamed as brightly as the huge white tiles on the kitchen floor. The scattered area rugs looked genuinely ethnic.

Tripp must have been an extremely well-paid baseball player.

My life didn't exactly include hanging out in McMansions. My own family barely escaped being trailer trash by virtue of living in cramped, run-down apartments instead of a mobile home. This kind of subdued *taste* was out of my realm, but I recognized it for what it was. I could *smell* it.

Even Penn's apartment had been nicer than what I was used to, but compared to Tripp's cottage, it was a dump. And I'd felt awfully out of place there. Here, I'd be afraid to walk barefoot because the calluses on my soles might scratch the floor.

Tripp opened the slider to a deck that hovered over the lake and deposited me on a chaise. Tall trees created a heavy canopy of leaves over the water and dappled the treated wood floor with coolness from the July sun.

It wasn't nearly as hot on the lake as it had been in town.

"I need to unload the car. Penn packed some food to tide us over until I can get to a grocery store. Stay here," Tripp instructed.

I offered to help. Self-preservation and all that. First of all, I didn't trust Penn making food for me, no matter how great the food in his restaurant was, and secondly, Tripp seemed to think I was on vacation or something.

"You're supposed to be off that ankle," he reminded me.

I stashed my purse under the chaise and leaned back. Closing my eyes, I let the silence seep into my bones and, in turn, absorb me.

"Here you go," Tripp said.

I started awake.

He stood over me, holding two glasses of iced tea. Lemon, like slices of sunshine, garnished the rims. I blinked the sleepiness from my eyes and realized I was thirsty.

"Thanks," I said as I took the glass from him.

He sat splay-legged in the chair on the other side of a low bamboo table from me. "Since we didn't get lunch, how about an early dinner?"

I hated repeating myself, but Tripp didn't seem to be hearing me. "I thought you were driving me home. My home. In Syracuse."

He covered his initial guilty look with that charming aw-shucks grin of his. "I'm not supposed to feed you?" Ice clinked as he took a long drink of his tea.

Fascinated, I watched his throat muscles ripple as he swallowed. The open collar of his spring-green shirt framed his tanned skin.

Unfortunately, my stomach answered with a rumble before I could respond to his question.

"Look," he said. He set his glass on the table and reached for my hand. "Your cousin is feeding your cat. You've called in sick to work with a legitimate excuse, so why can't you spend another night here with me?" His thumb caressed the center of my palm and, like steel on flint, sent sparks skittering every which way inside my body.

"I'd like to spend some serious time with you." His eyes glowed like warm honey. He sounded sincere.

I really wanted to believe him. I said the first thing that popped into my head. "I don't have any clean clothes."

Aw-shucks turned into a cute leer. "Don't wear any. I won't complain."

I looked rather pointedly at the smooth expanse of lake and then at the glass wall of his house.

"I've got shirts I can lend you. You look real nice in my shirts. And I do have laundry facilities."

He was worse than a serpent with an apple.

I thought about all the clothes I had back in Syracuse, just waiting to be packed for a fantasy week at a waterfront summer cottage.

But this was reality, and I wanted to stay. This was turning into the world's longest opera date—and I'd yet to hear a note sung.

"All right," I said.

He leaned across the table and kissed me. If I hadn't already conceded, I would have then.

He disappeared for a few minutes and then returned with a kiwi-colored T-shirt. "Here. Change into this, and give me your clothes. Including your underwear. I'll run a load of wash."

He was going to do my laundry?

He wouldn't let me up, so I made him stand between me and the lake with his back turned as I shimmied out of the dress he'd bought me and into his T-shirt. Then I removed my bra and panties. My face was hot, but he was right about my ankle. I'd been doing too much.

Letting him take care of me for a few more hours wouldn't hurt.

"Dinner's almost ready," he said, dumping a can of beer over the beef sizzling on the grill. Flames flared. The aroma of fire-seared meat and smoke drifted across the deck.

We ate steaks and some salad courtesy of Penn, with pears, gorgonzola, and candied pecans in a tangy dressing over mixed greens. Tripp also opened a bottle of wine, a ritzy-sounding Italian red. We ate on the deck. Tripp even lit a candle in the center of the table. Okay, it was citronella, but the ambience was there.

I loved being pampered. The wine made me drowsy, a potent combination with sun.

And we talked. I told him about my job as an executive assistant for a philanthropic foundation, which doled out money to various not-for-profits in the form of grants. He told me about growing up an athlete with a gay brother in a community where jocks ruled and homosexuality led to near-death beatings. Tripp was the reason Penn was still alive.

Daylight faded, turning the summer sky to the color of worn denim and the surface of the lake to crumpled aluminum foil. When the sun finally set, the sky blazed orange and reflected off the water and onto our faces. Tripp looked more like an award statuette than ever.

He dribbled the last of the wine into my glass, leaned back in his chair, and smiled at me.

"I've been picturing you sitting here ever since I met you. This is my favorite place in the world, and I wanted to share it with you."

"Why here?" I asked. I wasn't touching the rest of what he said with a ten-foot bat.

"Cooperstown," he replied without missing a breath. "It's the birthplace of baseball, or so it claims. But it's really rich in all kinds of history."

Oh boy. A bunch of stuff that was going to make me sorry I'd asked. "I came for the opera," I said as brightly as I could. "I didn't know about the baseball."

Or care.

"So are you really into opera?" he asked.

"I don't know," I admitted.

"You don't know?"

How could I explain? Well, it was definitely time to fess up. "Have you ever seen the movie *Moonstruck*, with Nicolas Cage and Cher?"

"Can't say as I have."

"My Grandma Judy loved movies. We watched movies all the time when I was growing up. Anyway, Cher and Nicholas Cage meet, and it was love at first sight. But see, she's engaged to his brother, so she can't get involved with Nicholas. So he tells her he'll leave her alone if she'll go to the opera with him. So she does."

"Are you engaged?" His tone was dark.

"What? No!"

"Just checking." He crossed his arms over his chest.

I waited for his grin, but it didn't come.

"What?" I asked again.

"So when Baird McKechnie asked you to go to the opera, you said yes because you think he has a great name and...?"

I merely looked at Tripp and said nothing.

Fireflies blinked behind his head. A mosquito landed on my arm, and I smacked it flat and gooey.

"Okay, Chelsea. Work with me here," he said. "What does *Moonstruck* have to do with you and Baird McKechnie? You want him to leave you alone? If that's the case, I think it worked."

"It was very romantic," I finally confessed. "The movie, not Baird."

"Why did you want romance with *him?*"

"I wasn't looking for romance with him...just...romance." I knew I sounded like an airhead. This was so difficult to explain. "It's like...a goal."

"Baird?"

"Romance! Leave Baird out of this."

Tripp scowled. "I'm having trouble understanding why you were looking for romance with a gay man."

"I didn't know he was gay."

"But you aren't attracted to him, so why did you go on a romantic date with someone you aren't attracted to?"

Because I hadn't met you yet.

"For the romance."

I figured he was a jock. That's why he never seemed to hear anything I said. "With someone you aren't attracted to." He shook his head. "You're really lucky this worked out for the best."

Well, I never got my romantic opera date, but hey, he was right. Things could have been a lot worse. Baird could have abandoned me in a place without Tripp.

He pushed himself away from the table and started gathering our dirty dishes. I stood to help. Grandma Judy raised me right.

"Sit," he said. "I want you off that ankle."

So I sat and savored the symphony of crickets, frogs, and other creatures in the balmy evening.

Tripp returned with another bottle of wine and placed it on the table next to the chaise. Again, I started to stand so I could move, but he scooped me off my feet before I got very far. He settled me on the chaise and then sat beside me.

Across the lake, lights wrapped the shoreline in a necklace of irregular yellow beads. Several bonfires threw orange onto the water's surface. An occasional wisp of wood smoke scented the breeze.

There were no lights on Tripp's side of the lake.

"So do you have neighbors?" I asked.

"I bought up several properties and had the buildings torn down. I like my privacy." He handed me another glass of wine. "And I like that there's no light pollution out here at night. Look up."

I tilted my head and saw what he meant. The night sky was stunning. Stars like the opening of *Star Wars* splayed across the nearly black expanse of the sky.

"The Perseids meteor showers are going on right now." His breath was warm against my ear, sending chills through me. "They don't peak for another couple of weeks, but if you look long enough and hard enough, you'll see a shooting star or two."

Was that his tongue exploring the outer rim of my ear?

He nibbled his way down the side of my neck. My hand trembled, and I was afraid I'd spill some of that great wine. He was in his mind-reading mode again, because he took my glass from me and set it on the side table.

Then he kissed me. His lips brushed against mine. Soft. Gentle. Exactly the way I liked. When he deepened the kiss, I was ready. He tasted of steak and dark red wine. I found myself melting against him. He smelled great—of lingering essences of his soap, the grilling meat, and the core of what I thought of as *eau de Tripp*.

He stretched out beside me. The two of us on that chaise lounge were very cozy and very snug. His hands moved up and down my back, while all I could do was cling to him. My breasts squashed against his chest. His erection pressed against my belly. But he didn't try to cop a feel. He didn't do anything you couldn't see in a G-rated movie. Only his mouth moved on mine.

I lost myself. I let the delight of Tripp's kisses sweep me out of Cooperstown, out of my body, out of the guilt, and out of the shame and the uncertainty that had plagued me my whole life. Nothing else existed except Tripp's tongue, his lips, his taste and scent.

"You are amazing," he whispered, taking a break from the action. "You're so unassuming. So genuine. I love kissing you. I love your muddy red dress, your sprained ankle, and your sexy red toenails."

He rubbed his nose against mine. My lips felt swollen. Although he'd shaved only a few hours earlier, the scruff on his face had chafed mine.

"Do you have any idea how often I've dreamed of having you here, grilling steaks, and spending a quiet evening just stargazing with you?" he asked. His whisper was still hoarse.

Well, since he'd just met me, I was willing to bet he hadn't dreamed about me all that much.

"You're real." He buried his face against my neck for a moment.

I didn't know about that either. Being real. I was firmly planted in my fantasy world.

His huge hands framed my face, and he kissed me again. He kissed each of my eyelids, the tip of my nose, my left cheek, and then the right.

"Amazing." His mouth covered mine.

My world lit up.

"What the hell is going on?"

The female voice was like ice water.

Tripp sat up. "Maura?"

Someone had turned on the deck lights. Probably the drop-dead gorgeous redhead, standing with her hands on her hips and glaring at us.

A taller, bulkier shadow emerged from the dark into the light. "You asked me to pick up Ms. St. John in Albany tonight. Last week."

It was Faboo.

"Fuck," Tripp said under his breath.

My thought echoed his.

Maura St. John.

Tripp Shaneybrook and Maura St. John, the supermodel turned actress. Who had tied with Angelina Jolie for most beautiful woman in the world two years running. Who stood in front of me perfectly coiffed and made up in cream linen blazer and capris with turquoise raw-silk shell, and strappy sandals.

Tripp positioned himself so that I wasn't in her direct line of vision. I still wore only his T-shirt, which had ridden up almost to indecency.

"I'm not into group sex, despite what you might have heard," Maura said. "So why did you invite me if you're...entertaining?" She sneered the last word.

Oh, I didn't like the sound of that at all.

"And here I thought you were going to propose this weekend." Maura St. John turned her back on us and let herself into the house. As if she belonged.

Tripp followed.

If he hadn't followed, things might have turned out differently, but he abandoned me on that chaise lounge on his deck the same way Baird had abandoned me in the restaurant. The way my father had abandoned me before I was even born.

Okay, maybe Tripp did very tersely tell me to stay put, but I am not a dog. There is an old Vietnam War movie with Jane Fonda and Jon Voigt, *Coming Home,* and Jane tells some soldier that a woman is like a dog: you need a license to prove ownership. That was pre-Women's Lib days for sure, but yeah, Tripp wasn't married to me. All I'd gotten from him were a couple of meals, a dress, a place to crash, a lot of words, and the most incredible kissing and sex I would ever have in my life.

At least that was all the stuff I tried to tell myself as I sat there nearly naked on his deck while one of the world's most beautiful women gave him what for on the other side of the glass wall.

Do not cry, I suggested to my eyes. I was so tense that I hurt, but if I relaxed at all, I knew I'd shatter. Grandma Judy always said, *"If it's too good to be true, it probably is."*

Yeah.

Faboo stood on the edge of the shadows. He was so big, he could have been threatening, but he'd been kind to me once.

"Faboo, could you drive me home? I'll pay you." I'd postdate a check. I figured if he could play chauffeur for Tripp's other women, he could do the same for me, only not on Tripp's ticket.

I was in a really bad spot. Both of my dresses and my underwear were in Tripp's laundry room, but I had my red sandals and my purse on the deck. I could leave.

Faboo didn't respond right away. I thought he might not have heard me.

"Where do you live?"

Okay, maybe he was tired. Albany to Cooperstown wasn't a real short drive, and Cooperstown was definitely off anyone's idea of the beaten path.

"Syracuse," I said.

Something flashed in his face. It might have been his teeth in a smile or the wireless phone receiver in his ear, but it was too dark to tell.

I swatted a mosquito on my calf.

"I live in Syracuse," he told me. "You can catch a ride home with me."

Finally. Something going my way. I was due. I was overdue.

"Can we leave now?" I asked. Even I heard the quaver in my voice. Men have a real aversion to crying women. I could have let go so very easily to try to manipulate him. But Faboo didn't deserve that.

He glanced through the glass window to where Tripp and Maura St. John were having a very intense conversation. "You're just going to sneak off on him?"

"I loathe scenes."

He thought about that for about two seconds, nodded, and said, "Let's go."

I pulled my purse from under the chaise lounge where I'd stashed it.

Pain lanced through my foot when I put my weight on it, but I figured it was only bothering me because the rest of me hurt so much, it magnified the physical stuff.

Faboo helped me off the deck and into his black SUV. I was grateful for the dark, because while Tripp's shirt covered me, it was far from decent.

Faboo didn't speak to me again until we got on the thruway in Herkimer. "Do you need to use the rest stop?"

"No, thanks." I replied. Only sheer willpower was holding me together at that point, and I didn't want to do anything that might crack my resolve not to get all emotional because Tripp's regular girlfriend had finally shown up. I'd seen pictures of Tripp and Maura St. John together on the covers of those tabloids lining supermarket checkouts. I just hadn't recognized him before, because Maura's stunning good looks weren't there to blind the eye to Tripp Shaneybrook's appeal.

After we passed the rest stop, Faboo decided to get chatty. "He's not such a bad guy."

"He's a great guy," I agreed. *Just not for the likes of me. I'm a drone. I can't even do an opera date right.*

"We played ball together for a lot of years."

"Yankees?" I asked.

"God, no." Faboo sneered. "We were with the Columbia Gems."

Greek. Pure Greek.

"Tripp's going into the Hall of Fame in a couple of years. Probably the first year of his eligibility. He's one of the best center fielders to ever play the game, right up there with Willie Mays, Mickey Mantle, and Joe DiMaggio."

I'd heard of a couple of those guys.

"He could sit back and be a retired baseball star, but he doesn't. He's got this organization, like Paul Newman, the salad dressing guy."

I'd never thought of Butch Cassidy as "the salad dressing guy."

"It's one of those not-for-profit groups. Camp Home Safe. It's baseball camp for kids who come from domestically violent homes. And not just boys, either, because girls live in abusive situations too. He spends all of induction weekend trying to get the retired players to donate so the kids won't have to pay. Some of the guys even volunteer to come and coach."

So Tripp was good with charity cases. Didn't I have firsthand proof of that?

"Ms. St. John, well, she heard about what Tripp was doing and offered to help. That's all."

"How stupid do you think I am, Faboo?"

"Hey." Faboo sounded nearly as offended as he had when I asked him if he'd played for the Yankees. "Not every professional athlete has a zipper problem. And how come people always blame the jocks when the Annies are the ones who flash their boobs at us, sneak into our hotel rooms, and in general don't behave like decent women?"

"Who's Annie?" I asked.

"Baseball groupie." I wanted to believe him about Tripp, but then even if Faboo were telling the truth, what difference did it make? Tripp Shaneybrook was a celebrity athlete who had women like Maura St. John taking numbers to be in his life. And then there was me, planning fantasy dates and falling flat on her face in the mud when opportunity presented itself.

Tripp belonged with Maura St. John, not me.

Faboo's cell phone rang.

Trepidation clutched at my heart, squeezing it until I thought I would pass out. "If that's Tripp—"

"I won't lie."

Faboo answered with his earpiece.

"Yeah, I got her," he said after a minute.

I couldn't hear anything, but I did notice Faboo wince in the green glow of the dashboard light.

"She asked me to drive her home, and since you seemed a little busy with Ms. St. John—"

I gripped the armrest and noticed the faint odor of skunk seeping into the cab of the SUV.

"You need to calm down," Faboo told Tripp. "And just you never mind where I'm taking her. If she wanted you to know where she lives, she'd have told you."

He disconnected the call.

I released a breath I hadn't known I was holding. "Thanks," I said.

"You need to call him back and tell him where you live," Faboo said. He tried to hand his phone to me, but I refused to take it. Maybe when I wasn't quite so...raw. In a decade or two.

We didn't speak again until I directed Faboo to the thruway exit closest to my house. Once we were off I-90, I told him how to get to my apartment. That was it. He didn't even walk me to my door—not that I expected him to or anything. I could see lights in the living room of my second-floor flat. I figured Caitlin was still there.

I thanked Faboo, climbed out of the SUV, nearly falling on my face as agony bolted up my ankle.

But I lived. That was me. Survivor.

Chapter Seven

I didn't like the look of my front door. It seemed off kilter, and the key didn't work right in the lock. I finally forced it open by leaning on it, only to discover the overhead lightbulb in the stairwell had burned out. I used the miniature flashlight on my key chain to illuminate my way to the top. I unlocked the upper door, only to be met by a shriek.

"It's me!" I called out, dodging a flying book. I did not need this kind of homecoming. "What's going on?"

"Chelsea!" Caitlin practically gasped my name. Only the dimmest of lamps lit the living room. "I thought it might be Spencer."

Everything in me stilled. "Did Spencer trash the downstairs door?"

Caitlin nodded. That's when I saw her face.

"Oh my God, Caitlin. Did he do this to you?"

Both of her eyes were blackened. Her right cheek was as swollen as my ankle. Bruises circled her neck, and what was left of her hair looked stretched, like snags in cheap polyester fabric.

"You bailed him out after he did this?" I snapped on the overhead light. Foggy meowed and wove figure eights between my ankles. The twenty-pound cat knew how to make his presence known. He knocked me into the little table where I kept my keys and purse, jabbing my thigh into a sharp corner. I scooped him up for a cuddle. I needed his unconditional affection.

Caitlin nodded. "I'm afraid you lost the bail money, because as soon as he got out, he came over here looking for me. He's back in jail for the time being."

If Spencer was back in jail, why was she still in my apartment? I mean, I love Caitlin and all that, but I really wanted to be alone and lick my wounds. I didn't want her problems. Not that night.

"You need to put that lard-ass cat on a diet," Caitlin said. She didn't like Foggy, and the feeling was mutual.

"Shut up," I said. The last thing I needed was someone maligning my kitty. Especially an expensive cat sitter.

All my credit cards—maxed. My checking account—empty. And then Spencer had to go after Caitlin again. I'd be paying interest on Caitlin's marriage for the rest of my life.

Spencer's family should have been paying, not me. Maybe his mother didn't like Caitlin, but she couldn't possibly condone what he'd done.

I limped to Grandma Judy's bentwood rocker and sank into its welcoming embrace. Foggy gave my cheek a kitty kiss.

"What happened to you?" Caitlin asked.

"Baird abandoned me," I told her. It was my turn for family sympathy. Her dilemma was old news—same story, new chapter. "And he's gay."

Caitlin perched on the peach-colored sofa, never leaning back, never getting comfortable, and always ready to flee. "Gay? You're kidding."

I shook my head. "The owner of the restaurant was nice enough to take me in," I said. "It was induction weekend to the Baseball Hall of Fame, so there wasn't a hotel room to be had." *Even if you hadn't maxed out my credit cards to spring your worthless husband out of jail.* "And I couldn't get a bus or limo or anything."

Caitlin's eyes narrowed. "So you landed on your feet like always. What else is new?"

"I sprained my ankle."

Foggy wound himself into a ball for a snooze on my lap.

Caitlin finally seemed to realize I wore only an outsize T-shirt and red sandals. "What happened to your clothes? Knowing you, you had a costume for this date."

"It's too complicated, and I'm exhausted." I didn't want to share my humiliation. I just wanted my bed. "I assume you're camped out in the guest room," I said.

Caitlin shook her head. "The air conditioner is in your room."

Great. Just flipping terrific.

My apartment, my bed, my air conditioner, and my turn. Her house had central air. If Spencer was in jail, then her place was perfectly safe.

I said as much to her.

Her eyes grew wide, and she shook her head. "Spencer's friends...they've already called my cell phone. Three times tonight. Not a word, but I can hear them breathing. They don't know where you live."

She had to be kidding. Spencer's cousin was my landlord. But Caitlin always had problems with long-range vision.

"Then don't answer your phone when the caller is a number you don't recognize. You should be at Vera House, not here." It was the local shelter for battered women. "Until then, you're moving into the guest room."

"But I'm hurt," Caitlin said, her annoying whine creeping into her tone.

"So am I." I extended my foot so she could see the swelling in my ankle and the bruises swirling across my foot and up my calf. The bruise on the side of my knee where I'd hit the gear stick in Tripp's SUV punctuated the sprained ankle.

"Oh." She didn't look impressed, and to be truthful, her face looked a lot worse than my foot and leg.

But the bedroom with the air conditioner was mine. Period.

She could stay with me. I understood why she might not want to be alone in her house, especially if Spencer's cronies were on the prowl, which was why she should have gone to the shelter. Or to her mother-in-law. Spencer's gang wouldn't harass Caitlin there.

In the end, her need to stay alive superseded my need for a solitary sob fest.

I hoisted my pet and retreated.

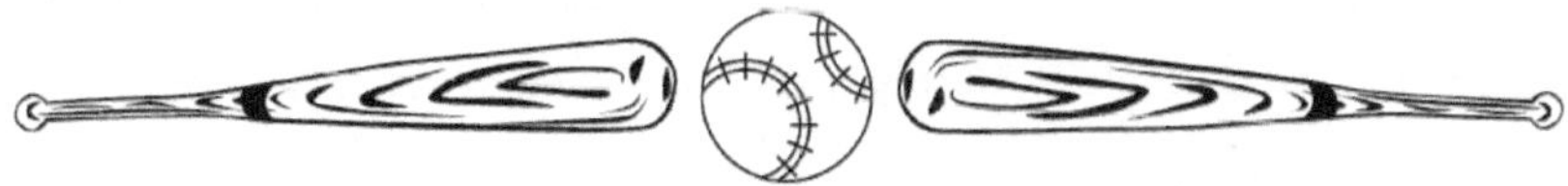

My sprained ankle was the subject of many oohs and aahs at the office. My boss, Jeanie Wexler, asked if I'd enjoyed the opera, and I gave her some sort of vague, noncommittal response.

I'd slept like crap but figured the fastest way to get over myself was to resume my boring life. So I put on a black linen suit, a pair of high, strappy black sandals, dug some change from my change jar, and hopped on a bus. I had a car, but I worked downtown, where parking was expensive and a hassle.

The Genevieve Hart-Darling Foundation kept a suite of offices on the sixth floor of an old building smack in the center of downtown. The rooms were tiny and oddly shaped, but the views were great.

I sat at my overburdened desk and shuffled the papers. Part of my job was to do an initial evaluation on grant requests and pass along likely candidates to Jeanie. Only two other people worked with me—Jeanie and a receptionist. I propped my sprained ankle on a banker's box of rejected applications and got to work reading. I was not in the mood to be social, but Haley, the receptionist—the very young receptionist—was in a chatty mood. I wished I had an office of my own, instead of shared space with a blabbermouth.

I tried to concentrate. I frequently wore earbuds and listened to music while reading, because Haley drove me crazy, but had forgotten to put them in my bag that morning.

"The Genevieve Hart-Darling Foundation," she chirped when the phone rang. "Let me see if she's available. One moment please." Haley punched the Hold button. "Are you available, Chelsea?"

It had taken months for her to learn not to say, "Sure, just a sec," to callers.

I nodded. No one I knew would be calling me on my work phone. My freshly recharged cell phone was on my desk. I could handle a business call.

I picked up the phone and punched the button for that line. "Chelsea Lyndon," I said to the dial tone. Haley must have disconnected the caller instead of pressing the hold button. Typical.

Midmorning, I came across an application—I was working on requests we'd received three to six months earlier—for Camp Home Safe. My heart seized for a minute, and I thought I was going to black out. I gulped in air and then skimmed the application. Yes, it was Tripp's charity camp. What were the odds of me finding that particular application in my pile on that particular day? The Coincidence Fairies must have been working overtime.

I grabbed the paperwork and hobbled into Jeanie's private office. I was going to be a professional if it killed me.

"I can't evaluate this application," I said, gripping the papers so tightly with sweaty palms that I wrinkled them. "I wouldn't be objective."

Jeanie seemed surprised but took the application from me. "Do you have some sort of personal connection?"

I nodded, willing the tears floating in my eyes to stay put. *No crying in baseball.* Or something like that.

"Thank you for your honesty," Jeanie replied. "Is everything all right with you?"

I so totally did not get into my personal life at the office. I mean, Jeanie and Haley knew I'd gone on an opera date to Cooperstown on Saturday. And they knew I had a cousin who had some personal problems. But that was all they knew. I didn't work for a social life or the free T-shirts Haley seemed to collect.

"I'm fine," I lied. I stretched my lips into a semblance of a smile and limped back to my desk to suffer out the rest of the workday.

At five o'clock, I waited until Haley left and then called a farewell to Jeanie. The delay garnered me an elevator to myself. I walked through the air-conditioned lobby and through the front door.

Tripp Shaneybrook, bigger than life, golden as a heathen idol, and muscled in diamonds, leaned against the fender of a black German-made luxury sedan illegally parked in the bus-stop zone. He looked great in a butter-yellow shirt with the long sleeves rolled to his elbows. Reddish curls peeped from the vee of his open collar. Navy Dockers completed the classy casual look. The late-afternoon sun glinted off his blond hair.

He straightened and uncrossed his arms as soon as he saw me.

My mouth went dry. My lungs hurt. My erogenous zones perked up and started begging. Fleeing in the opposite direction wouldn't work.

"How did you find me?" I'd never told him the name of the foundation for which I worked or even where I lived.

"Why did you run away?" he asked. His tone was bleak, and his honey-colored eyes were distant.

"Three's a crowd," I replied. "How did you find me?"

"You used my phone to call in sick yesterday. Why did you leave?"

"I came home."

"Yeah, well, I gave Faboo hell for that."

"He was going my way."

"Have dinner with me. Please."

I didn't know what to say. Tripp had certainly come after me quickly enough, even though that hadn't been my plan. I hadn't even told him where I lived.

"Is Maura St. John waiting for you at home?" Deal breaker.

Tripp grimaced. "No." His voice was a low growl.

I thought about all the reasons why Tripp and I weren't suited and about all the reasons I shouldn't trust my heart to him.

"Please, Chelsea. Give me a chance to explain."

Perspiration trickled down my ribs and spine like parades of insects. Okay, I owed him that opportunity. Not that an explanation would change anything.

He opened the passenger door of the car for me.

"Where's your SUV?" I asked.

"Cooperstown," he replied. "I do have more than one vehicle."

Oh. So he could have let me drive the sedan home the night he'd almost killed us.

A moment later, he slid into the cool interior next to me. The supple leather on the seats smelled fantastic, and was as smooth and rich as extra-virgin olive oil.

"Will your car be all right?" He was all politeness.

"I took the bus to work."

He signaled and then pulled into traffic, cutting off the bus whose stop he'd preempted. "Did you want to go home and freshen up or anything before dinner? There's plenty of time."

"What? I don't meet your standards?" I said before I thought. The only thing in my head at that moment was the memory of Maura St. John, who had been fresh and lovely even after traveling several hours.

Tripp seemed startled. "Is this about Maura?" he asked. He sounded tentative. "Because I owe you an explanation."

"You don't owe me anything," I lied. My heart was breaking all over again.

"I damn near fired Faboo for driving you home."

"Where else was I supposed to get a ride? Craigslist?"

"You were supposed to wait for me."

"While you were boinking your girlfriend? No, thanks. I have more respect for myself than that." At least, I tried to.

Why, oh, why did my imminent tears have to show up in my voice? I would never be one of those cool, collected, in-control women. I was too...frayed. "Turn right at this light," I said.

"I wasn't *boinking* Maura," he said. Now he sounded peeved.

Well, good.

"And she's not my girlfriend. You are."

"You forgot to tell her," I pointed out to him. *And me.* "Turn left at the next light."

He slid the car into the left lane and made the turn.

Why was I directing him to my house? The last thing in the world I wanted was for him to meet Caitlin.

"Where are we going?" he asked.

"I don't know," I grumbled. "There's an Irish pub not too far from here."

Except I didn't want a drink. I wanted peanut butter cup sundae ice cream. A half gallon. And a spoon.

"I know of a place," Tripp said. "It'll be quiet enough because it's still early."

"You know of a place? In Syracuse?"

"Yeah. I do stuff for the Saltboilers," he said.

"Who?"

"The baseball team."

Oh. Yeah. Syracuse has a minor league baseball team.

"Why?" I asked him.

"Because they're the Triple-A affiliate of the team I retired from, and they pay me to do stuff sometimes."

"Isn't that convenient."

He sighed. "You're really upset."

Upset? Upset? I was freaking devastated.

"Just tired."

I guess I was better at lying than I'd thought. I sure was feeding him line after line. Maybe this wasn't a good time to see him again. Not even twenty-four hours had passed since Maura St. John showed up on his deck. I was still aching, and even worse, I was still baffled as to why seeing them together had hurt so much.

Which was nuts. Completely and totally insane. I'd known the man a little over three days. The agony in my heart was disproportionate.

I couldn't help but wonder if it wasn't a sign. Then I convinced myself I was being ridiculous. Omens, signs, portends—they didn't exist in the real world.

"Yeah, I'm upset," I said, breaking the silence. "I'm tired of guys thinking they can use me. How are you any better than Baird McKechnie?"

"Ouch," Tripp said. "That was below the belt."

"Since you brought it up." I couldn't believe how bitter I sounded and how bitter I felt. "At least Baird never pretended—"

Tripp slammed on the brakes, stopping in the middle of a busy street in the middle of rush hour. "What the *fuck* do you mean by that?"

I'd heard Tripp drop the *f*-bomb before, when in the middle of the act, but I'd never heard him use it to express anger before. At least not to me. I guess I'd infuriated him.

Good. Why should I be alone in my misery?

He slammed the car into park. The honking horns of the drivers behind him didn't seem to faze him.

At least I had his undivided attention.

"If you're going to throw something like that out there, you'd better be able to back it up."

No problem. Whatsoever. "Baird never kissed me, never got me out of a single piece of clothing, and never...used me." Well, except to tick off Tripp's brother.

"Thanks a lot."

Yep. He was annoyed. Furious.

"You're welcome." He didn't hold the monopoly on sarcasm. "Move the car before someone rear-ends you."

He shot me a filthy look but slipped the transmission into drive and inched slowly ahead. At the first curbside opening, he parked.

I was in for it now.

Attack. Wasn't the best defense supposed to be a good offense?

"I'm sorry," Tripp said, taking me completely by surprise. His knuckles were white on the steering wheel. "I am so, so sorry that you got caught in the crossfire of whatever kinkiness my brother and Baird have going on, and I am even sorrier about Maura."

I blinked back some pretty persistent tears. He hadn't been too specific about Maura. I might have been an emotional basket case, but I was still astute enough to pick up on that.

"I never planned to ask Maura to marry me," he continued, when I didn't even sniffle in response. "I don't know where she got that idea."

I wanted to believe. Really, I did.

"Right now, all I want to do is kiss you. I really like kissing you."

"Ditto," I croaked. Stupid emotion clogged my throat.

"Then can't we go somewhere and kiss and make up?"

"My cousin is at my apartment," I said.

"Look at me, honey," he said.

I turned to face him.

"You're the only woman I've ever come after. You're the only woman I've ever wanted to make babies with."

Babies. Just what I didn't want to think about.

I thought I saw raw pain in his honey-colored eyes—a misery reflecting my own mood of the past twenty-four hours or so.

"It's too soon," I whispered. How could he know what he wanted with me? We'd just met.

"You just keep on telling yourself that, honey," he said. "You just keep telling yourself that it's too soon when you're hurting as bad as I am about what happened last night."

I had a rational explanation. "No one likes being used or being made a fool of." I spoke in a low voice, even though I wanted to shriek.

He sighed and then nodded. "I'd completely forgotten Maura had invited herself to Cooperstown. She claims she wants to help raise funds, but she wasn't there for induction weekend, now, was she? In fact, she was in Saratoga for opening weekend of the races. And you know what? I don't care. I didn't even care enough to go to Albany and pick her up myself."

Interesting.

"What do I have to do? Get down on my knees at the final game of the World Series and declare myself in front of millions of fans? Because if that's what you want, then that's what I'll do."

"Can't we just get to know each other?"

It didn't seem like a lot for me to ask. The three days of Cooperstown seemed as if they'd happened to someone else, like a movie.

His thumbs thumped the steering wheel. "Okay," he said. "On one condition."

"What?" I asked.

He lifted my clenched fist off my lap—my left hand—and massaged open my fingers. Then he slipped an enormous diamond solitaire ring over the knuckles of my ring finger. If the sun hit that stone just right, I could knock satellites out of orbit.

"If you don't like it, we'll get you another one," he said. "But I want you wearing my ring."

I wished I could have felt as if I was a fire hydrant newly anointed by a dog, but I couldn't. He was marking me as his territory, and it felt really good. Warm and fuzzy.

He must have noticed that the jewelry I'd worn in Cooperstown was silver. The diamond solitaire was set in white metal, and that pleased me to no end.

"Okay," I said, wanting to stare into the depths of the stone, but Tripp held on to my hand. Wearing his ring didn't mean permanent. Another Mama lesson.

"Can we seal this with a kiss?" He sounded plaintive.

"Okay," I said and leaned toward him.

Then I lost track of time and place—all that stuff, except for the console separating us. Stupid bucket seats.

Someone knocked on the passenger window, startling the daylights out of me.

"Get a hotel room!" a teenage punk with multiple face piercings and tattoos yelled. His cronies howled with laughter. They sauntered off down the sidewalk before I could gather enough wits to be frightened by them.

"He's right," Tripp muttered. He glanced at the dashboard clock. Then he looked at me. "You're a little overdressed, but that's okay."

He put the transmission in drive, checked his side mirror, and eased back onto the street.

Most of the traffic was gone now. Rush hour was not a big deal in Syracuse.

"Where are we going?" I asked.

"Our first date."

Chapter Eight

I'd never been to Saltboiler Stadium before. I barely knew there was baseball in Syracuse. My ignorance was about to change.

Tripp bought our tickets and then led me up the steep stairs into the stadium. My ankle protested with every step.

"Want a hot dog?" he asked.

"Sure," I said. While we were on line for our food, several people wearing staff badges greeted Tripp by name. Then an older man approached, a fan judging by his hat and T-shirt. He, too, greeted Tripp by name, held out a baseball card, and asked for Tripp's autograph. It was just like what had happened at the Cooperstown health center.

"My rookie card," Tripp said. He sounded happy.

Dear heavens, I was with a man whose picture had been given away with bubble gum.

We took our seats in the first row behind what Tripp told me was the visitor's dugout along the first base line.

We barely made it for the singing of the national anthem by someone of whom I'd never heard, and probably never would, unless she made it to the reject episode of some reality TV talent show.

Tripp explained the basics of the game to me while I ate my hot dog and drank my lemonade. I remembered some of the stuff from gym class in school, but apparently there were all sorts of nuances I was missing. Like ducking when a foul ball headed right straight toward me and people yelled, "Heads up!" Fortunately, my date had great hands and caught it without exerting himself. Then he turned and gave the ball to one of the kids sitting behind us. The fans in the stadium cheered. What was that about?

In the meantime, four ushers, two security guards, and several other staffers descended on me to make sure I was okay. I was fine. I was more than fine. I was with Tripp.

We held hands while he explained things to me. I couldn't remember the last time I'd held hands with anyone. It was incredibly...sexy. Tripp's hand wasn't like clasping a dead fish, the way I remembered hand holding from school. His thumb caressed my palm, massaged my fingers, and in general, was very erotic. I was getting really turned on.

A couple of fans asked for his autograph, and he was always nice to them.

At the end of the fourth inning, Tripp directed my attention to the scoreboard, where fans were being welcomed and were being wished happy birthday or anniversary. Then, in flashing lights for the whole stadium to see, *Chelsea, will you marry me? Tripp.*

We showed up on the screen courtesy of the stadium cam.

The crowd went wild.

I was stunned. I didn't know what to think, what to say, what to do. He leaned down and kissed me, which only encouraged the crowd's applause.

"You accepted my ring," he said, his huge palm cupping my cheek.

Well, no. He'd put the ring on my finger. A little different.

I reminded myself that I wanted romance. Okay, a scoreboard proposal was a bit of a cliché, but Tripp was trying without me even asking. Mama would have jumped at the proposal.

And that alone was enough to make me hesitate. I wasn't even going to consider the lost-condom fiasco—the one where I might be pregnant.

I concentrated on the field, trying to figure out what was going on there, because baseball seemed easier than trying to untangle my emotions. The third baseman particularly bothered me. He kept adjusting his...cup. Every player on both teams periodically checked to make sure he still had his private parts, but the third baseman seemed really enamored with his own balls, and because of that, he missed a few baseballs hit his way.

"If a woman kept grabbing her boobs the way baseball players keep grabbing their crotches, she'd probably be assaulted and then accused of asking for it," I said in a low voice.

Tripp choked on his lemonade. "Athletic cups get really uncomfortable. And the boys shift around a lot."

"I put my girls in their cups, and they stay put," I replied.

I liked sitting in the fading sun, holding hands with the man I loved—and yeah, I knew I loved him. I was just terrified that he'd break my heart. A man like Tripp Shaneybrook with someone like me? It just didn't jibe.

At the bottom of the sixth, with the setting sun glaring in our eyes, the third baseman with the athletic cup problem was at bat. He swung at a pitch, and the bat flew from his hands.

"Heads up!" the crowd shouted.

Fortunately, Tripp is very good at catching flying objects. Being a baseball spectator was downright dangerous. If that bat had hit me in the head, I could have been killed.

"We'll get him to autograph it later," Tripp told me.

The batter had other ideas. He came over and gestured for Tripp to return the bat. The crowd booed. The ushers, the security guards, and administrative staff descended again.

Again I assured them I was fine, just shaken a little. Tripp returned the bat to the third baseman. I'd wanted that bat.

"I'll get you another," Tripp promised. "The guys at this level have to buy their own bats, and they're custom made. That was a new one—not even any pine tar on it. Not cheap. I don't blame him for wanting it back."

Budgeting was something I could understand. Especially this week.

There were interns wandering around the stands auctioning a "game-worn" jersey in a pretty pink with teal numbers and piping, and I thought I'd like it. Raffle tickets, however affordable, weren't in my budget for the next couple of weeks. If not for my change jar, I wouldn't have had bus fare that morning.

I didn't have a baseball game costume, and if I were going to be engaged to Tripp, I'd probably be going to a lot of games.

Tripp must have seen me eyeing the jersey. "Breast Cancer Awareness Night jersey," he said, explaining the pretty pink color. "If you want one, I'll get you one with my number on it."

Wow. He really had a thing about me and his shirts.

I loved standing and singing "Take Me Out to the Ball Game" during the seventh-inning stretch. I was having a wonderful time just being with Tripp.

I was a little warm in my suit, so I took off the blazer. My bright purple blouse stuck to my ribs. I was glad I hadn't worn panty hose that morning.

My cell phone rang between the seventh and eighth innings. The theme from *Gone with the Wind* meant the caller was Caitlin.

I'd forgotten about her for a couple of hours.

I answered her call, hoping I could be circumspect around Tripp.

"Where are you?" she asked.

"At a ball game," I replied.

"I was expecting you home hours ago." She sounded nervous.

I wasn't used to checking in with anyone. I lived alone and didn't need to. "I'm fine. How are you?"

"I think I'm going to go home," she said. "Spencer is still in jail, and my place has central air. It's *hot*."

"That's a great idea," I said, meaning every syllable.

"My cousin is going back to her place," I told Tripp after I'd ended the call.

His honey-colored eyes gleamed. "Really?" He said it soft and sexy, sending shivers skittering through me.

"Yeah," I said. "Her place has central air. I have only a window unit in my bedroom, and she doesn't like my guest room."

"No kidding." His thumb increased the speed with which it traced circles on my palm.

We saw his proposal on the scoreboard repeated at the bottom of the eighth inning and kissed again for the few fans who were left. After the game, Tripp went in search of management to find me a bat to replace the one he'd returned to the third baseman. I didn't want that one anyway. It probably had athletic cup cooties on it or something.

Then we had to wait while management congratulated me on our coming marriage.

It was all very surreal. I never said I'd marry him. Everyone—including Tripp and maybe me—assumed my answer was yes. I was flattered. But I wasn't convinced. I wouldn't be the first woman to confuse lust with some other lasting emotion.

We stayed so late that we couldn't leave through the regular entrance, so had to go out through the offices. Tripp clutched my elbow as we made our escape.

"So, are you going to invite me back to your place or make me drive back to Cooperstown tonight?"

Who knew in what kind of shape Caitlin had left my apartment. Her house was spotless. Spencer demanded nothing less. That morning I'd noticed she hadn't been as diligent at my place. I preferred my own messes.

"Come home with me," I whispered. If he wanted to marry me, then he was going to have to learn the real me. The girl with her hair down.

Okay, maybe he'd already seen that, muddy dress, bare feet, and furious. But everyone has an in-between reality. The person who came out when one was home alone, watching movies, or reading, and the public persona was abandoned.

When we reached my apartment, he parked behind my clunker.

"This is a clock store," he said.

"I live upstairs."

He took my house key from me. A real gentleman. "What happened to your front door?"

It was late. It was dark, and the streetlight didn't cast much glow on my front porch. I'd tried to convince the landlord to install motion-sensor lights, but he was too cheap.

"It looks as if someone tried to break in. Maybe we should call the cops."

"It's okay," I said.

"It looks recent. Too recent." He'd pulled out his phone.

"It's okay," I repeated. "We don't need to call the cops again. It's been taken care of."

A lot more information than I'd wanted to share with him.

He inserted the key into the lock and had to jiggle and maneuver to get it to work. "You need to have this fixed." He sounded worried. "Give me the bat."

"I'll call my landlord in the morning," I lied as I handed the bat to him.

Actually, I'd probably have to pay to have it fixed myself or wring the money from Caitlin, who had no money except mine. Which was why neither one of us had anything at the moment.

Tripp finally got the door unlocked and opened. I hit the light switch at the bottom of the stairs. Nothing happened. I'd forgotten the light was out. Now I really was going to have to call my landlord. There was no way I could change that overhead bulb myself.

"I don't like this," Tripp said in a low voice.

"It's okay. Really. The lightbulb is blown. That's all. There's a little flashlight on my key ring if that will make you feel better."

I retrieved my mail, remembering at the last second that I hadn't been home from work yet.

"Want to give me my keys?" I said. "There's another lock at the top of the stairs, and it's easier if you know what you're doing."

"I'm a pretty smart guy," he replied and brushed by me so he could precede me up the stairs.

"There's a landing about halfway up. Then turn right," I told him.

He'd turned on my flashlight and led the way just fine. I locked the downstairs door and followed him.

A moment later we were in my living room. A light-sensing night-light kept the room from being completely dark, and Foggy meowed as if he hadn't been fed in days instead of a few hours. Or maybe he was just lonely. Caitlin wasn't much of a cat person, and Foggy was a people cat. He loved conning them for food.

I hit the wall switch, and my shabby but comfortable living room sprang into view. Caitlin had left things fairly orderly.

Foggy performed his routine between Tripp's ankles.

"That's Foggy," I said. "Sometimes known as Fog Feet."

"Fog Feet?" Tripp sounded amused.

"There's a famous poem about fog coming in on little cat's feet. Someone forgot to tell this cat that cats are supposed to be silent and stealthy. Move around on fog feet."

Tripp laughed. I didn't know if he got the joke, but he laughed.

I dropped my purse and my mail on the table near the front door. Tripp placed my keys there too. "Want something to drink?" I offered.

The apartment was stifling. So hot and closed up. I didn't leave windows open during the day when I wasn't home or at night, when I was sleeping. Grandma Judy didn't raise any dummies. Well, except Caitlin sometimes.

Tripp shook his head and reached for me.

And going to him was okay. Better than okay, because he started kissing me again, and I was lost.

Several moments later, when we stopped to breathe, I mentioned the air conditioner in my bedroom. He snapped off the living room light and suggested I lead the way.

I felt bad about closing the door in Foggy's face—he usually slept with me—but I was greedy and wanted Tripp all to myself.

I didn't turn on a bedroom lamp but made my way to the window unit and snapped it on. It roared to life.

We undressed each other in the dark, the lack of light adding to the sensitivity of my hands as my fingers explored his magnificent body.

Mine, I thought as I realized that marriage to this man would mean permanent access to his body, making love with him every night until death separated us.

Yeah, I was a marriage-is-forever kind of girl.

When our clothes were puddled together on the floor, we fell onto the bed. His body gave off heat like a sauna. I wanted to show him how much I loved him, so I started kissing my way down his chest, teasing his nipples, and using my tongue to taste and tantalize him. But when I got close to my target, he stopped me.

"Don't." He caught my face between his palms.

"I want to," I said.

"I don't like that," he said.

What guy didn't like oral sex?

He pulled me up until we lay face-to-face. His kiss was achingly tender.

Every time I tried to reciprocate, he evaded the gesture, my hands, and my mouth. And when I was on my back with my legs splayed to accommodate him, he leaned down and whispered, "I love you, Chelsea. Forever." Then he filled me, completely, leaving no room for loneliness or pain or even doubt.

I'd forgotten to set my alarm clock and woke up seriously late. Fortunately, my baseball all-star drove me to work, so I was only a little late getting to the office.

"I'll pick you up tonight," he said as he put a phone earpiece in his ear. "I need to go to Cooperstown, but I'll be back by five."

There went my hope for an intimate lunch.

Haley noticed my diamond right away. A rock that big was hard to miss. She squealed like a stuck pig, insisted I show Jeanie, and wanted to hear the whole story.

I kept trying to tell them there was no story, but Haley Googled Tripp and found photos of him on the Internet. With Maura St. John.

Oh boy.

"Your fiancé used to date Maura St. John!" Haley shrieked.

Yeah. I knew that.

"Why would he dump her for you?"

That hurt. A lot. I still wasn't comfortable with the thought that I was engaged to a man whose existence I hadn't even known less than a week ago. It was really weird.

"Maybe if I'd met him first, he'd have dumped her for me instead of you," Haley continued.

The day dragged. Between wanting to throttle Haley even more than usual and needing to be with Tripp again, I had no patience for the endless hours. Reading proposals for a wide variety of people wanting Genevieve Hart-Darling Foundation money wasn't exactly scintillating. But they paid me pretty okay to do it, and generally, I didn't mind. Living vicariously was my middle name. Immersing myself in other people's needs made my own life seem a little less pathetic.

I waited until Haley went to lunch to call my landlord about the downstairs door and the stairwell lightbulb.

"I'm so glad you called," Tanner said, sarcasm dripping from every syllable. "Your check bounced."

"What?"

"What part of bounced check don't you understand?"

I have a great apartment but a jerk for a landlord. The only reason I had the apartment was because Tanner was Spencer's cousin, so when I moved to Syracuse from Akron to be near Caitlin, Spencer helped me procure the place.

"When did you try to cash it?" I asked, a sinking feeling in my stomach. If he'd held the check—

"Yesterday."

Damn it! He'd held the check. Which meant that when Caitlin emptied my checking account, she'd taken the rent money too. *Okay, take a deep breath,* I admonished myself.

"I think I might be the victim of identity theft," I lied. Sort of. I'd been careless with my passwords and had been financially wiped out, so that was kind of identity theft.

The only difference was I knew the culprit. Had trusted the offender. If Caitlin had only paid the ER, I wouldn't have been nearly as furious as I was. But to max out my credit cards to bail her lousy no-good, two-timing Neanderthal husband out of jail—where he deserved to be for the rest of his miserable, low life, well... I didn't know how much longer I could enable her. Now my rent check had turned to rubber.

I didn't know what to do.

"That's not my problem," Tanner replied.

"Indeed it's not," I agreed. "Let me get back to you." I hung up the phone before he could zing me again.

It wasn't as if my rent checks always bounced. This was the first time. I'd been in that apartment for three years. Caitlin was going to have to come up with the money. Even if she had to get it from her mother-in-law. I punched in her home phone number, knowing she wouldn't be at work, not looking the way she did. Yeah, she worked. But Spencer took her paycheck. He controlled the purse strings in that family. She was going to have to do something, like cough up my rent money. Now.

"Hello?" she said.

"You bounced my rent check." I tried really hard not to shriek at her, but I was shaking with anger.

"What are you talking about?" Caitlin asked.

"When you emptied out my checking account, you took my rent money. I need it back. Now."

"How was I supposed to know that was your rent money?"

What? She couldn't be serious.

"What did you think was in my checking account? Play money?"

"How was I supposed to know it was earmarked for your rent?"

"Because that's what people use their checking accounts for!" I yelled, completely losing it.

I took a deep, cleansing, and calming breath. "I need the money back. Now."

"Where am I supposed to get it?" Caitlin asked.

"You work. You have a paycheck. You owe me."

"You know Spencer takes my money."

"Spencer is in jail. Take it from your household account or something. Ask your mother-in-law. I don't care where or how you get it. Just get me my rent money back."

Haley chose that moment to return from lunch. I turned my back on her.

"His mother hates my guts. You know that. And Spencer will kill me if I use his debit card to pay you," Caitlin sniveled. "He even checks the grocery receipts to make sure I'm not skimming."

"I'll kill you if you don't. It's your money too."

"I thought I could count on you," she said, sounding cool and defensive, as if I'd done something really awful and hurtful to her. "I guess I know where I really stand with you."

And she hung up.

There had to be some kind of irony in this somewhere. In the meantime, I needed to find six hundred dollars and find it fast.

Chapter Nine

At five o'clock, I sang my good-byes to Jeanie and Haley. The elevator had never seemed so slow in all the years I'd worked in the building. I jostled my way through the lobby. July humidity body-slammed me as I left the air-conditioned space for the great outdoors. Waves of heat shimmered off the baking concrete like a graveyard filled with restless ghosts. Every pore in my skin wept.

It didn't matter. Tripp was waiting for me.

Except I didn't see him. Or his sedan. Or his SUV. Maybe he had yet another vehicle that he hadn't offered to let me drive home the night he nearly killed us by falling asleep at the wheel.

But no golden god leaned against any fender.

Okay, every parking spot, including the bus stop areas, was crammed bumper to bumper. The city could have made a fortune had a meter maid been making rounds.

Maybe Tripp had to drive around the block. I stood near the curb, hoping he would hurry. It was blasted hot out there, and I'd worn slacks to work in case he wanted to catch another ball game. My ankle hurt like the blazes too. I was thirsty but didn't have the dollar and change for a bottle of water from the vending machine. And I didn't have bus fare.

I cursed Caitlin for putting me in this predicament.

I checked my cell phone to see if I'd missed a call. Nope. It was only five fifteen. Cut him some slack, I reminded myself. He had to drive in from Cooperstown, and it was rush hour. Not everyone in the world was as anal about punctuality as I was.

I wanted to shrug off my blazer. Perspiration cavorted over my body like ant-farm Olympics. My hair clung to the back of my neck and stuck to the sides of my face.

The crowds around me gradually thinned. Vehicles abandoned their curbside posts. My sunglasses kept sliding down the slippery slope of my nose.

No Tripp.

I checked my cell phone again. I didn't have his number, or I would have tried calling him.

Six o'clock.

The seed of a lump lodged in my throat started expanding. Growing. Thrived until it encompassed my chest too. I should have known better.

This wasn't driving around the block looking for a parking spot. This wasn't stuck in traffic, not in Central New York in July, when construction season was as bad as snow when it came to snarling traffic.

Nope. He wasn't coming. I was left standing on the street corner in the middle of downtown Syracuse, without bus fare.

I blinked back imminent tears. *It could be worse*, I reminded myself. At least I was in Syracuse. I had resources, including my own two—make that one and a half—feet.

I tried calling Caitlin, but my call went to voice mail. She was probably still sulking about my earlier phone call. Haley and Jeanie both lived in the suburbs. Walking home would be quicker. It was only a couple of miles. I'd even done it once or twice, indulging in temporary health kicks. Of course, the weather hadn't been past ninety in the shade, I'd worn sneakers, and I didn't have a sprained ankle.

Six thirty.

Ninety minutes was more than a fair shot. Tripp wasn't coming.

I stared at the diamond weighing down my hand and wondered if it was some kind of restitution for what his brother had done to me. Talk about taking one's paranoia seriously.

No matter. But I didn't want to walk flashing that rock. It was practically an invitation to be mugged. My fingers were swollen from the heat, so I had to really yank at the ring to wrest it free. I tucked it into my otherwise empty wallet just in case it was genuine. Yeah, I even wondered about that.

I finally slipped off my blazer and shoved it into my purse.

Fortunately, it would be daylight for hours yet.

I started walking. After ten blocks or so, I realized I wouldn't be able to keep it up wearing my sandals. My ankle screamed. I tried calling Caitlin again, leaving another voice mail. I didn't apologize. She didn't deserve an apology, and she definitely owed me more than six hundred dollars' rent money. Certainly a favor or two. Like a ride. At the very least. I could count on one hand the number of times I'd asked her for anything since Grandma Judy died. Including my most recent favor of asking her to feed Foggy—and then that had turned into me doing her a favor by giving her sanctuary.

I plodded onward. My red shirt clung to my ribs. A dark vee of sweat delineated my cleavage. My white slacks chafed my thighs with each step. I slipped off my red sandals—the ones Tripp had bought me in Cooperstown—and jammed them into my purse with my blazer. At that point I didn't care if the white linen got dirty or not.

The sidewalk seared the soles of my feet. Every pebble felt like a needle, and I needed to watch for broken glass where I stepped instead of paying attention to my surroundings. Not good, but I didn't know what else to do.

It took me an hour to get home. I hadn't been mugged, I hadn't sliced open my feet, and I hadn't fallen and further injured myself. Not bad considering what an emotional basket case I was.

The downstairs door was still wonky. The stairwell light was still out. Apparently Tanner wasn't going to do a thing until he had his rent money. I opened the upstairs door, greeted Foggy, fed him, and then shed the remainder of my clothes on the way to the bathroom.

A cool shower was just the ticket.

Okay, I didn't just cry. I howled. I think I scared poor Foggy with the force of my sobs, but I couldn't stop. I let the cold water sluice over me, washing away the salty residue of perspiration and tears and snot and all those other lovely emissions.

I felt beaten up. Every muscle ached, especially my heart. That felt ripped. Shredded. I thought about trying to convince myself that I was better off without Tripp, that our whirlwind romance had once again proven Grandma Judy right. *"If it seems too good to be true, it probably is."*

Despite all my efforts, I was turning into my mother.

I wept until I was completely dehydrated and the water went from cool to arctic. I stumbled out of the shower, banged my arm on the door, grabbed my pearl-white satin robe from the back of the door, and wandered into the kitchen for a bottle of water from the fridge. I avoided all mirrors. I knew my eyes, nose, and cheeks were red and swollen. I had never been a pretty crier. Ugly was more like it, with huge gulping sobs, hiccups, and drool.

I opened the refrigerator door and learned Caitlin had cleaned me out of bottled water. The empties stood on the counter, waiting to be returned for the deposit.

"Maybe if there are enough empties, I can ride the bus to work tomorrow," I told Foggy.

He blinked.

I opened the freezer to grab some ice cubes for a glass of tap water and noticed Caitlin had eaten all of my frozen dinners and my emergency stash of peanut-butter-cup-sundae ice cream. Only half a loaf of frostbitten bread remained. She'd even finished off my jar of Nutella.

I would never forgive her.

It was so much easier to focus on how angry I was at her than it was to think about Tripp, at whom I should be furious. That would probably come later. The hurt there blocked out everything else.

Dusk had settled while I'd been sobbing in the shower. I flipped on my living room light and plopped onto the sofa.

What now? I thought as I stared at the bat Tripp had gotten for me the previous night. *Probably ought to put that away so I don't have to see it every time I walk through the living room.*

The doorbell rang, startling a squeak from me. Foggy's fur shot out in six different directions.

If that was Caitlin, I was going to take the baseball bat to her.

Then someone started pounding on the downstairs door.

What if Spencer was out of jail?

Fear gummed up in my throat.

I tiptoed to the door, grabbing the bat from where it was propped next to the table holding my keys and my purse.

"Chelsea!" The voice was muffled, but it didn't sound like Spencer. His voice always had an undercurrent of mean, even when he was being allegedly nice.

Bang, bang, bang. "Chelsea, open up."

It sounded like...Tripp?

My heart did a little backflip.

"Who's there?" I called down the stairwell.

"Tripp. Open the door."

I dropped the bat and hurried down the stairs. I stumbled on the landing and banged my forearm on the rail.

"Jesus Christ, you scared me," he said as he embraced me. I thought he would fracture my ribs. His mouth came down hard on mine as he moved us inside and slammed the door.

"God, I've been so worried about you," he said when he finally stopped kissing me.

I bit my bottom lip to keep from blurting out, *You should be.* I was angry. I turned and started up the stairs.

"You're limping worse than you were this morning," he said. "What happened?"

I didn't answer, still not trusting my temper to temper my words.

"Where have you been?" he asked once we were upstairs. "I've been sitting outside for an hour, waiting for you to come home."

"I was in the shower." My words came out in a croak. My throat was still raw from all the sobbing.

He tilted my face toward the light. "You've been crying."

He led me to the sofa and forced me to sit. He tried to pull me onto his lap, but I was having none of that. I had a right to be upset.

"I don't have your phone number," he said. "I know that sounds really stupid, but we never exchanged numbers."

I nodded. I'd discovered that myself. He was right. It did sound stupid.

He took my hand—my left hand—and squeezed it. "Remember the meeting with Johnny and Wade that I missed on Monday? Well, Johnny stayed in town, hoping to get in touch with me. I hate asking the guys for money, even for a good cause like Camp Home Safe, but there you have it. I couldn't turn down Johnny after he'd stayed an extra day just to meet with me. I mean, these guys get hit up for money all the time.

"Anyway, Johnny wanted to do some fishing, and by the time I discovered there was no cell service in the middle of the lake, it was too late. I tried calling you at work as soon as I got a signal, but it was after five. So I tried calling your cousin—the one you called to look after your cat—and I have to tell you, she is not a nice person. She refused to give me your phone number, saying she didn't know me from Adam, which I respect, but then she refused to call you herself and give you a message for me."

So much for Caitlin not answering calls when she didn't recognize the number. My number was different. She was ignoring my calls just fine.

I closed my eyes. I'd always known Caitlin was petty, but to refuse to call me to give me a message smacked of fifth-grade antics.

"I'm so sorry." I felt his breath on my face. He kissed each closed eye. "Please don't cry."

"I walked home," I said.

He winced. "I'm so sorry. I got here as fast as I could." He rubbed my bare finger. "Where's your ring?

"I took it off, so I wouldn't be mugged."

"Oh Jesus." He pulled me close. "Was it bad?"

"It's not that far. You probably ran farther every day when you were still playing ball."

"But I was a professional athlete. And not on a sprained ankle. I am so, so sorry. I went to your office. I drove several routes looking for you. Why didn't you call a cab or your cousin or even take a bus?"

"Caitlin wasn't answering her phone," I replied. I sniffled.

"Oh, honey." He kissed my lips, so gentle, so tender. "Where's your phone? We're exchanging numbers right now."

I gestured at my purse on the table next to the door. He released me and went to fetch it.

My chest ached. I hated that I had doubted him. But then again, tell that to the blisters on my feet.

He programmed his number into my phone, then checked my number and punched it into his phone. When he was done, he placed both devices on the coffee table and reached for me again.

His thumbs rubbed my cheeks. "You cried because you thought I'd pulled a Baird on you." His voice was full of wonder. "Oh, God, somehow I will make this up to you. Have you eaten yet?"

Uh-oh. I was the hostess here, and I was broke. The most I could offer him was tap water and cat food.

I shook my head.

"Are you up to going out for a burger or something?"

I shook my head again. I couldn't face putting on another bra or slipping my feet into another pair of sandals. I couldn't face my face in a mirror.

"How about we order in a pizza?"

"Are you buying?" I tried to inject a teasing tone, but it fell flat.

"Of course." He looked worried.

"I don't have anything to drink," I said. "Haven't had a chance to hit the grocery store."

Well, it was true. I hadn't. Even if I'd had money or a usable credit card.

"We can get some pop with the pizza."

"The phone number is on a magnet on my fridge." I didn't even have the strength to walk to the kitchen and get the number for him.

He made the call, went downstairs to get the food, and paid. I finally roused myself enough to put paper plates and napkins on the dinette table.

I loved my dinette. A large poster of Janet Fish's *Spring Party* that I'd bought from a Boston Museum of Fine Arts catalog when I was a teenager dominated the room. I'd decorated the small space in colors pulled from the poster. Vividly hued place mats from an import store and colored pressed glass and Fiestaware I'd picked up at yard sales and flea markets over the years. It was a happy, cheerful room, even at night.

Foggy begged for pizza, but I ignored him.

"You're awfully quiet," Tripp said after devouring his second greasy slice. "Are you still upset with me?"

"I had a bad day."

That was a freaking understatement.

"And I didn't help it."

I didn't respond. I was angrier at Caitlin than I was at Tripp. I didn't know what to do about my landlord. Asking Tripp for the missing rent money was out of the question. This wasn't his problem; it was mine. And hadn't he just finished telling me pro athletes get hit up for money all the time? Well, I was one person who wasn't going to be hitting him up for anything.

I nibbled on the end of my slice, and my stomach knotted. Which was weird. Maybe if I had chips and dip...

"Are you okay?" Tripp's tone was sharp.

I swallowed the speck of pizza and nodded.

"You just turned real pale." He eyed me like a scientist examining something under a microscope.

"I'm not a hundred percent," I said. Heck, I wasn't even 50 percent.

"You think you might be pregnant?" he asked.

I wanted to forget about that. "I'm not pregnant."

"Are you sure? Have you gotten your period?"

Heat burst into my cheeks. I didn't care if it was the twenty-first century. There are some things I wouldn't discuss with men, and my menstrual cycle was right up at the top of my list.

"Not yet," I muttered.

"Then you don't know." He sounded so solemn. Concern clouded his caramel eyes.

"I know it's a really wrong reason to get married." All I had to do was think about Caitlin and Spencer. Mom and the sperm donor I'd never known. And the father she'd never known. Bad marriages were in my genes, especially when the bride was knocked up.

"What are you talking about?" He sounded peeved. "No kid of mine is going to be a bastard."

Wow. That simple statement explained a lot.

"Love child." I wasn't going to lie about my heritage. Just because the love part wasn't exactly true didn't make me a lesser person. "Grandma Judy called us love children."

He waved me off. "That's not what I meant. I meant fatherless."

"Fine," I said.

"And if you're not pregnant now, I can take care of that." He grinned at me, but it seemed a little strained. He must have realized he'd practically said the only reason he wanted to marry me was because I might be pregnant. "No problem."

"Do you have any children?"

He seemed taken aback by my question. His brow lowered. "None that I know of," he admitted. "Listen, I wasn't a saint all those years I played ball. But I've never been careless."

I nodded. I knew he was...experienced.

"But I've always wanted to be a dad. At least two kids. Maybe three. What do you say?"

How nice of him to include me, especially since he planned to use me as the incubator. He was retired. He could deal with them.

Then it struck me. Marriage to Tripp Shaneybrook meant I probably wouldn't need to work. I could be the full-time cookie-baking mom of my fantasies. The mom I'd never had.

Oh, I was too tired and too drained to think about any of this. We'd stayed up way past my usual bedtime last night, I'd gotten in more exercise by walking home than I'd had in the past year, and I was emotionally battered. I just wanted my bed.

"Let's set a date," Tripp said. "What kind of wedding do you want? That's going to be what determines the date."

I'd planned my fairy-tale wedding so many times—I had a file somewhere. Me in an amazing gown, carrying white roses, Caitlin as my matron of honor, and the reception looking like either the *Spring Party* poster in my dinette or the reception in *Mamma Mia*, right down to being held on a Greek island.

Tripp probably could afford that. I couldn't.

"What kind of wedding do you want?" I asked.

"One that makes me your husband forever. Other than that, it's your day."

"Yours too." I followed up with a quote from the priest in *The Princess Bride*, but it seemed to go over Tripp's head.

He helped himself to another slice of pizza. "I don't care about getting married. It's being married that matters."

Whoever said jocks were shallow never met Tripp.

If I married him, every day of the rest of my life was going to be a fantasy come true. Did I need the pomp and the party? Nope. Not a minute of it.

"Something small, then," I said. Then I remembered the man had baseball teams in his past. "Do you have a lot of people to invite?"

"Just my brother," he said. "The only time the rest of my family—cousins and all that—contact me is when they want something. How about you?"

"Just Caitlin," I said. "We grew up together. Promised each other we'd stand up for each other in our weddings."

Tripp made a face. He wasn't a Caitlin fan, and I didn't blame him.

"Maybe Baird could give me away," I said, trying to infuse some humor.

Tripp finished off the last slice of pizza. "He already did. His loss, my gain. How are you going to handle being his sister-in-law?"

I shrugged. "I've already told you, there wasn't anything between us."

"Just checking." He eyed my plate, where grease congealed like an extra layer of cheese on the top of my pizza, and the only sign that I'd tried to eat was a bit of fraying at the very tip. "Aren't you eating?"

"Not hungry. Too tired." I was *never* not hungry.

He covered my curled hand with his own huge warm one. "You're like ice. That can't be good. Why don't you go on to bed? I'll clean up here."

I wanted to argue, but I couldn't keep my eyes open. "Thanks," I said.

I didn't bother with a nightgown. When he finally came to bed, the first thing he did was rub some kind of lotion on my poor abused feet. It was so sensuous, I moaned.

He slid under the sheet with me and curled around me. I'd turned on the air conditioner for him, because despite the record-tying heat, I felt chilled through to my marrow. The warmth of his bare chest felt heavenly against my frosty back. He stroked my outer thigh in a purely nonsexual way, just petting me as he would Foggy. There was no mistaking his erection pressed against my backside, but he didn't try to do anything about it. He just held me, as if he knew I was confused and needed some time to figure out exactly what I was thinking and feeling.

"Sleep, honey," he murmured in my ear.

Chapter Ten

Tripp must have set my alarm clock, because the next thing I knew, it was buzzing. I didn't want to move. The room was just the right temperature for snuggling. Tripp's hand cupped my breast, thumb flicking an already taut nipple. I wondered if the erection nudging my backside was the same one from last night. He nuzzled the side of my neck, and I sighed.

"Can you take fast showers?" he whispered.

"Yeah." It came out more of a moan than a word.

"Oh, good."

His hand slid lower, as low as I wanted it to go. "Move your left leg forward," he instructed.

I did.

He thrust. The breath whooshed out of my lungs as he filled me. I groped for something to hold, something against which to brace myself. My headboard—swirling brass circles, just waiting for my curling fingers.

Oh God, I thought he'd already done everything he could to make me realize just how sexually innocent, inexperienced, and inept I was.

"Hold on." His breath was hot against my ear. One of his hands gripped my hip. The other burrowed between my thighs. Seeking. Seeking. Finding...

Bingo.

"You okay?" he asked me once I could breathe again. His heart pounded against my back. He was slick with perspiration and smelled faintly musky.

I nodded, not sure if I'd ever find my voice again. The clock indicated I was running late. Again. Except he'd drive me to work, so that would make up the time.

Outside the bedroom door, Foggy yowled for his breakfast.

I reached for my robe.

"What happened to your arm?" Tripp's tone was sharp.

I glanced at two new bruises. "I must have knocked against something. I think I fell on the stairs last night."

"How's your ankle? I don't suppose you'd call in sick again today."

I shook my head as I slipped the pearl-colored satin over my arms. I stood. My legs trembled and were barely able to support me.

"You could give notice," he said. "You do realize you won't have to work once we're married."

I glanced down at him, still sprawled across my bed. He'd crossed his arms over his head. Tufts of reddish hair sprouted from his armpits. His eyelids were droopy with sleep. His muscled chest looked formidable and comfortable. His shoulder scars were barely visible in the dim light. I wanted nothing more than to crawl back into bed and rest my head there.

"It occurred to me," I admitted. "But I like my job."

He just stared at me.

"If I marry you, it's not for your money," I said.

"If?" His brows rushed together in a scowl.

"Okay, when." *There.* I finally said I would marry him.

"What's wrong?" His voice was very soft.

"I'm off balance," I told him. "It feels too soon. I feel as if you're rushing me, and I don't trust what I feel for you."

Foggy threw himself against the door.

"I need to get moving." I turned my back on Tripp and went about my morning.

He joined me in the shower. "To save time," he claimed.

Yeah, right.

Then I was really running late. No time to dry my hair. Fortunately, I'm a wash-and-go kind of woman, so showing up at the office with wet hair wasn't a rarity.

Tripp watched me put on my makeup as he sipped a cup of coffee. He offered me a cup. But I declined. The man actually made coffee in my kitchen. He certainly was useful.

"I think we need to have a serious conversation," Tripp said. "You sure you have to go to work?"

I nodded.

"Then we'd better leave right now, or you're never going to make it."

I fielded a nasty call from Tanner as soon as I got into the office.

I called Caitlin before Tripp arrived to take me to lunch. She finally had the decency to answer my call.

"Why didn't you give me Tripp's message yesterday?" I asked.

"Who is Tripp, and why should I play secretary for you?" she countered. "After everything you said to me yesterday, you're lucky I answered the phone today."

I inhaled deeply and mentally counted to ten. "Because it was an important message."

"So who's this Tripp guy?"

I was afraid to tell her, afraid she would act as if she were as entitled to his assets as she was to mine. And that was something else I needed to do: change the passwords on my accounts and cancel her access to my credit cards.

"Look, Tanner is getting antsy about his rent money. You need to help me out here," I told her.

"It's not my fault your rent check bounced," she insisted.

"Yes, it is, and I can't afford to pay two month's rent when you've maxed out my credit cards on top of everything else."

"Tell Tanner to get the money from Spencer," she suggested.

"I don't think so, but you could," I countered.

"Tanner doesn't like me." She sounded sullen.

I understood where Tanner was coming from.

Tripp walked into the office then, bringing the sunshine with him.

"I have to go now," I said, using my most professional voice. "I'll speak with you later." I disconnected before she could say anything.

"Hi, honey," he said.

"I can't leave until Haley gets back."

"That's okay." He perched on the corner of my desk. "How's your morning going?"

"Okay." I smiled. "I'm a little tired, but I'll survive."

"You'll catch up on your sleep this weekend," he promised. "We'll go to the lake, okay?"

Oh my. I was entering a life where people went to the lake for the weekend.

"Sure," I said.

"If you want night life, there are things to do."

"Why would you think I want night life?" I asked. I really wanted to sit out on his deck and pick up where we'd left off on Monday. "I'm not a party girl, so if you're expecting arm-candy function from me, you're going to be disappointed."

He cupped my cheek. "I don't think you could ever disappoint me, and don't underestimate yourself. You are definitely arm candy."

He might have kissed me then, but Haley returned from lunch. I stood, slung my bag over my shoulder, and walked to the front of my desk.

"Hi, you two," she chirped. Her eyes went wide at his gorgeousness. She tossed her long blonde curls over her shoulder and smiled in a predatory way.

I wondered if she'd always worn her skirts that short and tight.

"Congratulations, Tripp. Nice rock." She gestured toward my hand.

"Thanks." Tripp sounded sincere, but the pressure of his hand on the small of my back told me he wanted out of there.

"See you in an hour," I said.

Tripp kissed me on the empty elevator. "Wanna go home for a quickie?" he asked.

I could barely walk as it was, and I didn't mean my ankle.

"Food," I said. I hadn't eaten in a long time, and I was more than a little light-headed.

We ducked into a cramped sandwich shop, where I ordered a chicken Caesar wrap, and Tripp chose a hamburger. We walked to a small triangle of a park and found an empty bench. The heat hadn't broken, but the spray from the fountain cooled us.

Tripp had just taken a bite of his burger when his phone buzzed.

I'm going to have to get used to constant interruptions, I told myself. Nothing would be sacred if I—when I—married a former baseball star. I hoped I'd be able to handle it without being too testy.

And that's when I knew I wanted to marry this man more than I'd ever wanted anything in my life.

"Hello?" He said. A deep vee formed between his eyes. "No, I think you have the wrong number." His caramel-colored gaze met mine as the tone of his voice grew cautious. "Yes, I know Chelsea Lyndon. Who wants to know?"

I inhaled sharply. Now what kind of game was Caitlin up to? I reached for the phone, but Tripp twisted away from me. The South in his voice thickened.

"Well, now, Caitlin, it seems I called you yesterday to give a message to Chelsea, and you didn't accommodate me. So I guess we didn't start out our relationship on a real good tone. I mean, since we're going to be family and all, maybe you should apologize to her."

I heard Caitlin's shriek from where I was sitting.

Tripp held the phone away from his ear, made a face, and then handed the unit to me.

"Caitlin," I said, "I hope you're feeling better really soon, because Tripp wants to get married right away. And you're going to stand up for me when I become Mrs. Tripp Shaneybrook. So you really need to take care of yourself and get over...that *flu*."

"What flu? Why didn't you tell me you were getting married? Chelsea! This is so exciting. We need to go dress shopping, book a church, a reception hall, and—"

"I can't talk about any of that right now." I interrupted her bubbling plans to spend more of my money. "Tripp and I are going out of town this weekend. Can you feed Foggy for me? And you need to rest so you'll look stunning in my wedding pictures. The flu always leaves you looking...battered."

"Oh." She finally caught on.

"But I promise I won't get married until you're feeling a hundred percent better. Talk to you later." I hit the End button and returned the phone to Tripp.

"She didn't sound sick to me," Tripp said. He took a big bite of his burger.

Eventually, he was going to have to know all about the sordid side of my life but not today.

"I think the news of our pending wedding perked her right up." I sounded like my great-grandmother. Good grief.

But listening to Caitlin rattle on was a real eye-opener.

"You know what you said last night about being married is more important than getting married?"

He nodded. His mouth was full.

"You're right," I blurted. "Caitlin was just spouting off about dresses and churches and reception halls, and I realized I don't want any of that."

The very thought was making me hyperventilate. In another minute, I'd have to stick my head between my knees to keep from passing out.

"Okay," he said. "I don't need any of that stuff. I just want to be married."

It was hard letting go of my *Mamma Mia* wedding dream, but then I'm no Meryl Streep.

"Small," I said, now wishing I didn't have to include Caitlin. "Private."

"Private is good," he agreed.

"Do you get hounded a lot by fans?"

He shrugged and gnawed off another bit of burger. "Not too much anymore. When I was playing and we were in the home city, then yeah, privacy could be an issue. It's calmed down since I retired."

"If you want something big and splashy, we can do that," I said, my stomach clenching at the thought. "For your image and all that."

Why hadn't I thought about this sooner? He was famous. His fans might have expectations.

Like Maura St. John. She was an expectation. Beautiful. Glamorous. Famous. Chelsea Lyndon was none of those things.

"The only image I gave a damn about is that of Tripp Shaneybrook, family man. Will you stop worrying? I'm old enough to know what I want."

My cell phone chose that moment to ring. Whatever happened to the day when a woman could go to lunch and be unfettered?

I glanced at the screen and recognized Tanner's number. I put the phone back in my purse.

"Aren't you going to answer that?" Tripp asked.

I shook my head. "It's my landlord. I'll call him later."

"You really need to get that door fixed."

"Will we be living there?" I asked, trying to deflect him.

The question startled him. "Of course not."

"Then what's the problem?" I bit into my wrap. Lettuce crunched. Dressing dribbled.

"You're living there right now. That's the problem. That door and the burned-out light aren't acceptable. Call him back."

"I'll call him later," I repeated. I really didn't want to get into the rubber rent check in front of Tripp, because that would lead to all sorts of awkwardness, which would eventually lead back to Caitlin and her situation. I had my pride.

He studied my face, as if looking for my motive. I chewed and grinned. Of course, my insides were shaking.

"Do you think your brother would cater the reception?" I blurted out, desperately needing to change the topic.

"Well, I'd like him to stand up for me, not cook," Tripp said.

"I meant his restaurant."

"I knew that." He wiped his hands on a napkin, wadded into a ball, and pitched it into a nearby trashcan. Two points.

My cell phone rang again. I ignored it.

Tripp didn't look happy, but short of reaching into my bag and snatching the phone, there wasn't much he could do.

"So what are we doing tonight?" I asked, a little too brightly, because his eyebrows arched. "Are the Saltboilers playing?"

"You want to go to a baseball game?" He sounded surprised.

"Sure." I figured there were going to be a lot of baseball games in my future, so I may as well figure out what it was all about sooner than later. Besides, it had been nice, just sitting there while holding Tripp's hand. I could forget about everything else going on.

"Okay," he said.

We held hands as we walked back to my office.

"I'll pick you up at five," he said, brushing a stray lock of hair off my cheek. "Honest."

"Can't wait," I said. And it was true.

"Where's your baseball player?" Haley asked as I entered the suite.

I ignored her. As soon as I got to my desk, I turned my chair so that my back was toward Haley and called Tanner.

"I don't have your money yet," I said in as low a voice as I could. "I'm working on it."

"Hey, Chelsea!" Tanner said. His tone was...different.

Every instinct I had sat up and shrieked, *Danger, Chelsea Lyndon, danger!*

"I read in the newspaper that Tripp Shaneybrook had proposed to someone at the baseball stadium the other night. What a surprise to hear it was you. I'm landlord to the celebrities."

Oh, fudge buckets. Caitlin. I definitely needed to have a come-to-Jesus with that girl.

I didn't say anything.

"In fact, I'm going to have to raise your rent."

"I have a lease," I replied through stiff lips.

"You bounced your rent check, which invalidates the lease," Tanner said. "Read the fine print."

"I didn't bounce the check," I whispered, my voice shaking. I had no idea if what he said was true or not. "You didn't cash it in a timely manner."

"Plus," he continued, quite leisurely, as if I hadn't spoken at all. "I'm going to have to charge you interest for every day you're late." He named an amount that made me gasp.

"That's usury. Take me to court, and see how far you get with that."

"And I hear my cousin isn't very happy with you either."

Everything inside me froze. I'd always thought Tanner knew Spencer was scum. Now I wasn't so sure. And frankly, Spencer scared me. A lot.

"Your rent money went toward bailing Spencer out of jail the last time he beat on Caitlin." My furious whisper shook. "And that's who tried to break down my apartment door, so maybe you ought to try getting the money to fix it out of him."

"Kind of hard to get money out of man who's in jail," Tanner replied. "It's a lot easier to get it from my tenant who's engaged to a future Baseball Hall of Famer. I mean, how much was Shaneybrook pulling down his last year? About ten mil is how I recall it."

Ten mil? As in million? Dollars? A year?

My thoughts squealed, although I did manage to swallow the one threatening to escape my throat.

I splayed my knees and thrust my head between them. The room still wouldn't stop spinning.

"This has nothing to do with Tripp," I said.

"Sure it does," Tanner replied. "Because it has to do with you. That's how it works, chickie. I want my rent money, and I want my interest. It's in *your* best interest to see that I get them both."

I hung up on him and then sat up way too quickly. Little white pinpoints of light danced around the office.

Haley was looking at me as if I'd sprouted a second head. I hoped she hadn't overheard any of my...negotiations with Tanner.

I never should have told Caitlin that I was getting married. Tripp and I should have gone to the courthouse on my lunch hour, gotten our license, and eloped over the weekend.

It wasn't too late. We could do that. Tomorrow. If I wasn't going to do the Greek island thing, eloping would work.

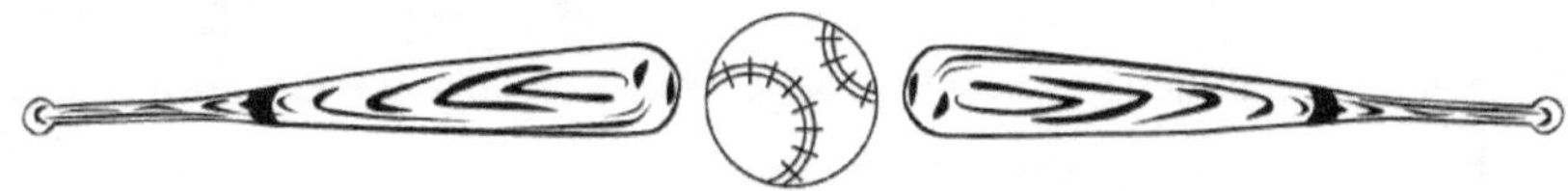

"What's wrong?"

It was the bottom of the first inning, I had my hot dog and lemonade, my feet were propped on the top of the visitor's dugout, and I was trying to figure out what was going on out on the field. It was a lot easier than thinking about Tanner, Spencer, and Caitlin.

How could a man who'd known me six days know me well enough to realize that something more was wrong? Most of the time I was with him, something was wrong. Besides me.

Ten million.

My brain couldn't wrap around that number, not as a salary. The Genevieve Hart-Darling Foundation dealt with big money all the time. But it was a foundation, an organization formed for philanthropic purposes. A business. Not a paycheck.

"Nothing," I said.

Ten million wasn't wrong. It was just...a lot. Not that it was my concern anyway. It was Tripp's money. *His* headache. I just needed to scrape together enough cash to make the bounced check good plus pay the next month's rent. At the inflated rate.

I shuddered and bit into my hot dog. I really wanted one of those helmet sundaes, thick with hot fudge, peanuts, and faux whipped cream. Guess that meant I was stressed.

"Don't tell me *nothing*." Tripp sounded peeved. "I can tell."

I took another bite of my dog and then chewed. And chewed. And chewed some more. The roll turned to sawdust in my mouth. I sipped some lemonade to help.

"Chelsea." He voice held a warning.

I swallowed. Checked my teeth with my tongue to make sure there was no residual roll goo clinging to them. Smiled at him. "Remember I told you my cousin was having some problems with her husband?"

He nodded.

I turned back to the field. I couldn't look him in the eye and...prevaricate. "She's still having problems."

"Is this the cousin with the flu?" he asked.

"Yeah."

"Is there anything I can do to help?" he asked.

I shook my head. "Caitlin knows what needs to be done."

Just like I knew I needed to get to the bank and revoke her access before my paycheck next week. Maybe tomorrow's lunch hour. Unless Tripp and I went to get our marriage license. I'd need to excavate my birth certificate from the bottom drawer of the file cabinet in my guest bedroom.

Tripp and I held hands as the Saltboilers beat the Rollers. It was late when we got back to my place. I still had to pack for the weekend.

"I need directions to your house," I said as I waited for him to unlock the downstairs door. "But not on the thruway. The back roads." I didn't have money for tolls. Then I wondered if I had enough gas in my car to make the drive.

"Why?" he said as he struggled with the lock. The door finally opened. The street lamp caught a white oblong shape on the floor of the entry. Tripp picked up an envelope and handed it to me. "I'll pick you up after work, just like always."

"I don't want to get stuck in a strange place without my own wheels," I said. I followed him up the stairs. The lightbulb still hadn't been changed. Damned Tanner.

Tripp dropped my keys on the table at the top of the stairs and then stooped to pet a vocal Foggy.

"That really hurts my feelings," Tripp said as he stood upright.

"I'm sorry." I rested my palms on his chest. Foggy circled my ankles, still voicing his feline woes. "I...need that, okay?"

Tripp shook his head. "No, it's not okay. It's insulting. You make me feel as if visiting me is being trapped and you need your secret escape route."

Well, that was a little dramatic but not far off what I was feeling.

"Humor me," I said.

"I'll give you a set of car keys when we get to my place."

The gas tank on my clunker was probably empty anyway.

"What's the envelope?"

I'd forgotten about it. Clearly, it wasn't regular mail, or it would have been in my mailbox. I opened the flap and slid out the single sheet of paper.

Tanner. Playing landlord.

I quickly read a basic summary of what he'd told me on the phone: my rent just doubled because the rubber check had broken my lease, and he was charging me a usurious amount of money of interest for each day he didn't have his money.

My head went light. I swallowed hard and refolded the letter.

"Is everything okay?" Tripp asked.

"Sure," I said.

"You're hiding something from me," he said. "What's going on?"

I wanted to tell him. I really did. But I didn't want him to think his ten million a year was why I was with him. His ten million a year had nothing to do with anything. At least on my part.

Tanner, maybe not.

"What's the letter?"

"From my landlord."

Some of the tension left his body. "Is he going to fix the door and replace the lightbulb this weekend?"

"Probably not."

"Then what?"

"He's raising the rent."

Tripp completely relaxed. "Not an issue. I mean, we're not living here once we're married."

"Right." And that was the truth. I liked my apartment but not that much.

"So when is your rent going up?"

Here was the tricky part.

I shrugged. "Does it matter? Aren't we getting married sooner than later?"

He lit up like a Christmas tree. "I'd love that! Hey, you want to get naked?"

"Hey, I need to pack."

"You'll be naked most of the weekend." He waggled his eyebrows, and I giggled. When was the last time I was relaxed enough to giggle with a man?

Apparently he realized it too, because he caught me close and kissed me.

"We're going to be okay, yes?" he asked.

I nodded. "We're going to be perfect."

So much for packing right away. Fortunately, I'd been planning a weekend at the edge of some body of water all my adult life. I knew exactly what I wanted to pack and knew exactly where it was.

When I finally got to sleep, it was almost two in the morning.

But it was worth it.

Chapter Eleven

The next day, Jeanie called me into her office after lunch. "Do you have any idea what you're going to do after you get married?" she asked.

I stared at her. "Um, Tripp wants to start a family."

Jeanie smiled. "I meant about working."

"Oh. Yes. I will probably give my notice." I couldn't see me commuting from Cooperstown in January. If we ended up living in Cooperstown. "Lots of notice," I assured her.

"Well, there might be a conflict-of-interest issue," she said.

"Oh. Because of the camp and fund-raising," I said, finally getting with the program. Dread filled my throat. "Do you want my notice now?"

I really hoped she'd say no. I loved my job.

"I don't want you to leave, but under the circumstances, it might be for the best."

Okay. I knew it wasn't personal. Jeanie had to do what was right for the foundation. That was her job. But it still hurt.

"Sure," I said. "Is two weeks okay?"

"Not really given the circumstances…"

Oh, how I hated the way she said that. *"Circumstances."* As if I'd embezzled some of old Genevieve's money or something.

"You have vacation time coming," Jeanie reminded me.

Ice water. She'd thrown me into the Arctic Ocean in January. "Are you saying you'd like me to clean out my desk?"

She had the grace to blush. "Unfortunately. There really is a perceived conflict of interest."

I blinked back sudden tears. I wasn't ready for this. I always thought that when I left the foundation, it would be on my terms.

But I nodded with my chin up and shoulders square and thanked Jeanie for her time.

Fortunately, I didn't have a lot of me at my desk. A coffee mug. A couple of paperweights. But no photos, no humorous knickknacks, or pampered plants. Three years ought to have shown more accumulation.

I dug through my drawers, looking for anything I might have forgotten. The only things I found were a spare pair of panty hose, two tampons, and a small sewing kit. I didn't even need a box.

It wasn't five o'clock yet, but I was done. Finished. I said good-bye to a bewildered Haley and then closed the door softly behind me.

I waited until I was in the lobby before I called Tripp.

"Hey, honey," I said, smiling so he wouldn't hear the tears standing guard in my eyes. "I'm done at work. We can start the weekend early."

"What happened?" Tripp asked me twenty minutes later, as I buckled my seat belt.

My voice didn't betray me. "You're a conflict of interest, so rather than wait for me to give notice after we get married, they asked for my resignation now."

He squeezed my hand but didn't say anything, and I was grateful. I wasn't ready to talk. It was still too raw.

I'd forgotten how beautiful Tripp's lake house was. How serene. I tried to picture myself living there and couldn't.

We sat on the deck, drank a toast to ourselves, and then sprawled on separate chaises to enjoy the afternoon.

"I was going to quit anyway," I said.

Tripp said nothing.

I glanced at him. His sunglasses hid his eyes. "Now I'll have time to plan the wedding."

"There is that," he finally said.

So this was the rest of my life. Lounging around without purpose, drinking wine in the afternoon, and holding hands with my wonderful husband. It wasn't a bad way to spend time, but it seemed kind of pointless.

Maybe we should start our family right away. That would keep me occupied. But having a baby because I was bored felt like a lousy thing to do to a kid.

Tripp's thumb traced the lines in my palm. I watched the play of the shadows from the overhead trees on the foiled surface of the lake. Periodically, a motorboat would zoom too close to the deck, but mostly the afternoon was quiet.

We chatted about nothing consequential, as if the topic of my job was taboo.

"Want to watch a movie or something?" Tripp asked after we'd eaten supper.

"Sure." Movies were like comfort food for me. Grandma Judy watched movies all the time. Movies let us escape the hideous monotony of our sad little lives.

"You will get used to it. The not working thing. It's tough at first. When my shoulder injury—" He broke off and shook his head, as if he'd revealed too much.

I shrugged as if it didn't matter. Don't most women dream of marrying a rich man and never working again?

"If you want to cry, I've got one good shoulder."

I was saving my tears for something more important. Crying over losing a job I no longer needed seemed self-indulgent.

"Maybe later," I said. "What movies do you have?"

I was right about his collection consisting of lot of action adventure flicks. But he also had a lot of baseball movies, including my personal favorite in that genre, *Bull Durham.*

He didn't argue with my choice. We curled up together on his oversize sofa.

"That's what I'm going to do to you," he whispered during the scene where Costner paints Sarandon's toenails red. "I even bought the red nail polish."

He nibbled on my neck.

After the movie, we took our wine out to the deck. Tripp and I shared a chaise. "How are you doing?" he asked, massaging my nape.

"I feel kind of...lost," I admitted. "Like there's a big hole inside me."

"Is there anything I can do? I'm a good listener."

I shook my head. "No, let's just cuddle."

Sparks of light flickered through the night sky.

"Make a wish," he whispered in my ear. "You're supposed to wish on shooting stars."

I closed my eyes and wished for Tripp.

"Did you make a wish?" I asked him.

"Sure did," he said, grinning. "I wished I could keep you naked all weekend."

"Go for it," I said.

On Saturday, Tripp called Penn to set up a meeting to discuss catering. He didn't tell Penn what event he wanted catered.

"Let's surprise him," he said.

Oh boy. Penn had already called me a skank and a floozy. Heaven only knew what he'd call me when he saw me wearing Tripp's ring.

We decided on a small wedding in Cooperstown, as soon as we could manage it. Shaneybrook's would cater it. Neither of us was particularly religious. We were both Protestants, although not the same sect. A justice of the peace would work fine.

Faboo showed up late in the afternoon followed by Josh from Shaneybrook's, who arrived with a ton of food. Faboo noticed my ring, congratulated us, and asked us if we'd set a date.

Then Tripp's agent, Marty Fiscoe, showed up. That surprised me. Tripp wasn't an active player. Why did he need an agent?

I excused myself to use the bathroom. I stopped in the kitchen on my way back to the deck. Josh had laid out the food buffet style. There was no sign of him anywhere. That's when I heard my name. I didn't mean to eavesdrop, but I did.

"You're getting a prenuptial, right?" Marty asked. "I mean, Kelsey seems like a sweet enough girl, but you need to protect your assets."

He couldn't even get my name right.

I hadn't even thought of a prenup, but Marty was right. I wasn't marrying Tripp for his money. And I didn't plan to divorce him ever, because like my cousin, I believed marriage was forever. Caitlin deserved credit for trying to make her marriage work. Too bad it might end up killing her.

I rejoined the men on the deck. "I want a prenuptial even if Tripp doesn't."

Tripp seemed surprised. Everyone was always hitting him up for money. He probably wasn't used to someone refusing to take his money.

"You have assets?" Faboo asked.

"That's none of your business," I replied, smiling at him. "By the way, thanks for the lift to Syracuse Monday night."

More people appeared. Baseball people. Tripp's former teammates. I got a taste of another aspect of what my future life might hold: ex-jocks hanging around, drinking Tripp's alcohol, and eating his food. Most of them arrived with women. Tall, thin, tanned, and glamorous women. I felt like a ragamuffin in my shorts and camp shirt.

I fought an urge to go change into something a little less casual, slap on some makeup, and run a brush through my hair.

But that wasn't me. Yeah, I costumed up for events, but that was because I led a very rich fantasy life. Cold reality was there hadn't been that many events in my life. And the quality of my clothes was bush league compared to these majors.

I tried playing hostess, but I wasn't very good at it. I felt more like a servant, fetching wineglasses, wiping up spills, and pointing out the bathroom. I was loading silverware in the dishwasher when Maura St. John arrived. The other guests greeted her as if she belonged.

I thought the woman had a lot of nerve to show up after Monday night. But then, I really didn't know how Tripp had handled her, did I? I'd run off with my tail between my legs. Which seemed like a good idea again. Except Tripp had forgotten to give me the promised spare keys to his car, so I was as stuck as I ever was. I had a feeling Faboo might not be so accommodating a second time.

I finished in the kitchen.

"I'm staying at Otsego Manor," I heard Maura tell another willowy redhead.

I walked through the throng on the deck and sat on the foot of Tripp's chaise, because there wasn't another available spot. All the other chairs on the deck were in use, and my ankle throbbed.

Tripp reached for my hand, smiling as if he were glad to see me. "Where have you been? I want to introduce you around to people."

I stretched my mouth into a smile.

"Hey, everybody," he announced. "This is Chelsea." He held our joined hands over our heads. The diamond in my ring caught the setting sun and sent prisms of color across the deck, tattooing startled faces. "We're getting married, and none of you are invited to the wedding."

Several people laughed, thinking Tripp was joking.

I watched Maura. She didn't flinch, but her eyes did widen. Then she looked at Tripp with such sadness and such longing, I almost felt bad for her.

A few women eyed the ring—it was kind of hard to miss—and exchanged looks that I didn't bother trying to interpret. I just wanted all these people gone.

"So how did you two meet?" the blonde hanging off Marty's arm asked. "I didn't realize you and Maura had broken up."

"I didn't realize Maura and I were ever together," Tripp muttered.

"She's here," I replied in the same tone.

His brows rushed together. "Do you want me to ask her to leave?"

I was torn. I didn't want to embarrass her, but then, could someone be embarrassed who'd shown up at her ex-boyfriend's house knowing he didn't want her there?

"It's okay," I lied.

"It's not okay," he said.

"So how did you meet?" Marty's blonde asked again.

My face heated.

"At the restaurant," Tripp replied.

Well, that was true.

"My brother's significant other introduced us," he continued. "I took one look at her and knew I'd met the one. In fact, we're celebrating our one-week anniversary today." He leaned over and planted a chaste kiss on my mouth.

"A week? You've got to be kidding," some other female said.

They might be glamorous, polished, and poised, but I had better manners.

So I sat there with Tripp, holding hands but not clinging to him, not the way the other women clung to the men who'd brought them.

I tried to ignore Maura as she flitted from group to group. Tripp didn't seem to be paying any attention to her either. He laughed and was easy with his guests. I smiled until my face hurt and kept on smiling.

A couple of the men had gone to the dock to puff on cigars, and the pungent smoke drifted our way. Someone had lit the citronella candles and tiki torches lining the railing. The scent suffocated me.

"I need another beer," Tripp announced. He released my hand and made to get up.

"I'll get it," I said, scrambling to my feet.

"But your ankle," he protested.

Said appendage was still slightly swollen, and the bruises had morphed from black-and-blue to something that could confidently march in a gay pride parade alongside Tripp's brother.

"I'm fine," I assured him. I needed a breather.

I went into the house and stepped into the bathroom to gather my wits. I'd had no clue he was throwing a party, and I didn't like it. I don't mind impromptu, but this gathering seemed less than spontaneous. My first clue should have been Josh's arrival with all that food.

After several moment of breathing deeply and wishing my nose wasn't quite as sunburned as it was, I forced myself back to the mob. I grabbed the last two bottles of Moonsinger from the refrigerator.

When I returned to the deck, my gaze sought Maura St. John like a mosquito scouting blood. There she was, sitting on the foot of Tripp's chaise in the spot I'd vacated.

He no longer sprawled but sat up, as if trying to keep distance between them.

I was tempted to exaggerate my limp but didn't. I didn't want Maura to see me as vulnerable.

I handed Tripp his beer.

"Thanks, honey. Come on. Sit down." He scooted farther away from Maura as if making room for me.

"We're not done with our discussion, Tripp," Maura said. "I'm sure business will bore Kelsey."

"Chelsea," I corrected her as I twisted the cap off my beer. "As in Clinton. You know, the former president's daughter?"

"Whatever. Tripp and I have business to discuss about some grant applications for Home Safe. Something I'm sure would just bore you to death, so why don't you go wash some dishes or something?"

Tripp grabbed my free hand and tugged me into his lap. "Then Chelsea definitely needs to be here. Don't you do something with grants, honey?"

"I worked for the Genevieve Hart-Darling Foundation," I replied.

Candlelight masked Maura's reaction.

Tripp squeezed my hand. "Didn't you evaluate grant requests or something?"

I nodded, wishing I was anyplace else than where I was.

I didn't mean Tripp's lap. I loved sitting there. I meant on that deck surrounded by people who seemed to have more money than manners. Why couldn't they all just leave, so Tripp and I could hold hands, talk, and watch the sky for shooting stars?

"By all means, then, stay." Maura's tone seemed strained, but that may have been my irritation coloring my perception. "You wouldn't happen to know the status of our grant application to Hart-Darling, would you?"

I shook my head. "I turned it over to my boss as soon as I realized what it was. I wasn't sure I could be impartial."

"Her integrity is one of the things I love about her." Tripp's hand tightened on mine.

"Of course." Maura's smile was wooden. She stood. "I guess that explains a lot. You're marrying your way into a grant." Her voice was sharp. Loud.

Several people glanced our way.

My cheeks grew warm. *No scene, no scene, no scene.*

"No, I'm marrying a wife," Tripp replied. His tone was no longer cordial. His aw-shucks grin disappeared. "Anything else she can do is just icing on the cake." His clasp on my hand turned into a grip.

Maura studied him with her glossy mouth slightly open. Her pale pink tongue visibly flickered. "Do you want me to resign from the board?" she asked in a very low voice.

"I don't even know why you're here." His tone was cold. Frigid. "The only reason I haven't asked you to leave is because of the work you've done on the board. But if your behavior gets in the way of our working together, then that's not a bad idea."

I shivered, and his anger wasn't even directed at me.

Maura nodded, stood, and walked away. That wasn't an answer I could understand, but I never was very good at reading live people. Give me a movie, however, and I could process the hints, absorb the foreshadowing...

"Sorry about that," Tripp muttered. "I made things real clear to her on Monday, but I guess Maura got to where she is by sheer persistence."

What could I say to that?

"So do you have these...gatherings often?" I asked.

He shook his head. "I'm sorry. I should have warned you. This is the board of the camp, and we always get together the Saturday after induction weekend, which is when we raise most of the funds for the following year."

That explained why Josh had shown up with all the food.

And Maura. She was on the board.

"Any more surprises?"

"Snuggle a little closer," he suggested.

I didn't need to get any closer to know what he was talking about. "That's no surprise at all."

"As soon as everyone leaves, I'm going to make love to you right here on this chaise," he whispered against my ear. "Ever done it outdoors?"

My insides clenched. "Can't say as I have."

"Good. Just don't drink too much and get sleepy on me, okay?"

Tripp introduced me to the members of the board as they came over to greet him. Most of them were former baseball players. Faboo, of course, I already knew, but some of the others had great names too: Mookie, Pudge, and Boomer. I just love great names.

Neither Tripp nor I got up from the chaise again. I decided to ignore most of what was going on around me and study the sky, looking for the meteor showers Tripp had promised me. Someone turned on the deck lights, diminishing the purity of the night sky and drawing villages of mosquitoes.

"There's one," Tripp said. His voice low was nearly inaudible in the party din.

I felt all warm and squishy inside. He'd also been looking for shooting stars.

"I saw it too," I whispered.

He tightened the arm he had draped around my waist. "Rather watch the sky than party?"

I nodded.

"Good. Me too."

I figured the difference was that he was all partied out, while I'd never learned the art.

I thought his guests would never leave, but eventually, as the food and the booze petered out, so did the stamina. Even professional athletes had to sleep sometime.

Faboo was the last to leave. Tripp asked him to shut off all the lights and lock up behind him.

Four in the morning. I was barely holding on, and I'd dozed a bit, using Tripp's chest as a pillow. The drool spot was evidence.

Neither Tripp nor I had moved from the chaise.

"Next time you plan a party, warn me," I murmured.

"In about twelve hours," he replied. "Penn will be here to plan our wedding reception. Consider yourself warned."

He unzipped my shorts and splayed his huge hand across my abdomen. "And in about three minutes, I plan to be partying very deep inside you."

Just like that, my sleepy languorous body melted.

I didn't understand it. I'd never been this sensuous before. When Tripp was involved, all my senses heightened.

While his mouth ravished mine, he freed his penis from his shorts, rolled on a condom, and wiggled me out of my shorts and panties.

"How's that ankle feeling?" he whispered. "Think you can ride?"

There was only one way to find out.

I straddled him, planting my feet on either side of the chaise. The ankle twinged, but it could bear my weight.

"Oh, yeah," Tripp breathed, as I slowly, millimeter by millimeter, lowered myself onto his burgeoning erection. His eyes closed. Amazement altered his features. "Honey, since you don't want kids right away, could you go on the pill or something?" he asked. "I'd really like that a lot."

"I plan to call my GYN as soon as I get back to Syracuse," I said as I sank completely down on him.

There are no words to describe the sensation. My skin was stretched tight, adding to the pleasure of having him inside me.

He unbuttoned my camp shirt and then released the front clasp of my bra. My breasts spilled out. He curled upward and captured a nipple between his teeth. Sharp pleasure spiraled through me.

With Tripp, I was wanton in ways I'd never known I could be. Being outside on the chaise was far different from the time I'd been on top in the bed. For one thing, I had better control because my feet were flat on the wide planks of the deck.

I didn't understand why I was drawn to this man. It wasn't his golden good looks, his aw-shucks grin, the dual dimples in his cheeks, or his amazing athlete's body. Those were mere physical things—the results of spontaneous combustion when two sets of genes merged.

He seemed to cherish me. Treated me as if I were valuable, fragile, and worthy. All of those things were new to me.

He didn't like my slow, teasing pace and grasped my hips to take charge. And that was okay by me.

"Touch yourself," he said. "Like I showed you before."

I wasn't comfortable with his request. But I did it because it really felt fantastic. His fingers were otherwise occupied.

His eyes were open now, watching me. "Kiss me," he said.

Oh, now there was a real hardship.

I leaned forward and brushed my lips against his.

"Uh-uh." His tongue plunged into my mouth, mimicking what his cock was doing deeper inside me. His hands left my hips. One rested on the small of my back as my ass retained the new pace he'd set. The other toyed with a nipple.

My orgasm was sharp, sudden, and frightening in its intensity. When it was over, I was as limp as three-day-old tossed salad. But Tripp wasn't through with me yet.

Limp made me pliant. He was a man on a mission. Impossible as it seemed, he increased his pace and the depths of his thrusts. I thought I would split in two. Finally, he thrust upward while pulling me down, went tense, and held himself rigid. I could feel every twitch as his orgasm forced a harsh cry from his throat.

He clutched me close, nearly cracking my ribs. His breath was a harsh rasp, in and out. "Chelsea," he managed to whisper.

He was in better shape than I.

"No matter what happens, I need you to know you're important to me."

I didn't think anything of it at the time, although I probably should have.

"I am going to marry you. We're going to settle down, have a couple of kids, and live happily ever after."

It worked for me. I could almost believe.

I slowly eased myself off him, not wanting a repeat of the lost condom. He winced. I winced. Maybe he'd been a little too...vigorous.

I shivered. The night had grown a bit chilly. Dawn wasn't far off. He pulled me down next to him. "Let's sleep out here," he said.

I was too tired, too weak, too sated to argue.

Chapter Twelve

Stupid birds. All that chatter and cooing and just in general being inconsiderate to those of us trying to sleep.

I was stiff. I was cold. I was huddled next to Tripp, who still wore most of his clothes, having freed only what he needed to have sex with me. My butt was bare. My shirt was open and hanging from my shoulders.

Tripp snored lightly on the top of my head. The sky was a rosy pearl color, and but for the birds, everything was still. No breeze ruffled the overhead leaves. No motorboats or Jet Skis marred the surface of the lake.

My panties were still wrapped around my right ankle. My shorts were under the chaise. Who knew what happened to my red sandals?

Something plopped into the water.

I padded barefoot to the railing to peer down at the lake. Only widening ripples in the otherwise still water proved I wasn't hearing things. In the distance, a mother duck followed by five ducklings drifted, their bodies creating vees in the surface of the lake.

I decided to get a cup of coffee and enjoy the calm before reality.

"Good morning." Tripp came up behind me and nuzzled my neck, startling me. I hadn't heard him stir, much less cross the deck. His unshaven chin scraped my skin as he kissed me. His hands cupped my breasts.

And he rubbed his morning erection against my bottom. Given our height difference, this was not an easy task.

"I saw you standing here and had the greatest idea," he murmured in my ear right before his tongue traced the outer of rim of it. "Good thing I had a condom in my pocket."

I leaned back into him. All he had to do was touch me, and I was ready for him. "What idea is that?"

"Lean over the railing, like you were a minute ago." He pinched a nipple.

I was beginning to get an idea of what he wanted. Good thing the deck railing was relatively new, very sturdy, and splinter free.

I'd been premature in donning my shorts. Tripp corrected that. His arm snaked around my waist.

"Hold on, honey." He probed between my legs. I caught my breath as he slowly penetrated. By the time he was fully seated, I swear my eyes were bugging out of my head. "God, you're so tight," Tripp groaned as he withdrew ever so slightly.

I swear he filled me so completely I didn't have the lung capacity even to sigh.

"You okay?" he whispered and then nibbled on my earlobe.

I nodded. I was incapable of any other response.

He started thrusting, slowly at first. I gripped the railing. The wood creaked from the strain of holding me upright as Tripp made love to me.

The sensations swirling through me were as emotional as they were physical. I tried to imagine waking up like this every morning but couldn't wrap my mind around it.

"Come for me," he said, his voice a harsh rasp.

One of his hands left my hips and burrowed to find that little orgasm push button. He increased his pace as his finger stroked me.

My climax started in my toes. They seemed to curl every time he withdrew and then straighten as he pushed. The soles of my feet grew warm. The heat flickered up my calves, weakening my knees and burning in my thighs. I must have moaned or something.

"That's right," Tripp encouraged me. "That's right. Come for me."

Impossible as it seemed, he increased his pace yet again, slamming into me almost violently.

I fell apart. My nipples seemed to grow painfully sensitive. Every muscle in my body shook. I heard a high-pitched keening and realized it came from my own throat.

Tripp thrust one final time and then held himself taut, fully embedded. I couldn't tell where my contractions ended and the spurting of his cock began.

He didn't move. He just rested against me, pinning me to the railing. His breaths came in great gulps of air, hot against the side of my neck. His legs trembled as badly as mine did.

We fell to the deck.

He winced and then muttered, "Holy crap."

"Yeah," I agreed, still trying to catch my breath. I wondered how we would ever top the perfection we'd just created.

"You're trembling," he panted.

"So are you." I was gasping for air.

He kissed my cheek. "God, we're amazing together. Isn't it great to know that we're the best lovers each other will ever have?"

Heat filled my face. I already knew—had known from the start—that he'd ruined me for anyone else. I'd had no clue that he felt the same about me.

"Every bone in my body aches," he said. "We should have gone to bed last night instead of sleeping on the chaise."

I drew my index finger down his sternum. I was fascinated by the reddish whorls of hair covering his chest. This was probably the first time I'd seen him in really good light, which was unfiltered by shades, blinds, or curtains. The sun was fully over the horizon, throwing sharp shadows across the deck. We lay in full sunlight.

My fingers traced the silvery scars on his shoulder.

He tensed. His Adam's apple bobbed as he swallowed hard.

"What happened?" I asked.

"Surgery." He bit out the syllables.

"Want to talk about it?" My question was hesitant because of the waves of negativity rolling off him suddenly, threatening to smother me.

"Not particularly."

Okay. I could relate to that. He'd hinted that whatever happened had ended his baseball career. Haley had mentioned something when she'd Googled him, but I hadn't paid attention.

I stretched to kiss the scars, but he jerked away from me.

Not okay.

I extracted myself from his now lackadaisical embrace. "I could use some coffee," I said, purposely keeping my tone bland.

I brushed a twig off my bare butt and pulled on my clothes.

"Chelsea," Tripp said to my back.

My fingers fumbled with the buttons on my camp shirt. I needed a shower. I kept my back to him.

"Honey." He climbed to his feet, wrapped his arms around my waist, and tried to get me to relax against him.

"I need coffee," I repeated. "I need to shower. What time is your brother coming?"

"Three," he replied. He rested his chin on the top of my head. "I'm sorry. I don't like talking about...my surgery. It's really difficult."

"That's okay," I lied. "You'll tell me when you're ready. Right?"

I'd always thought that when I fell in love there would be no secrets, that the world would be bright with light chasing away shadows and cobwebs.

But then, I had my own secrets I didn't want to share with Tripp, didn't I? But not because they shamed me—at least, not solely—but rather, because my secrets were leeches, waiting to latch on to his bank account. Everyone wanted a piece of Tripp Shaneybrook. Everyone but me.

He let me shower alone. I put on a lettuce-green sundress for our meeting with his brother. No makeup. Nothing could hide my sunburned nose and forehead or the paleness around my eyes from wearing my sunglasses.

Tripp showered and wore khakis and a green golf shirt. He usually wore button-down shirts. I didn't like the golf shirt look on him. It wasn't...real.

Penn was half an hour late. Things were still slightly tense between me and Tripp. We sat at the round wrought-iron table on the deck with our coffee in our dressy clothes, pretending all was well.

It wasn't.

Penn, of course, had shown up with food. Restaurant food, not opera food. Although I was beginning to suspect those opera sandwiches had been a bit of a "screw you" to Baird. He referred to the food as samples for Tripp's event.

"Chelsea and I are getting married," Tripp told his brother. "Will you stand up for me?"

Dislike slid across Penn's face. A week ago, the man had called me a skank and a floozy.

"Pregnant?" he asked, snide dominating his tone.

"I wish," Tripp replied. "The sooner the better. I want to be young enough to enjoy my family."

"I hope you're making her sign a prenuptial agreement," Penn continued as if I weren't sitting right there next to him at the table.

"She hopes so too," I replied as sweetly as I could. "You know, instead of blaming me for what Baird did, you ought to try blaming him."

Tripp frowned at me and shook his head.

Oh, dear. Chelsea was being naughty. "Excuse me," I muttered as I pushed away from the table. I walked into the house with as much dignity as I could muster.

My eyes burned, and something caught in my throat.

I stayed in the bathroom for a few minutes, dashing cold water on my eyes and resolving that I wouldn't cry. Not in front of Penn and not in front of Tripp.

When I felt a little more in control, I rejoined them. I didn't want to. I'd much rather get in a car and head home. I didn't belong in Tripp's world, only his bed. Which didn't say very many nice things about me, did it? It was glaringly obvious to the people who knew him best, like his brother and agent.

But now wasn't the time for that conversation. I would go through with this meeting with Penn with a smile on my face if it killed me.

"I just don't like the way she latched on to you," Penn was saying as I crossed the kitchen.

"She didn't latch on to me," Tripp replied. "I took one look at her and fell head over heels. She's the one who's been trying to slow things down."

"Head over heels? With *her*?"

He didn't know me. How could he be so judgmental?

Tripp saw me through the slider and motioned for me to rejoin them. I grabbed a fistful of paper napkins on my way out.

"These hors d'oeuvres look great," I said as I took my seat at the table.

"So are you getting married and having the reception in Syracuse?"

"Someplace around here," Tripp replied. "It's not so far from Syracuse that people couldn't make the trip."

Who would I invite other than Caitlin, my matron of honor? Jeanie, the boss who'd asked for my resignation? Haley, the coworker I loathed? Too bad the video chain store was gone. I could have invited the clerks from the local franchise.

What a pathetic little life I lived.

"Small," I muttered. "Nothing fancy."

"You can do small and still be elegant," Penn snapped.

The temptation to ask if his defense of *small* was from personal experience was strong, but I refrained. For Tripp's sake. If Penn got too out of line, Tripp would handle him, just as he'd done last week.

I hoped.

"What's available around here?" Tripp asked.

"Plenty. Are you looking for a church? A hall? You need to be more specific."

"Greek island," I muttered under my breath.

"No church," Tripp said. "Civil ceremony." He reached for my hand.

I stared at the tray of appetizers Penn had brought.

"Look, boys and girls," Penn said, sounding exasperated. "I'm not a wedding planner. I'm a chef. I run a restaurant. I cater. I'm not closing the restaurant to cater your reception. You guys need to come up with some kind of plan."

"We have a plan," Tripp said. "We're getting married as soon as possible, and you're catering."

"Hire a planner." Penn slammed his book shut.

"A planner will turn it into an event," I blurted. "We don't want an event. We want… We just want to be married."

"Then elope."

He was right. In more ways than one. If we eloped, I wouldn't have to worry about buying a dress, wouldn't have to wait for Caitlin's face to heal, and wouldn't have to feel inferior when my side of the venue was empty and his was as full as the home team's stadium on opening day of the World Series.

Was I pathetic or what?

"What about Doubleday Field?" Tripp asked. "Think we could rent that?"

"Not this season." Penn crossed his arms over his chest.

"Too big," I chirped. My throat was tight, my vocal cords taut. "Penn's right. We should elope. We can get our license tomorrow, elope the day after."

I knew there was only a one-day waiting period in New York State, because Caitlin had followed Spencer to Syracuse from Akron when she found out she was pregnant. They'd eloped.

Then I decided there was only way to get what I really wanted, and that was to speak up.

"Did you see *Mamma Mia?*" I asked. "That's what I want."

Tripp and Penn exchanged a look, and Penn shuddered. "Not an ABBA fan. Is she always this high maintenance?"

"I'm not high maintenance," I protested.

"She's perfect," Tripp added.

Well, not perfect, but wasn't that sweet of him?

"I want simple and small. No fancy floral arrangements. No hideously fancy food."

Penn shuddered again. "Baked ziti and macaroni salad at the fire barn?"

"No mayo." I was firm about that.

I picked up one of the savory tidbits he'd brought for us to sample: gorgonzola on a slice of pear. It was simple and not tortured. I closed my eyes as I savored the textures and contrasting flavors.

"You have great food at your restaurant," I said, remembering last Saturday night and all the taste treats Tripp had provided me. What little bit I'd managed to eat last night was pretty amazing too. None of it explained the opera sandwiches. "I had your shrimp in mango salsa over black beans the other day. That would be fabulous for a reception."

Penn seemed mollified. "How many people?" he asked.

Tripp reached for my hand. "Not many."

"Ten?" I said.

Penn choked. "Ten?"

"Small," I said.

"Ten?" He looked at Tripp, who shrugged. "You're serious."

I nodded.

Penn leaned back in his chair and studied me. "Then why don't you just get married here on the deck?"

Tripp leaned back in his chair and studied his deck, as if seeing it for the first time after a long time away. "That's not a bad idea."

The deck was shaded, getting only dappled sunlight, and it was close to the lake. It was beautiful in a New York State sort of way. But it wasn't my fantasy.

It was Tripp's. I was already coming into this relationship disadvantaged. If I couldn't get married on my terms, I wanted to get married in neutral territory.

Someplace unsullied by memories of Maura St. John.

"It's pretty here," I said. "But—"

"I take it that's a no."

Eloping was really starting to appeal to me. Or postponing until we lost interest. Because I still didn't and still couldn't believe this was happening to me. I was the girl ditched in a restaurant by her date, not the one swept off her feet by a celebrity athlete.

I didn't say much the rest of the meeting with Penn, except that whenever we decided to go through with the thing, I'd like a tapas reception. Lots of hearty appetizer-type things. He liked the idea a lot. Claimed to be intrigued by it. Said he'd get back to us with a menu.

After Penn left, we devoured the food he'd brought. He was an amazing chef. I wasn't much of a cook, but I loved great food.

"Why don't you want to get married here?" Tripp asked.

"Because my first memory of this place is of Maura St. John interrupting our stargazing," I replied. I wasn't going to start lying to him just to appease his feelings.

"Oh. Then you don't want to live here?"

No, I didn't want to live there. I supposed I could get used to being there in the summer, but Maura had tainted the place with her beautiful poison.

"Not particularly," I said.

"Oh," was all he said. "Do you want to live in Syracuse?"

I shook my head. "Where do you live?"

"Uh, here."

"Year-round?"

He nodded.

"Oh."

His turf. I didn't like that.

For some reason, I'd expected him to live in a big cosmopolitan city. In a penthouse or something, not in a small house on a small lake near a small town like Cooperstown. Maybe he wasn't as rich as Tanner claimed despite Penn and Marty's insistence on a prenuptial agreement.

I could deal with marriage to a poor man a lot easier than I could deal with the concept of ten million a year.

"I can live in Cooperstown," I said. "I don't know what the employment opportunities are, but I can deal."

"You don't need to work. I can afford to support you."

"Then what would I *do*?" I asked.

He waggled his eyebrows.

"All the time?" I laughed. "Not even you are that good."

"Are you challenging me?" His eyes lit like candles in amber glass. "Are you questioning my prowess? My masculinity?"

I pretended to ponder the question.

For about ten seconds. Which was all his ego could handle.

He leaped from his chair, pulled me from mine, tossed me over his shoulder caveman-style, and carried me into the house, up the stairs to his bedroom.

Sex is a great avoidance technique.

Chapter Thirteen

I woke up feeling crampy. Icky. Bloated.

Sure enough, as I discovered when I went to the bathroom, I'd gotten my period. I hoped I hadn't ruined Tripp's sheets. He had great sheets. A really high thread count. Not only had he spoiled me for sex with anyone else but also for sleeping on cheap sheets ever again.

We'd slept after a slow, languorous lovemaking session. A perfect Sunday afternoon fantasy. Except it was evening now, and the weekend was nearly over. Of course, there was no reason for me to hurry home, except to feed Foggy. Poor guy. He sure was getting short shrift these days.

I was at loose ends. No job and an apartment from which I'd probably be evicted. Yeah, I worried about my belongings. Tanner wasn't exactly concerned about the law. Otherwise, he wouldn't be blackmailing me. Because his alleged late fee was extortion.

I jumped into the shower to wash away the stickiness of sex, of my period, and of my mood. I'd just rinsed my hair when Tripp joined me.

I shouldn't have been surprised, but I was. Startled, that was. After my heart abandoned my throat for its regular spot in my body, I assured Tripp I wasn't pregnant.

"I'm sorry," he said, and I knew he meant it. Water ran down his golden skin as if he were a god trapped in a fountain. "I'll just have to try harder. Keep doing it until we get it right."

I smiled.

He cupped my face in his massive hands and very gently brushed his lips against mine.

I slid from his grasp. "Not now," I said. "I have my period."

"So?"

I wrinkled my nose.

"Prude." He laughed, but he left me alone, concentrating on his own shower. I didn't wait for him but finished my own ablutions and then left. I needed to call Caitlin, and if he was in the shower, I'd have privacy to speak freely.

Fortunately I had the two tampons from my desk drawer in my purse. I dressed in khaki capri pants and a white camp shirt and took my cell phone onto the deck. I'd missed two calls from Caitlin. The calls were only fifteen minutes apart. She'd called while Tripp and I were making love.

I sat at the table, where remnants of Penn's samples deteriorated. *We should have cleaned up before we went upstairs,* I thought. I wondered when the urgency for sex would fade into routine. I hoped it never would, but how long could two people sustain the intensity flaring between me and Tripp?

Caitlin didn't answer my call. I knew she wasn't making love with her husband. Hopefully, Spencer was still in jail.

I slipped my phone into my pants pocket and started clearing away the mess on the table. It seemed like a sin to throw away all that elegant food. But the bugs had been at it. And it had been sitting out in the heat for hours. The slices of pears had turned brown and smelled faintly rotten.

Tripp joined me once the table was clear and cleaned off. Suspicious guy timing.

"Want to go out for dinner?"

I shook my head. I wasn't that hungry.

He caught my hand. "That's one of the things I love about you. That you'd rather spend a quiet evening at home with me than go gallivanting around, hoping to be seen with me."

"I'm really not a social person," I said. "I'm not comfortable in a crowd."

For all my romantic fantasies, this was true. It was one of the benefits of my job too. No huge pool of coworkers to have to deal with day in and day out.

"What about you?" I asked.

He shrugged and rubbed circles with his thumb on my palm. "I like my privacy. I had enough of being in the spotlight when I was playing ball." He yanked on my hand and drew me into his embrace. "I appreciate that you want a small wedding. We should probably make a guest list. Work on that kind of stuff tonight."

I didn't want to think about the wedding. I wanted to think about tomorrow, Monday morning, and what I would do.

"Can we go back to Syracuse tomorrow?" I asked. "I want to get Foggy and bring him here. Start packing."

Deal with my cousin and my landlord.

"Think your cat will like it here?"

"He'll adapt," I said. "You don't mind, do you?"

He shook his head. "Foggy is a nice cat."

My cell phone rang then, the theme from *Gone with the Wind* letting me know it was Caitlin.

"Chel?"

I could barely hear her. "What? What's wrong?"

"Help." The word was less than a whisper.

I whirled away from Tripp and went into the house.

"Where are you?" I knew my question sounded sharp, but Caitlin—

"Your. 'Parmen."

"I'm calling the police." My voice shook from the ice in my veins.

"No. Kill me."

I thought I heard a sob, and then the phone went dead. I tried her cell but was kicked right into voice mail.

"What's wrong?" Tripp stood behind me.

Oh, how I wanted to lean into his strength and share this hideous burden of family with him. I couldn't. It was too awful. Too shameful. I didn't trust his love for me enough.

"I need to go to Syracuse now," I said. "You told me you'd give me a key to your car when we got here. I need it now."

"I'll drive you," he said. "You're shaking like a leaf."

"Stop trying to control me!" I shouted. "I'm adult. I handled my life just fine before I met you. I can handle it now. Give me the car keys."

"I'm not trying to control you," he protested. "I'm trying to take care of you." He looked kind of pissed.

Tough.

"By keeping me prisoner here? By choosing when and how I can come and go?" I held out my hand. "Keys."

"You're the one who wanted to stay in tonight," he pointed out.

I struggled not to burst into tears. He hadn't seen me cry yet, and I wasn't going to sob on his shoulder now. I didn't have time. I needed to get to Syracuse. To Caitlin. All my talk of tough love was just that: talk. I couldn't let Spencer kill her. She was the only family I had in the whole world.

I squeezed my eyes closed. "Please, Tripp."

"Okay. You can drive." He dropped the keys into my palm. "But I'm coming with you."

Spencer and Caitlin had started out that way. *I'm just looking out for you.* Who gave anyone the right to determine what was best for anyone else?

Tripp must have seen my determination. "If you don't want me in the car with you, I'll only follow you," he said. "You're upset about something, and I'm worried about you."

I wasn't used to anyone worrying about me. I was the worrier, not the worry-ee.

"Fine!" I snapped. I tossed the keys back to him. "Let's go." I'd figure out what to do with him once we got to Syracuse.

"What's going on with your cousin?" he asked once we hit the thruway.

I was grateful he'd waited until then, because the roads winding out of Cooperstown were scary enough in the daylight. At night, they were like something out of the *Twilight Zone*.

"My cousin is having problems with her husband."

"You've mentioned that before." He said nothing for a heartbeat or two. "Don't you think it's time I met your family?"

"Not a good time right now," I muttered.

How could I tell a man who ran a baseball camp for kids in violent homes that my own cousin—my only family—lived in one of those homes.

Things were too complicated.

Still, I was glad he was with me, which was stupid. I didn't like that he'd manipulated me with his concern, so how could I be grateful he was driving me into the thing I so desperately wanted to hide from him?

He addled my brains. He had from the first.

Well, I had time to figure out how to ditch him before we got to Syracuse.

That was a good thing about the distance between Cooperstown and Syracuse: all that time.

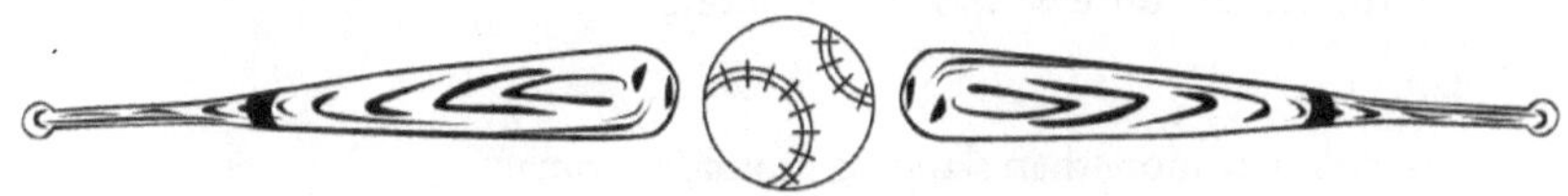

"I'm calling the police," Tripp said. His phone was in his hand.

I snatched it away from him. "No."

We sat in his car, parked in my driveway, where my poor clunker leaned drunkenly to one side on flat tires. My front door mirrored the angle, the hinges ripped from the frame.

Who had let Spencer out of jail? I thought about suing someone. I normally didn't think in those terms, but remembering Caitlin's frail voice put foreign ideas in my head.

And Foggy. What about my cat? If the upstairs door was in bad as shape as the porch, who knew what had happened to my pet?

My hands were shaking when I seized Tripp's phone. Heck, my whole body vibrated like a trailer in a tornado.

"Wait here," I whispered.

He snatched the phone from me and started punching numbers. "Like hell. We're both waiting here, and I'm calling 9-1-1."

Spencer would kill Caitlin.

My teeth started chattering.

"You'd better tell me what's going on." Tripp's tone was one I'd heard only twice before: when he'd pinned Penn against the wall by the throat for calling me a skank and when he'd told Maura St. John she'd better leave his party. It was a dangerous tone and one I'd never expected to hear directed at me.

"Spencer...Caitlin's husband...he...hits her sometimes."

Tripp winced. Then I noticed a bulge in the side of his jaw pulsing in a shaft of pinkish light from the street lamp. "Possible domestic disturbance at two-eleven Wadsworth," he said into the phone. He patiently answered all the questions the operator asked him.

"Bastard," he said once he was off the phone.

"Yeah," I agreed.

"This looks like more than slapping around a woman."

I didn't say anything.

"Is that what happened to the door last week?"

I nodded.

Tripp used some pretty colorful profanity. I'd never heard cuss words mixed up in quite that manner before.

"You *knew* he was this violent, and you *stayed* here?"

It wasn't as if I had resources to stay someplace else, but I didn't want to get into the whole financial fiasco with him. Not just tonight, either.

"He's in jail." I looked at the door and very much doubted that. "He's supposed to be in jail."

"Yeah, right."

I turned on him. "Well what is she supposed to do? She doesn't have any options other than the criminal justice system. It's not her fault it sucks."

"No, it's not."

I could feel waves of black rage pouring off him. Tripp Shaneybrook was furious.

A cop cruiser pulled up to the curb silently with no emergency lights announcing its presence.

I tried to get out of the car again, but Tripp's arm crossed my breasts, pinning me to the seat.

He unrolled his window with his free hand and beckoned to the officer getting out of the cruiser.

A second car pulled behind the first one. I remembered reading that budget cuts forced cops to ride solo. No one was going to approach a car without backup.

Sure enough, weapon drawn, the cop approached Tripp.

"I called in a possible domestic disturbance," Tripp said. He released me and placed both of his hands on the steering wheel, where the cop could see them.

Now that the cops were there, there was nothing I could do. Tripp had neutralized me with his phone call.

"This is my apartment," I said. My voice rattled like the aforementioned tornado-besieged trailer. "My cousin called me. Said she was here. Said she was hurt. Her husband—Spencer Madison—*was* in jail for beating her up. That's my door." I gestured toward the porch.

The cop shone his flashlight in my face as I spoke.

"Can I see some ID, ma'am?" he asked.

Very polite, our Syracuse police.

"Yes." I pulled my purse up from the floor and dug through it for my wallet.

When I looked up, the cop had his gun pointed at me. My heart galloped.

"Sorry," I muttered, realizing he thought I might be going for a weapon. I pulled my license out of my wallet and handed it to Tripp to hand to the officer, who shone the flashlight in my face again as he checked reality against the photo. And the address.

He handed my license back to me. "Wait in the car."

I started to argue, but Tripp shot me a look that shut me up.

The officer went back to his car. I saw him on his cell phone. Probably checking out my story of Spencer.

"Let him do his job," Tripp said.

I was antsy, wanting to go into my little nest and see what had happened and wanting to find my cat and give him a big hug.

It took the two cops forever to finish up whatever they were doing in their cruisers and then use their flashlights to illuminate their way up the stairs to my apartment.

Tripp held my hand. He didn't say a word. He just gripped my hand in his.

I watched as the lights came on in my apartment, room by room, as the cops checked it out. I found myself gripping Tripp's hand in return, using him as an anchor.

"I would have been okay," I said to him. "See? There's nothing there."

"Don't." His voice was a low growl.

I heaved a sigh. I hated waiting. Every light in my apartment must have been on at that point. I hoped my closets were in order, because I was certain the cops were checking out every inch.

Finally, one of the cops came down stairs and approached Tripp. "You can come up now," he said.

I was out of the car before he could finish the sentence.

"You might want to take a look at those tires," Tripp said to the cop in a soft voice. Maybe he thought I wouldn't hear him.

But right now, I didn't care about the car. Cars were nothing but money pits. I ran up the dark stairs—Tanner still hadn't replaced the bulb. I stumbled, banging and scraping my shin on a riser.

Tripp was right behind me and helped me up.

I stopped at the top of the stairs. The second police officer stood there, talking on his cell phone. Beyond him was destruction.

I covered my mouth with my hand to keep from crying out. Tripp's presence was behind me, firm and unyielding. Had he not been there, I would have burst into tears.

"Don't touch anything," the officer broke away from his phone call to tell me.

"My cat," I managed to squeak out through my nearly paralyzed vocal cords.
The cop shook his head.

"Foggy," I croaked, scanning the overturned bookcases, the spilled CDs, DVDs, and VHS cassettes in the designated dining room.

A huge dark spot stained my pale peach sofa. The baseball bat lay under the coffee table.

Blood.

I started moving through my apartment. My nest. Violated. I felt so very unsafe and violated. My pretty Fiestaware—the original stuff, not the re-pro—lay in shatters on the dark hardwood floor, the bright colors reduced to chalky-edged shards. At least my *Spring Party* poster was intact on the dinette wall.

"Foggy? Here kitty, kitty, kitty."
Tripp's huge hand closed over my elbow.

I never should have left Foggy here for Caitlin to care for. She was unreliable at best and unable to care for even herself. What had I been thinking?

More blood splattered the beige stucco in the hall. But I couldn't think about Caitlin or about what Spencer might have done. He was supposed to be in jail. Which meant he hadn't done this. Which didn't mean he wasn't behind it.

And Caitlin wasn't here. She'd either lied to me or had left after calling me.

"Foggy!"

Pots and pans were strewn on the kitchen floor. A bloody dish towel was in the sink.

Stubborn tears leaked from my eyes.

My apartment—my *home*—was a crime scene.

"Foggy, kitty. It's Mommy."

I found him in the bathtub. Blood matted his fur, but his body rose and fell with his breathing.

"Foggy!" I wanted to stroke him and check his soft body for wounds and broken bones, but I was terrified I'd hurt him even more.

"Call your vet. Tell him we're coming in," Tripp said.

"There's an emergency hospital in the strip mall up the street," I said as I knelt on the floor next to the tub. My hand hovered over soft gray fur. "Foggy?"

Oh God. I didn't have the money to pay the hospital, and they would want their money up front. I didn't have a credit card Caitlin hadn't maxed out. I had nothing. My cousin had destroyed my entire life.

I couldn't take it any longer. I burst into tears.

Tripp dropped to the floor next to me, put his arms around me, and pushed my face against his chest. I sobbed while he held me. He didn't murmur *There, there, everything will be okay,* or try to console me in any way. He just let me cry. I clutched his shirt.

"I can't take him to the vet," I finally muttered. Well, squealed. Dogs in the neighborhood would have no problem hearing me. "Caitlin maxed out my credit cards and emptied my bank account."

"Don't worry about that." Tripp's voice was rough.

"If it wasn't for Foggy, I wouldn't ask—"

"You don't have to ask," Tripp interrupted. "Of course we'll take your cat to the vet. Want me to get a towel to pick him up and hold him?"

I nodded.

He helped me stand. I caught a glimpse of my face in the bathroom mirror, but for once I didn't care that crying made me look like the *Creature from the Radioactive Lagoon.* There were more important things here at stake than my silly vanity. Like my cat's life.

Tripp found my linen closet without a problem and handed me an oversize aqua-colored towel.

I wrapped it around Foggy as gently and as carefully as I could. He growled a little, but I spoke softly to him, reassuring him that I would take care of him.

Tripp draped his arm around my waist and helped me walk to the front of the apartment.

"The cat is hurt," he told the officer. "He needs a vet." He then gave the officer his phone number and walked me down the stairs.

I cradled my poor cat, who was swaddled in a towel, as if he were a baby. It felt very odd.

The downstairs cop was waiting. "The tires have been slashed," he confirmed. Tripp once more repeated his phone number and then opened the car door for me. He fastened my seat belt before closing the door and walking to the driver's side.

What would I have done without him? If I'd come to Syracuse alone the way I'd wanted?

Chapter Fourteen

I directed Tripp to the closest veterinary hospital. Once inside, he took over so I didn't have to do anything except answer a couple of questions in a monotone: Foggy's full name, age, breed, and type of injury.

The technician on duty took Foggy from me as gently as I had cradled him. Tripp led me to the waiting area, where I promptly burst into tears again.

"I'll pay you back," I sobbed as he pulled me onto his lap.

He held my face against his chest, resting his cheek on the top of my head. "Don't be silly," he crooned. "You're not paying me back."

I heard an edge in his tone, but I was too upset to care about his mood.

He simply held me like that, curled on his lap with my face hidden in his strength, as we waited. And waited. And waited.

My tears eventually ceased. The tech brought a box of tissues to me. I mopped up, keeping my face averted from Tripp.

Throughout it all, I heard and felt Tripp's phone vibrate, but he ignored it as he tended to me. If it was the police calling, they'd be ticked, but I was so grateful for his attention. His care.

I was a pathetic fool.

I tried to climb off his lap, but he held me firm. "Relax," he murmured. "I've got you."

Yeah, he had me, all right.

I was starting to feel uncomfortable, as if I needed to hit a bathroom and deal with circumstances. Thank goodness I still had an extra tampon from my desk in my purse. I was also starting to feel a little crampy. I needed a pain reliever, a fresh tampon, and someone to tell me how my cat was doing.

I told Tripp I needed to use the restroom, so he let me up. I took care of business, swallowed acetaminophen from my purse, and splashed cool water on my face. No sense repairing my makeup. I would only cry again.

When I came out of the restroom, a couple of men—detectives by the look of them—had joined Tripp in the waiting room. Tripp was answering questions.

"Have you found my cousin?" I asked. "Is her husband back in jail?"

Tripp stood and let me sit. He perched on the arm of my chair and held my hand. I really wanted him to go to the restroom or something so I didn't have to air my family's filthy laundry in front of him.

Judging by the expression on his face, that wasn't going to happen.

Caitlin was in the hospital, allegedly found and driven there by Tanner.

As if I believed that.

His story, according to the detectives, was that he'd come over to fix the door and replace the hall lightbulb and found the apartment in shambles and Caitlin badly beaten, blah, blah, blah.

I wasn't trying to downplay Caitlin's injuries or her condition. I'd heard her tale too many times. The only difference was this time I hadn't been the one to drive her to the emergency room.

I wondered how she was paying for this visit.

I surrendered my cell phone to the detectives—Caitlin's calls and voice messages were logged. I answered questions until the blueness of my face qualified me for a role in *Avatar*.

Spencer had destroyed my home and my belongings. I assured the detectives I was pressing charges, even if Caitlin wasn't. I didn't need money to do that.

After two hours, the vet came out. "Ms. Lyndon?" he asked.

Tears welled up in my eyes as I scrambled to my feet. "How's Foggy?"

"He was pretty badly beaten. There was a lot of internal bleeding, but I'm cautiously optimistic."

I sagged, but Tripp was there to prop me up. "Can I see him?"

"He's heavily sedated right now," the vet explained.

I nodded.

"You should probably go home and get some rest." The vet echoed the detectives' advice.

Tripp gave the technician his phone number in place of mine. I was so glad he thought of that, because it never would have occurred to me.

Tripp had remained mostly silent throughout the evening. He helped me into his car again. "We should go to a hotel for the night," he said.

Right. We couldn't stay at my crime scene, and I didn't want to be in Cooperstown while Foggy was in the hospital.

What would I have done without Tripp?

He checked us into one of the chain hotels off Carrier Circle. I wasn't paying a lot of attention to much of anything. Numb made me dumb.

When we got to our room on the fifth floor, he tossed a paper sack on the king-size bed.

"That's for you. I figured...." Pink stained his cheeks.

I peeked into the bag. Tampons. My face burned. So that was what he'd been doing with the clerk at the front desk. Taking care of me when I was too stupid—and broke—to do it myself. How completely humiliating for both of us.

"Thanks," I muttered and fled with the bag into the bathroom. Just in time to avoid catastrophe.

When I came out, Tripp was sprawled on the bed, hands behind his head, staring at me. He'd unbuttoned his shirt. The tails flopped outside his trousers. He'd also kicked off his shoes. The soft hotel lighting flattered his sun-streaked blond hair and his even features.

"You okay?" he asked.

I nodded, still embarrassed by his purchase.

He patted the mattress beside him.

I wasn't exactly paralyzed, but my limbs felt leaden and too heavy to move.

"Chels, we need to talk."

Here it comes, I thought, dread clumping in my throat. I twisted my engagement ring, readying it to return to him.

Now that he'd gotten a glimpse into the real life of Chelsea Lyndon, Chelsea Lyndon was history. Tears prickled in my eyes again, which surprised me. I thought I'd already sobbed away all body fluids.

I perched on the edge of the bed.

His lips formed a grim line, and the side of his jaw did that pulsing thing again. Yeah, he was angry.

"Thank you for paying the vet," I said. My voice warbled like a drunken bird.

He scowled. "Talk to me. Tell me what's going on."

I hung my head. I couldn't look at him. I didn't know where to begin. This wasn't a movie where a few clips could reveal backstory. This was my life. My poor, pathetic reality.

I had to start somewhere. "Remember last weekend?"

Had it really been only a week? Last week I'd been employed, had a home, a pet that adored me, and was mostly cheerful. Now I was homeless, jobless, my cat was at death's door, and I was miserable. All because I'd trusted Caitlin. I'd trusted Baird, and most foolishly of all, I'd trusted Tripp. I'd let myself love him.

At least he hadn't abandoned me at the veterinary hospital.

"Remember I tried to buy that dress and none of my credit cards worked?" This was so humiliating. I couldn't look at him, so I studied the carpet. Nice neutral pattern. Looked fairly clean too.

"Spencer had beat up on Caitlin. She emptied my checking account and maxed out my credit cards to pay for the emergency room for her—and to bail Spencer out of jail."

"Why was she able to access your accounts?"

I grimaced. I felt so foolish. "Because Spencer doesn't give her any money of her own even though she works, and I thought she might need...an emergency fund. I never thought she'd...wipe me out by bailing him out of jail."

He didn't say anything else. Okay, I was stupid. But Caitlin was my only family, and I was all she had too, besides that jerk she married.

"Then, when I got home Monday night, I found out Spencer had come over to my place where Caitlin was staying and tried to beat in the door. He broke bail, so I lost all the money. They arrested him again. Then when I called the landlord to fix the door, I found out he'd held my rent check, and when he went to cash it, it bounced. Because Caitlin emptied my checking account. So he wouldn't fix the door or replace the stairwell lightbulb and decided to start charging me a daily late fee that's probably illegal. And he decided to raise the rent, because he said bouncing the rent check was the equivalent of breaking my lease."

I sneaked a glance at Tripp.

He just watched me with no expression at all on his face. I wished he'd say something, even if it was just, "How stupid can you get?" But he didn't even sigh.

"Then Caitlin told Tanner—my landlord, who is Spencer's cousin—that I was going out with you. And Tanner knows who you are. That's why he decided to charge me a daily late fee. It's usurious, and I can probably have him arrested or something, but the bottom line is Caitlin, Spencer, and Tanner have all decided you're going to support them."

"So you've had no money at all for a week?"

"Just some loose change in a jar."

"Why didn't you say something?"

"It wasn't your problem."

"Look at me."

I really didn't want to, because I was afraid of what I'd see. Contempt. Disgust. There were a myriad of emotions that could be ascribed to this situation. I couldn't bear to have him look at me the way he'd looked at Maura St. John.

He shifted, and the mattress moved with his motion. "Please look at me." His tone was neutral.

I swallowed hard and turned my head.

His expression was solemn. "You're right. It isn't my problem."

I flinched.

"It's your problem. Just because we're getting married doesn't make it my problem."

He still wanted to marry me?

"But honey, we're supposed to be a team, and you shut me out. That hurts."

I thought I must be dreaming.

"Why didn't you tell me any of this before now?"

"Because I'm not my mother, my grandmother, or even Caitlin." My voice was doing that trapped-rodent squealing thing again. "Grandma Judy, who raised me and my mom, well, they always latched on to a guy and expected him to support them, and in between men, well, things were pretty awful, and I'm not like that. I support me. I take care of me."

I was sniveling. How completely attractive.

Hardly.

"I'm going to overlook the insult you just gave me because you're upset about your cat," Tripp said as he reached for me.

"I'm not a freeloader," I said as I buried my face against his shoulder.

"I know that, but I want to take care of you. I was raised that way. A man takes care of the people he loves. Now, that doesn't mean I'm going to take care of your cousin and her mess, but you? You're the most precious commodity I have."

Well what could I say to that, even if I could get a sound past the gooey lump in my throat?

"Okay. Here's what I'm suggesting we do. You do. Just a suggestion. Let me take you to the bank tomorrow, and you take your cousin's name off your accounts. And you call your credit card companies and do the same thing."

All things I'd planned to do this week but hadn't gotten around to doing.

I nodded.

"Then you should call your landlord, and tell him you're moving. We'll pack up your stuff and move it to my place. Let me pay him. Please. Just to be free of him."

I didn't like that and shook my head. "Caitlin should pay him. I told him to get his money from Spencer."

"Maybe that's why Caitlin is in the hospital right now."

I was an awful person. A completely wretched person. I was more concerned about my cat than about my cousin, and now my anger might have killed Caitlin.

"I know," I whispered. "But where do I draw the line between my life and hers?"

"Here," Tripp told me. "The line is here. We will help her when she's ready for real help, but you can't enable her anymore."

I slumped against him. He understood. He didn't think I was the worst person in the world.

"Instead of staying with you, she can go to the battered women's shelter."

"She won't go. She says only indigent women or women with children can go there, not middle-class people whose husbands make plenty of money and who live in the more affluent suburbs."

"That's not true. My camp does work with all kinds of people, and most of them have been in shelters of one sort or another." He pulled out his phone and made a note. "You want a cup of tea or something?" he asked.

Right. As if I needed caffeine or a diuretic at that point.

I shook my head.

"Feeling a little better?"

I nodded, then shook my head, and then shrugged. Confessing my woes to him had been liberating, but I was still sick with worry about my cat and Caitlin. I still didn't like being financially dependent on Tripp.

He cupped my cheek in his enormous hand, his thumb rubbing as if to erase salt tracks of my tears. "Okay," he said. "Brace yourself, because now you're going to get it."

He spoke in such a mild tone that I didn't catch his meaning right away.

"What the goddamn hell were you thinking?"

Huh?

Tripp was...yelling. At me.

He left the bed and started pacing the room.

"Are you out of your mind? *It could have been you.* You wanted to just drive back alone and waltz up those stairs, and God only knows what you would have found."

His rage paralyzed me. I felt like the chipmunk Foggy had once terrorized, unable to move and my little heart racing so fast it could have burst from my chest.

"Have you ever seen what a baseball bat can do to a woman?" Tripp's complexion was pale, then brilliant red, and then pale again. His expression was livid. "How do you think I would have felt if I'd followed you and found you beaten to within an inch of your life?" He seized my shoulders in a painful grip and pulled me to my feet. "It could have been you."

His honey-gold eyes glowed like twin flames. Nostrils flared. His lips had thinned to parallel blades, but that didn't stop his mouth from coming down on mine. Hard.

Then he thrust me away.

I sank to the bed.

"It could have been you." His voice went hoarse. His eyes were brilliant, as if tears...

Nah. No man was going to cry over me.

He raked his fingers through his hair. "It's bad enough you were keeping all this...crap from me, but when I stop to think that you could have been..."

I didn't say anything. I couldn't. I was stunned.

"Don't you *ever* keep something like this from me again. Do you understand? You have taken twenty years off my life tonight."

"I'm sorry," I squeaked. "I'm not used to having to think about someone else when it comes to my personal life."

His hands fisted at his sides.

"And it's my family. It's just my...reality."

"No." The word was harsh. "That is *not* your reality. I don't believe in hitting women. Hell, I don't believe in hitting anything except baseballs. Hitting women isn't something a man does. Women are supposed to be treasured and adored. Loved. Naked. In bed."

I could feel his anger leaving. "Pregnant?"

"Oh, yeah," he agreed. "Or at least trying to get pregnant."

The hint of his smile faded.

"When I was in double-A ball, a long time ago, one of my teammates, Perry Whitlaw, got hooked up with a woman." A touch of the South shaded his voice. "A groupie. Thought he was in love. Well, I've never seen love like that before or since. I hope to hell I never do. He found her with another player, and... Well, it wasn't pretty. A bat can do some pretty serious damage."

He stopped, staring at the carpet as though the movie of his memory was playing in the warp. "Even if she'd told Perry she loved him. Even if she was married to him, he didn't have the right to hit her. And she had kids too, and they had to see their mama all beat up like that."

That explained a lot. Like why he'd started his camp.

I left the bed and wrapped my fingers around his bicep. It was like holding a rock. "I didn't mean to worry you."

Tears definitely sparkled on his pale lashes.

"I would die if something happened to you," he whispered. His pain was there, stark and raw, gleaming from his eyes like hidden treasure revealed.

I stood on tiptoe and brushed my lips across his. "I'm new to this relationship thing. Be patient."

He nodded. "Me too."

And I believed him. Because I believed him when he told me he hadn't been in a real relationship with Maura St. John. He'd let her go too easily for it to have mattered to him.

Maybe it was just sex talking. But I couldn't imagine the lovely Ms. St. John not putting out and putting out well for a famous baseball stud. If Tripp was a famous baseball stud. I kept meaning to Google him, so I'd know exactly with whom I was dealing. I just never seemed to get around to it.

I rested my hands on his shoulders and tilted my head to look up at him. "I love you," I said. I wasn't sure I'd ever actually told him that before. Now seemed like a good time to start. "I never meant to hurt you. I was trying to protect you." Maybe that sounded stupid, but it was the truth.

"You're not supposed to protect me," he growled.

"Why?" I asked. "Isn't wanting to keep each other safe a two-way street? Isn't not wanting to see you hurt something I should feel?"

He glowered.

"I feel the same way about you as you say you feel about me," I continued. "Maybe I don't want my family hitting on you for money, and maybe I don't want you twisted up in knots about my safety, okay?"

I leaned in to kiss him again. His lips softened beneath mine. I dragged the tips of my fingers over his bare chest. His copper-colored nipples tightened in their nest of curly reddish hair.

His breath whistled between his teeth.

"Don't start something you're not willing to finish," he warned me.

Not a problem.

I kissed him again, a little deeper this time but still softly. His lips were slightly chapped, and he smelled of his wonderful soap. I half expected him to take control of the kiss, but he didn't. Apparently it was my turn to seduce.

And that was okay. I started it. I could finish it. Or I could just stand there and kiss him all night.

Kevin Costner defined the perfect kiss in *Bull Durham,* starting with long, slow, and deep.

It had to be a baseball thing.

Tripp didn't touch me at all. I guess all the kissing and making up was going to have to come from me. Because he was the one upset, and I'd upset him.

Sounded fair to me.

His skin was so soft and so smooth. It stretched over muscles as hard as diamonds. I brushed a fingertip over the scars on his right shoulder. He didn't stop me. He just stood as still as bronze trophy on a shelf.

I pulled his shirt off his shoulders. It puddled on the floor like butterscotch syrup on a sundae. The fine gold hair covering his arms glinted in the diffuse light. I gently kissed each pale line marring his shoulder and ran my tongue over the slightly raised scar tissue.

He flinched. That was his sole reaction. I mean, besides his breathing getting a little rougher and a little weightier.

I inhaled deeply, savoring the lingering traces of sage from his soap and the faint tang of summer sweat—the unique aroma of Tripp. Pure aphrodisiac.

And the taste of him. A feast. Savory, sweet, and nutritious, healing all the hurt inside me.

I explored every contour of his chest with my mouth, using lips, tongue, and teeth. The effect of my ministrations prodded my stomach.

My fingers shook as I unbuckled his belt. As I undid the button at the waist of his Dockers. As I slowly eased down his zipper over the bulge distorting the front of his pants. As I reached into the soft, warm cotton jersey knit of his boxers and found him completely aroused.

I pulled down his pants, letting them pool around his ankles. His belt buckle clanked like a pathetic bell. Then slowly—so slowly—I eased my fingers under the elastic waist of his boxers, caressing the taut, smooth flesh of his hips.

My knees gradually bent as I lowered his underwear. I pressed my mouth to the spot where his rib cage ended.

He groaned then. His fingers tangled in my hair.

I kissed my way down to his navel, rimmed it with my tongue.

"Chelsea." His voice held a hint of warning as I dropped to my knees.

The soft, vulnerable skin beneath his navel quivered as I worked my way down his treasure trail. The tip of his erection brushed the underside of my chin.

Tripp slid his hands to my armpits and yanked me upright. "No."

My head fell back, exposing my throat to his growl. "You told me not to start anything I wasn't willing to finish."

"And I meant it. But not like that."

I was confused. A little hurt too.

He stepped out of the clothes tangled around his ankles. Stood there naked, aroused, and proud. "Get rid of the tampon and bring a towel," he told me in a soft voice.

Heat bloomed in my face. Okay, we were getting married. We were adults. He was going to know when I had my period. And Tripp was a virile man. He liked sex.

I liked sex with him.

So I went into the bathroom to comply with his requests. A promise was a promise. I'd started this interlude. It was up to me to see it through.

CHAPTER FIFTEEN

I discovered new bruises while in the shower the next morning. Probably from stumbling on the stairs in my haste to find my cat.

The first thing I'd done upon waking was borrow Tripp's phone and call the vet. Foggy had made it through the night. His condition was improving.

I called Caitlin while Tripp showered, but she still didn't answer her phone. Probably had it turned off due to hospital regulations. Maybe I could convince Tripp to take me to visit her. They had to meet sometime.

Tripp was not a dawdler. He didn't need to check the morning headlines, weather forecast, or sports scores on the television. He didn't need to fuss around doing anything. He showered, dressed, left a generous tip on the bureau, and we went downstairs to the hotel restaurant for breakfast.

We discussed our plans for the day over coffee, toast, and melon.

First on his agenda: the county courthouse to get a marriage license. Which meant we had to go to my apartment to retrieve things like my birth certificate, my bank records, and more clothes. Then we needed to make some phone calls, possibly get on the Internet, and visit my bank...

My head spun. I wanted to make a list of everything we had to do. But he input it all into his phone.

So we went to my bank and closed my checking account. Tripp paid the overdraft fees while I wanted to cry. I felt so inept, even though I wasn't the one responsible for the mess.

"We're getting married this week," he told me. "We'll open new accounts in your new name."

He just assumed I'd become Chelsea Shaneybrook. Well, it sounded good, so I guessed I would. It wasn't as if I had college degrees or other important bits of history under the name of Chelsea Lyndon.

Before we went to my apartment, we stopped at a mall and went shopping. Or rather, Tripp went shopping. In a sporting goods store. He bought a baseball. I thought that was kind of odd, but I really didn't know much about baseball players, active or retired.

The police were at my apartment when we arrived. I showed my driver's license, and they let me in once I explained what I needed. They were really nice about it.

Tripp stood in the living room while I gathered clothes, my strongbox with all my important papers, my credit card files, and asked if I could take the *Spring Party* poster off the dinette wall. That poster epitomized every dream I'd ever had, and I wanted it with me to remind me there was always hope.

Tripp said nothing as he helped me lug everything downstairs. The poster was too long for the trunk of his car, so Tripp put it in the backseat.

We drove to the offices of the Genevieve Hart-Darling Foundation, where I picked up my final paycheck, which included accrued and unused vacation pay. He drove around the block while I ran in and out.

Of course, now I had no way to cash the thing, because I'd closed my bank account, so we opened a joint account at his bank. His name alone was enough for me to cash my checks.

I couldn't believe how being a jock star simplified things.

Our trip to the county courthouse was a bust because Tripp didn't have his birth certificate, so we couldn't get our marriage license. Neither of us was happy about that.

Another phone call to the vet informed me I couldn't take Foggy home for several days. I shuddered to think how much this was costing and then tried not to think about money.

Then it was time to visit Caitlin. We drove to the state teaching med center, where she'd been taken. Tripp held my hand as we walked into the gloomy space.

She looked so very small against the white sheets. Her head was bandaged, and the exposed parts of her face were bruised and swollen.

I winced.

"Hi," she said.

"You look like hell," I said.

"At least he didn't break my jaw." The words were garbled.

"That's looking on the bright side," I replied. "This is Tripp."

He moved into her line of vision. "Hi, Caitlin," he said, his voice low.

"Welcome to the family."

"Thanks."

Awkward silence. I didn't know what to say to her. Maybe I shouldn't have brought Tripp with me. I should have left him in the cafeteria or something.

He must have read my mind, because he squeezed my hand and told me he'd be in the waiting room.

But even after he left, I didn't know what to say to Caitlin.

She didn't have any such problem. "Cute and rich. You always seem to have all the luck. He good in bed?"

"I'm not discussing my sex life with you," I said.

"Good in bed." She sighed. "You're glowing."

"Look," I said. "We don't want to wait to get married. And it looks as if you're going to be here for a while."

"Yeah."

"I'm sorry," I said, because I was.

"Hey, I don't blame you. If I had someone that hot and that rich panting after me, I'd hurry up and get the ring on my finger too."

She didn't get it. That was why she had ended up with Spencer.

"Sorry about your place," she said. "But Mr. All-Star can replace your stuff."

A lot of the stuff destroyed were irreplaceable antiques. And Foggy couldn't be replaced.

"What happened?" I asked.

"I don't remember." She closed her eyes. "The doctors say I may never remember. That I won't ever recall the events leading up to the head trauma. I guess Tanner found me when he came by to collect his rent. Really, you should know better than to cross anyone in Spencer's family."

I wanted to grab her by the shoulders and shake her. It was as if she lacked a common-sense gene or something.

I decided to change the subject. "So, are you going to Vera House?"

"A counselor's been in," Caitlin replied. "I don't know what I'm going to do."

"You're not considering going back to Spencer?" I shouldn't have been surprised. This might be the worst he'd even beaten her, but it certainly wasn't the first time.

"Well, I thought maybe I could come live with you and your rich boyfriend."

"No." I didn't prevaricate at all. If I wasn't firm from the very first, I'd end up with her around my neck. I loved Caitlin, but Caitlin had to learn to do for herself.

"You are so selfish. You always have been," she pouted. "Look at me. I'm stuck here in the hospital. You're getting married without me. I don't dare go home, and now you're telling me I can't stay with you."

I inhaled deeply and braced myself to say the things I should have said to her years ago. "Stop blaming me for your bad decisions. I'm not going to take responsibility anymore."

She acted as if I'd hit her. I suppose in a way I had. I'd always coddled her far too much, a habit learned from Grandma Judy.

Spencer wasn't going to change. Caitlin wasn't going to change. I had no control over either of them. The only thing in the whole world over which any of us has control is our own attitude. And over the past week, my attitude had undergone some serious revisions. It had been gutted and left like an empty snail shell. I was slowly rebuilding my reality.

Caitlin needed to do the same, but she wasn't going to do it on my back. Not again.

"I'm moving away from Syracuse," I told her. I didn't tell her that I'd be only a couple of hours away. I needed space to recreate my sense of security. Space and distance.

Of course, Caitlin read it as I was abandoning her. That was how she'd suckered me into moving from Akron to Syracuse in the first place.

"How can you do this to me? I need you right now."

"I can't be your crutch. I'm not abandoning you, but I can't be your crutch. You need to learn to stand on your own."

"What about your job? Your apartment?"

"I quit my job, and you know perfectly well what happened to my apartment." *Spencer and a baseball bat.* But I didn't say that part aloud. "I don't have my cell phone right now," I said. "The police confiscated it because of the phone calls from you so they can pinpoint the time line of the attack."

"He didn't *attack* me."

"You're in a hospital bed with a fractured skull!" I practically yelled at her. "He took a baseball bat and whacked you with it. Caitlin T-ball league!"

She didn't say anything. No comeback. Very unusual for Caitlin.

I closed my eyes. Old habit wanted to reach out to her and assure her that I would do whatever I could to help her. It was time to let go. Helping her really meant teaching her to stand on her own. Leaving Spencer. Creating a new world without him, and temporarily without me.

"I can't help you until you start helping yourself," I said as quietly as I could.

It's called tough love for a reason.

But Tripp was right. If I'd been there in my own apartment, it could have been me in that hospital bed now, because Spencer in a rage is Spencer completely out of control. Caitlin and I could survive better alone.

She still wouldn't answer me.

"I'll call you later," I promised. "And you have Tripp's number if you need to reach me."

Tears blurred my vision as I made my way to the waiting room. Where Tripp awaited me with open arms.

"I'm so sorry, honey," he whispered as he held me close.

"I told her," I said. "I told her that I'm moving away and that she has to go to Vera House and get help. That I can't keep bailing her out."

"You did the right thing."

"What if he kills her next time?"

"What if he kills you?"

Our next stop was my landlord's office. This was not my idea. I would have been delighted to simply mail a check to Tanner, but I guess Tripp wanted to have a come-to-Jesus moment with the would-be extortionist.

Tripp carried the bag from the sporting goods store with him. I wondered if he were going to bean Tanner in the head with it. I thought it was a great idea.

Tanner's secretary told him we were there, and he came out of his office acting all noble and charming.

"I'm here to pay my rent," I said. I assumed Tripp had his checkbook.

"Just how much does she owe you?" Tripp asked, sounding charismatic.

Tanner named a figure that was triple my usual rent.

I felt the blood drain from my face.

"So I double that for this month and next month?" Tripp asked. What was it Scarlett O'Hara kept saying in *Gone with the Wind?* Butter wouldn't melt in his mouth.

Tanner shot a glance at me and nodded.

"And this is because the bounced rent check broke the lease?" Tripp continued.

"That's right." Tanner was practically drooling. "I'm a big fan, Tripp."

Tripp smiled. "So the lease is broken. Can we get that in writing?"

Tanner glanced at me again. "Um, I delivered a letter to Chelsea the other day. You got it, right, Chels?"

I nodded. He'd slipped it under my door while I was at work. I still had it in my purse, thinking maybe I'd sue him for usury or something.

"Good," Tripp said. His smile morphed from charm to aw-shucks. The dimples framing his mouth deepened. He pulled the baseball out of the bag and wrote something on it. "How do you spell your name?" he asked Tanner.

Tanner's eyes grew wide as he replied and watched Tripp write his name on the ball.

"Chelsea will be moving out by the end of the month, but I've included an extra month's rent. Here you go," Tripp said, extending the ball to Tanner.

"Oh, wow, Mr. Shaneybrook, I mean Tripp. An autographed ball."

Tripp shook his head. "No, that's your rent check. Come on, Chelsea. We need to get going."

"But...but..." Tanner sputtered. He turned the ball over in his hands. I could just see the words, *Pay to the order of Tanner Madison* and a series of numbers below Tripp's signature.

Tripp practically dragged me out of the office.

"What was that about?" I asked when we got back to his car.

"Well, I figured if he was going to jerk you around over a bounced check—the first one you've ever had—and one that was caused by his own cousin, well then, we could jerk him around a little."

I still didn't get it.

"Not to toot my own horn or anything, but in a couple of years, my signature on a baseball could be worth a lot more than the amount he claims you owe him. Now he has a dilemma—does he cash the check or keep the baseball?"

"Is that legal?" I asked.

Tripp nodded as he pulled into traffic. "I called my accountant this morning while you were in the shower. He made arrangements with the bank to honor the check for six months. If Tanner doesn't cash the check in six months, then the check itself is void. And yes, that's legal too."

We stopped at Shaneybrook's for dinner before going home. I was too wiped to think about planning a meal, buying groceries, cooking, and cleaning.

I kept seeing Caitlin's face, the hint of expression that seeped through bandages and bruises, and I felt like a worthless human being. Grandma Judy guilt nailed me every time.

Penn fixed us something light—the late July heat and humidity only added to everything else that was wrong. Lemony, garlicky grilled chicken and fresh steamed green beans fit the bill.

I loved the restaurant more each time I visited. Penn or someone had created a classy, casual feeling. Combined with the world-class food, it was a recipe for success. I couldn't understand Tripp's allegation that Baird McKechnie wanted to sabotage it.

"Penn," I said, acting purely on impulse. "I want you to see something."

Tripp shot me a quizzical look. He had no idea what I was talking about.

"Car keys, please," I said as I held out my palm. I still didn't have my own set.

Tripp handed them over.

The Shaneybrook brothers followed me out of the restaurant to Tripp's car. It was seven o'clock, but there was still plenty of light outside. The sun was a huge, juicy mango dripping across the western horizon.

The car chirped as I used the remote to unlock its doors.

There, in the backseat and slightly dusty, was my prized poster from the Boston Museum of Fine Arts: Janet Fish's *Spring Party*.

I pulled it out of the car. "This is what I want for a wedding reception."

He stared, as did Tripp. My gut told me Penn would understand—if he was the one responsible for the ambience of the restaurant.

No one said a word for several moments. "May I keep this?" Penn finally asked.

I shook my head.

"I meant borrow. So I can study it."

Oh. That was different. "Of course."

He looked from the poster to me. "This explains a lot."

I hoped that meant something good.

Tripp carried the poster to Penn's apartment, while I returned to our table and Penn brought out bowls of freshly sliced peaches accented with raspberries for dessert.

"Is that okay with you?" I asked Tripp when he rejoined me. "Our reception—our post-wedding party being like that?"

"Of course," he said. He smiled.

Watching him smile was like watching the sun rise in the morning after a night filled with bad dreams.

It was almost dark by the time we made it to the lake house. We rode in silence. I didn't have a clue about what Tripp was thinking, but I was brooding about Caitlin and the wedding. I guess I'd always thought that since my wedding day was supposed to be *my* special day, that everything would be exactly as I wanted it. Okay, I knew the Greek island was out of the question. That was why Janet Fish painted *Spring Party* for me. Right? And part of those dreams included Caitlin.

I guessed I was going to have to settle for the man of my dreams instead of the wedding of my fantasies. But I couldn't shake the sense that Caitlin was getting cheated on a lot of different levels.

"Wanna watch a movie?" Tripp asked as soon as we finished hauling in the stuff I'd retrieved from my apartment.

"Sure," I said. Movies were definitely in my comfort zone.

"How about this one?" He held up a DVD of *Mamma Mia.*

"I thought you hated it," I said.

"I said I've never seen it. I am emphatically not an ABBA fan, and this really sounds like a chick flick." He made a face.

"Where did you get it?" I asked. I knew we hadn't stopped anywhere he could buy it.

"Your living room floor," he admitted. "I'm curious about what you want for a reception."

If I hadn't already fallen butt over teakettle for this guy, I would have done it right then.

"Why don't you get us something to drink—wine or something—while I get set up?" he suggested.

I found a bottle of sauvignon blanc in the back of the refrigerator, pulled the cork, and poured a couple of glasses. Tripp made a toast, and we cuddled up together on the sofa to watch Meryl Streep, Pierce Brosnan, and Colin Firth sing and dance their way across Tripp's wide screen.

"You know," he said during one number, "the story isn't bad. The movie might be tolerable without the music."

He kissed the tip of my nose to soften the critique.

Finally, the wedding reception. The meal out on the patio, with the embroidered linens, candles, and vases filled with flowers plucked from the mountainside. Nothing elaborate, just bright and vibrant in its simplicity.

"Maybe we could go to Greece on our honeymoon," he said.

Everything in me stilled. Greece had always been my ultimate fantasy destination. "Are you serious?" I whispered.

"Well, they don't play baseball there, but other than that, isn't it one of the cradles of civilization? Sure, I wouldn't mind going."

I thought my heart was going to beat its way out of my chest.

"Besides," he said, "I can see you'd really like to go."

How did I ever meet this wonderful man? What had I ever done to deserve this kind of adoration?

We finished watching the movie. By the time it was over, the wine and the emotions of the past twenty-four hours or so had caught up with me, and I was more than ready to go to bed.

I kissed Tripp good night while he watched some cable sports network to catch up on baseball scores.

I kept thinking about Caitlin as I brushed my teeth and washed my face.

What if we got married in Caitlin's hospital room? Penn could come to Syracuse for the day to stand up for Tripp, we could get the hospital chaplain—if there was such a being—and we could exchange vows right there. Caitlin didn't need a fancy dress, a hairdo, or makeup. She just needed to witness the most important day of my life.

I pulled on one of Tripp's T-shirts and started down the stairs to discuss this whacked out idea with him. I was midway down when I saw someone on the deck.

Maura St. John.

I froze where I was, hopefully hidden by the shadows.

She rapped on the door and then let herself into the house.

"What are you doing here?" Tripp asked.

"I need to see you."

Tripp leaped off the sofa. "You shouldn't be here."

She moved closer to him, and he backed away until he was against the breakfast bar separating the kitchen from the living room. She dropped to her knees in front of him and reached for his fly.

Tears scalded my cheeks.

"No!" He leaped over her head. "Get out of my house right now. As far as I'm concerned, you just tendered your resignation from Camp Home Safe."

Some of the tightness in my chest eased. I struggled not to whimper.

"I need to talk to you. I need your help."

"I'm marrying Chelsea just as soon as we can get a license," he told her. "I doubt there's anything I can do for you."

Maura stayed on her knees, as if in prayer. Tears glistened on her face. "Why her? She's…a little white-trash nothing!"

"You're the one acting like a trashy nothing. She's got more class in a little toenail clipping than you'll ever have in your life."

Tripp couldn't be talking about me. Yet it seemed he was.

"I'm pregnant."

Tripp reacted as if she'd kneed him in the privates.

He got off easy compared to what her words did to me. Eviscerated.

"What does that have to do with me?" His voice was hoarse and full of nasty undertones. "You're not going to try to tell me I'm responsible."

She didn't say anything.

"I don't believe you," he said. "I think this is just another of your manipulative games, and guess what? I'm not buying."

I sank to the step and pulled my knees to my chest, trying to make myself as small and as invulnerable as I could. I knew I shouldn't stay there, hidden and eavesdropping, but I couldn't move. I could barely breathe.

"You're a decent man," she whispered.

"You wouldn't know decency if it came up and spit in your eye, would you?"

"You'll do the right thing. I know you will"

"That's right. I will. The right thing is marrying the woman I love, who is upstairs, asleep in my bed. A woman who cares more about me than about what she looks like with me. She's as honest as the day is long and as uncomplicated as a summer day. She never tries to impress me or anyone else. She just is, and I am so damned lucky I found her."

"Your brother told me the truth," Maura interrupted. "That Baird brought her here to make Penn jealous and then dumped her at the restaurant. She's a tool. Not worthy of you."

"I'm saying this just one last time. Get out of my house before I call the sheriff and have you arrested for trespassing." He turned his back on her.

She got to her feet and lurched toward him. "Please, Tripp, I love you. I know I can make you love me and the baby."

Tripp pulled his phone out of his pocket. "Have your lawyer call my lawyer." His tone was arctic. "I want DNA testing as soon as possible. I don't believe you for a minute, but just in case you're telling the truth for once in your pathetic life and it is my kid, you can bet you won't have custody. Now you have ten seconds to get out."

She lifted one arm, reaching for him. Even from my distant vantage point, I saw his jaw do the pulsing, throbbing thing.

Finally, as silently as a ghost, Maura slipped out of the house.

Tripp stood rigid for several moments. Tense. Angry. When he did move, it was to the sliders, which he locked, and then he savagely drew the blinds, blocking out the night. Then he went to the breakfast bar and braced his hands against it, his head hanging. His broad shoulders moved with his heavy breathing.

I wanted to go to him and comfort him, but shock limited me. My heart beat, my lungs inhaled and exhaled, but my body was capable of no more.

He punched the counter. "God-*fucking*-damn it."

I must have made a sound then. A squeak startled out of me or something, because he slowly raised his head and looked in my direction. Our gazes clashed.

"Tell me you weren't there the whole time," he said.

"I'm sorry. I didn't mean to eavesdrop. I was on my way down to talk to you when she came in."

He slumped, as if all his bones suddenly melted or he didn't have the strength to stand upright. He raked his fingers through his hair.

"Fuck."

"I'm sorry," I apologized again.

"I'm the one who should apologize to you," he replied after a painful pause. "I should have known Maura would pull this kind of shit."

I buried my face against my knees, letting the soft cotton of the T-shirt absorb my tears. All I could think about was Maura having Tripp's baby, the baby he'd told me he wanted to give me. I was jealous. I was hurt. I was devastated.

I stayed like that until Tripp squatted next to me on the bare wooden step. He rubbed my nape. "C'mon. Let's go to bed. To talk. Okay?"

I didn't know if I could do that. I was growing fond of my little fortress in the dark corner.

"Please."

I lifted my face. He'd turned off the downstairs light. The only illumination came from his bedroom, where I'd left on the light.

He didn't look so trophy-like in the gloom. He looked...tarnished. And I hated that I thought that way about him. Until I realized he looked human, and that made me feel better. I'm only human after all, and it would be a lot easier to spend the rest of my life with someone as flawed as I than with a trophy.

He helped me stand. We walked to the bedroom with our arms around each other. Then he sat me on the edge of the bed and stood in front of me.

"Sit down," I said. "I hate it when you tower over me."

He sat. He reached for my hand and toyed with my engagement ring.

"I don't think I'm the father of her baby," he said, cutting through the crap. No prevaricating. One of the things I most loved about him. "It's been too long...six months at least. And even then, I was always real careful with her. A lot more careful than I've been with you, that's for sure. Safe sex isn't just about birth control."

That was supposed to make me feel better?

I untangled my fingers from his and scooted up to the headboard so I could lean against it.

He collapsed onto his back, placing himself lower than me. He stared at the ceiling.

All I could think of at that moment was the old joke about the differences between a whore, a mistress, and a wife: the whore said, "Faster, faster"; the mistress said, "Slower, slower"; and the wife said, "Beige. We ought to paint the ceiling beige."

Yeah, I wasn't good in a crisis.

My chest was still tight. Every beat of my heart still felt like a sucker punch to the gut, and every breath burned like bronchitis.

"What if her baby is yours?" I finally asked.

"I doubt she's even pregnant," Tripp said. "She just likes to be the center of attention and will do just about anything to get it."

"But what if she is pregnant, and it's your baby?" I wasn't anything if not persistent.

"If she is, and if it's mine—I'm telling you, I swear to you that it's almost impossible that it's mine—then I'll fight her for it. I wouldn't let her keep a goldfish she won at a carnival." He turned his head and looked at me instead of the ceiling. "I'm sorry. I know that impacts you, and you should have some say. But a kid shouldn't have to suffer because its parents are idiots."

I nodded. "My grandmother raised me and Caitlin for that very reason."

Tripp reached for my hand again. "You are amazing," he whispered.

I didn't feel amazing. I felt beat up. Still stunned.

The image of Maura St. John dropping to her knees in front of Tripp and reaching for his fly was branded on my retinas. "So do most women greet you on their knees?" I asked around what felt like shards of glass in my throat.

He didn't turn his gaze away from mine. "They tend to."

I nodded just once.

"I don't need that from you," he said, his voice soft. "You don't need to impress me with your sexual skills. I'd rather kiss you than have you give me a blowjob."

Actually, I didn't have any sexual skills. I was just in love with him. Crazy in love with him.

The bedside lamps threw shadows over the even planes of his face. He rubbed the center of my palm with his thumb.

"I don't know what I ever did to have you drop into my life," he said. "But I thank God for you every day. Sometimes, when you're sleeping, I watch you, and I can't believe that you love me. That you're going to share the rest of your life with me."

It had never occurred to me that Tripp would be just as amazed by me as I was by him. I didn't consider myself amazing at all.

"We're going to be okay," he assured me. Or maybe he was trying to convince himself. "You do understand what happened here tonight?"

I nodded. If Maura loved him a tenth of how much I loved him, no wonder she was willing to humiliate herself the way she had.

Tripp closed his eyes and heaved a sigh. "I told you I don't believe in hitting women, but I came close tonight."

I remembered the way his shoulders had tensed after she left.

"And what you said to me, right after we first met, about notoriously promiscuous professional athletes. Well, that stung too. Except I outgrew that a long time ago. But tonight, when she showed up, got on her knees, it brought it all back. Cheap, empty sex. Get off. Get out. I felt so...empty."

I wasn't sure I wanted to hear all this.

Of course he had a past. He probably wasn't born a magnificent lover but had practiced just like he had his batting and fielding.

"The thought of her having my baby when I want to get you pregnant makes me sick. From the moment I first saw you, I've been imagining my baby pushing out the front of your clothes. A little girl with your gray eyes and dark hair calling me Daddy."

Wow. That was pretty vivid.

"I took one look at you and fell in love. I knew right away that you're the woman I've been waiting for."

"Let me guess. It was the mud."

"No, the bare feet," he said. His smile seemed sad. No dimples, no aw-shucks. He raised my hand to his mouth and kissed the center of my palm, the spot he always massaged when he held my hand.

I realized the tightness in my chest was gone. Breathing didn't hurt.

"It was your sense of being lost, a little out of control, but not wanting any help. Not expecting anything from me or anyone except Baird, whom you expected to do the right thing."

Had it been only ten days ago? It seemed like a lifetime.

"You believe people will do the right thing—not necessarily the thing you want them to do but to be honorable. Like with your landlord and your cousin."

I didn't know who he was talking about. He must have had me confused with some other Chelsea.

"You do love me, don't you?" he asked. He sounded as if his whole life were dependent on my answer.

I nodded. "Maybe too much."

He tugged on my hand, repositioned his hand until it wrapped around my wrist, and then pulled me to him.

"Never too much," he whispered. "You can never love me too much."

He kissed me. Softly. Gently. At least at first. It was like the very first time he'd kissed me in Penn's bathroom last Saturday. I'd been covered in mud and was hurting in my heart as well as my ankle.

He twined his fingers with mine, sliding his between mine on both hands.

"Forgive me," he asked.

"There's nothing to forgive you for," I said. "Whatever happened between you and Maura happened before you met me."

Didn't mean I had to like it, but I couldn't hold him responsible for things that happened pre-me.

"You want me to lose the tampon and get a towel?" I asked.

"Only if you want to," he said.

His erection prodded my belly.

I wasn't the only one wanting.

I kissed him lightly on the mouth and then rolled off the bed. "Give me a minute."

Chapter Sixteen

It rained that night. The patter of the drops hitting the roof woke me several times. I wondered if the windows were closed and then remembered I wasn't home, and Tripp had central air. I hadn't seen an open window all week.

The morning dawned gloomily. I awoke before Tripp, slipped out of bed, and took care of business in the bathroom. Before I went downstairs, I pulled on my swimsuit, followed by one of Tripp's T-shirts. I opened the blinds to the deck.

The rain had stopped, but the clouds were gray layers of dust bunnies scuttling across the sky. The hour was still early enough for the air to be cool, and the humidity only made it clammy instead of sweaty.

I started a pot of coffee.

Not getting ready for work felt as weird as not being in my own territory. I had no car, no phone—exactly like my first weekend in Cooperstown. I was a prisoner.

I didn't think Tripp was purposely isolating me, not the way Spencer tried to cut off all of Caitlin's options, but the similarities didn't sit well with me. Even a set of keys to one of Tripp's vehicles would have made me feel better.

The fragrance of coffee filled the kitchen. I poured myself a cup, using one of Tripp's boring mud-colored mugs. I couldn't wait to integrate my own sunshine-yellow oversize mugs into his dull repertoire. My Fiestaware might have been history, but I still had plenty of cheerful dishes and other household items to contribute.

I looked around the living area with a critical eye. Naturally, everything was dim, given that the room was built to depend on natural light to showcase its beauty. It looked professionally decorated, like something in one of those high-gloss magazines. But magazine pictures were two-dimensional, and I was definitely a three-dimensional kind of girl. I craved light and color. One of the things I loved most about my apartment was the east-facing front porch off my living room and the French doors that let in the sunrise every morning.

All the beige and blue in Tripp's living room was depressing.

He should have let his brother decorate his house. Penn's apartment was full of color, textures, and light.

I opened the sliders and stepped onto the puddle-pocked deck. Everything was wet. Even the spider webs spun between the railing posts captured raindrops like crystal beads on a necklace.

The sun started erasing the clouds. Fog rose like steam from the lake. I stood at the railing and sipped my coffee. A family of ducks glided across the silver surface of the water. I decided to join them. I pulled the T-shirt over my head and draped it across a chaise.

"Hello," Maura said.

Coffee sloshed out of my mug and scalded my hands. I turned, feeling vulnerable in my skimpy two-piece swimsuit. I said nothing. I had nothing to say to this woman.

"I used to wear his T-shirt and drink my morning coffee out here too," she said as she came up the steps from the driveway. "You're only temporary."

God, she was beautiful, even with dark circles beneath her turquoise eyes and fine lines marring the corners of her mouth. This morning she wore a pale green capri suit with a silky cream-colored shell beneath the short-sleeved blazer. Her trademark corkscrew red curls cascaded down her back.

I could never look that good even if I had her money.

I wrapped my fingers around my mug, making sure she could see the diamond on my left hand. I brought the mug to my mouth and sipped. I wasn't going to argue with her.

Desperate people frighten me.

She wasn't looking at my hands but at my legs.

"I'm pregnant," she said.

"Congratulations," I murmured, breaking my silence.

A sneer twisted her features. "That's all you have to say?"

I shrugged. There were a lot of things I could say, but I felt sorry for her. I didn't need to goad her. I could have. Verbal sparring with Caitlin all these years had given me a potent ability to wound with sarcasm. But I felt bad for Maura. I know how I would have felt if I'd been dumped by someone I loved.

"It's Tripp's baby." She practically spat the lie at me. I knew she was lying as well as I knew my own name. I believed Tripp, and if he said he didn't think it could be his child, then it wasn't his child.

"Then DNA testing won't bother you," I calmly replied.

"What will you do then?" she snapped.

"Pray for your child," I said. "You don't strike me as a very maternal type. And if Tripp is the father, then he's going to want to be an active father. I guess I need to brush up on my cookie-baking skills."

Nonexistent cookie-baking skills.

"It doesn't bother you?"

"Not nearly as much as it seems to be bothering you," I lied.

Because, yeah, it bothered me. I didn't know if I could be gracious about it, and I knew for certain I didn't want to share Tripp with this woman on any level. I wanted her out of our lives, because she was the type—every instinct I possessed screamed it—who would never leave Tripp alone, not if there was a link like a child binding them.

Maura pulled out her cell phone.

"What are you doing here?" Tripp stood behind the slider's screen. "I thought I told you to leave."

I would have flinched if someone addressed me in that brutal a tone of voice, but Maura barely acknowledged his presence. She was intent on reading her text messages or something.

Tripp stepped onto the deck. He wore nothing but his navy jersey boxers.

That got Maura's attention. She stared at him as if she were a starving woman, and he was a carton of her favorite ice cream. I saw her breath hitch.

The sun chose that moment to burst through the gloom, homing in on Tripp like a spotlight. His hair flashed gold. The award statuette was back.

"I... Please, be reasonable," she replied. "Arguing isn't going to solve anything."

"There's nothing to solve."

I flinched, and his ire wasn't even aimed at me.

"Either you have your lawyer contact mine, or I'll have mine contact yours. We are done with face-to-face dialogue."

If I hadn't been watching her so closely, I wouldn't have seen her nostrils flare and wouldn't have seen the ever so slight tightening of her lips.

She pocketed her phone, turned, and left the deck without another word.

Neither Tripp nor I moved or said a word until the sound of her car on the road faded.

"How long was she here?" Tripp asked.

I sipped my coffee before answering. "Not long."

"Did she upset you?"

Of course she upset me! I wanted to scream, but I shook my head. "I gave her something to think about."

He arched an eyebrow, but I shook my head. He didn't need to know every little detail of my devious brain.

I felt quite proud that I'd behaved myself, hadn't goaded her, insulted her, and belittled or demeaned her.

"Want some coffee? The pot's fresh."

We drove to the county seat in Oneonta to get our marriage license. I also insisted on getting duplicate keys to both of his vehicles made. Tripp agreed without a murmur.

When we got home, I borrowed his phone to call the vet to check on Foggy, who was doing as well as could be expected, the vet assured me. Then I called the med center to speak to Caitlin. Who wouldn't speak to me.

I handed Tripp's phone back to him. "What if we got married in Caitlin's hospital room?" I asked. Everything that had happened with Maura had pushed the idea out of my head until just then. "Penn could come to Syracuse for a morning or an afternoon, couldn't he? Then we could have our reception at a later date." Right about now, never would have been too soon.

Tripp sat on the edge of the sofa. He used the remote to flick through channels almost as fast as the speed of light. How could he even tell what was on?

"If that's what you want."

"And I want to sign a prenuptial before we set the date."

"My lawyer's working on that," he told me. His gaze was glued to the television. He'd found a baseball game. "We're supposed to sign it tomorrow."

I stood in the kitchen and looked around. I was restless. I wasn't used to inactivity. I'd worked hard for the Genevieve Hart-Darling Foundation. I used to clean my apartment, watch movies, play with my cat, and hang with Caitlin when Spencer would let her. I'd had a life.

Now I was an appendage—unless I learned to like baseball real fast.

I told myself it could be worse. He could have been a football fan. Except maybe he was. Even I knew that it wasn't football season yet.

"Want some iced tea?" I asked.

"Thanks, honey," he replied rather absently. He leaned back and watched the game. "Come sit with me."

I brought glasses of tea and placed them on coasters on the coffee table.

I sat next to him. He draped his arm around my shoulder and pulled me closer. One long, deep kiss, and then the commercial break was over. The game was on again.

Fortunately, baseball was the kind of sport where you can actually hold a conversation while watching the game.

"I need to get my phone back from the Syracuse police," I said.

"I'll get you a new one," he replied. "A super phone."

"I need to get the tires fixed on my car."

"I don't want you driving that rattle trap," he said. "It's too small and too old. I bought you something safer. We pick it up tomorrow."

Was anything about me right?

"Do you just throw money at things to make them better?"

"If I think it'll work." He grinned. "You're cute when you're ticked off at me."

"I want to choose my car and my own phone."

That seemed to startle him.

"I need something to do," I continued. "I've always worked."

"Well, I've been thinking about that," he said. "Camp Home Safe always needs help." Aw-shucks was all over his face. "I think it would be a great thing if my wife was involved in my work too."

I might have warmed to the idea if Maura hadn't suggested it first, when she accused Tripp of marrying a grant writer.

"So, since the Saltboilers are in Louisville, want to drive to Cortland tonight and watch the Single-A Crowns?"

The next morning, we drove to Syracuse. Tripp added me to his phone account and bought me a super cell, complete with a wireless earpiece. Another store at the mall yielded a tablet computer for my new job as a grant writer for Camp Home Safe. Then we picked up my new gas-guzzling high-end luxury SUV. Black.

That vehicle was a sin.

I donated my old car to an organization that disburses monies to charities and named Camp Home Safe as the recipient.

Tripp seemed awfully pleased.

Then we met with his lawyer, where I was supposed to sign a prenuptial agreement. His lawyer was shocked that I didn't have a lawyer. I'd never needed one. Both Tripp and the lawyer insisted I read the document thoroughly, even though I trusted Tripp. Independent witnesses watched me read it.

"The only thing that's missing is that I get his privates on a gold platter if he cheats on me," I said.

The lawyer blanched.

Tripp grinned. "Okay. Add it." He pushed the papers back to the lawyer.

I'd meant the comment as a joke. But as the words left my mouth, I realized that Tripp could pull a Tiger Woods on me, and I'd be stuck. Even if I volunteered for his camp, I'd still be out of the workforce. Which could make me unemployable—a woman without current job skills. If something should happen to us, I needed to live.

The whole thing scared me.

So I reread the document, paying a lot more attention to certain aspects.

Yeah, there was a provision for a flat million dollars if the marriage ended through no fault of my own—in other words, if Tripp ended the marriage. If I ended it, I would get nothing.

How awful that we were dealing with a marriage ending even before we spoke our vows.

Then I thought that if I ever found out he was cheating on me, and he didn't want to end the marriage so he wouldn't have to give me a million dollars, I was screwed too.

"I want another clause," I said, my voice barely working. I couldn't believe I was doing this. "If I have proof that Tripp is unfaithful to me, and I chose to end the marriage for that reason and that reason alone, then I want the same money I get if Tripp opts to end the marriage."

I hated this. Hated, hated, hated this.

Then I thought about all the notoriously promiscuous professional athletes out in the world.

"No. I don't want a million dollars," I amended. "I just want enough money to live on until I can start supporting myself again."

Tripp and his lawyer stared at me as if I'd sprouted a second head. I didn't want Tripp's money, but I didn't want to be in Caitlin's shoes either. Or Grandma Judy's slippers. "And he should be one hundred percent fiscally responsible for any children."

"Put it in," Tripp told his lawyer, his gaze never leaving my face. "Make sure the definition of unfaithful includes oral sex."

The lawyer sputtered.

I nodded as I pushed the papers across the desk.

"How soon can you make the changes?" Tripp asked. "She refuses to marry me until she signs one of these."

"Tomorrow?" the lawyer offered.

"Five tonight?" Tripp suggested.

The lawyer never blinked. "Of course."

"Good." Tripp smiled at him.

I guessed Tripp paid this firm a lot of money, and they would jump through fire to keep him happy.

I knew the feeling.

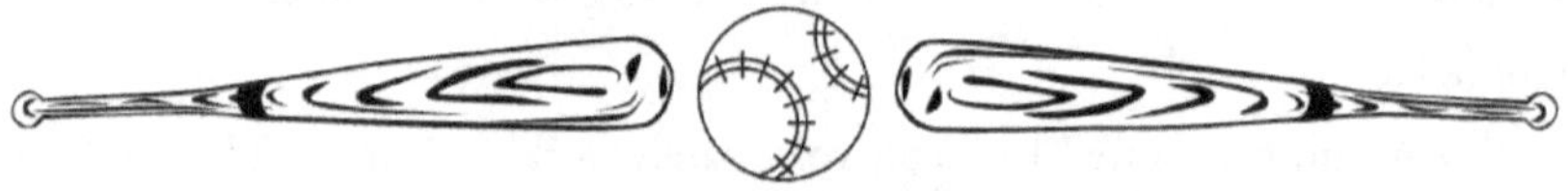

We stopped by my apartment. The crime-scene tape was gone, but the door still hung askew. The stairwell light was still out. A lot of people were boxing up my belongings.

Everything inside me froze. "What's this?" I asked.

"I didn't want you to be bothered, so I hired someone to come in."

I was...furious.

Strangers. In my home. Going through my things. Touching my stuff.

"No," I said. My voice shook. "You can't just barrel in and take over. We've already discussed this."

We stood in the middle of the living room, shafts of sunlight from the tiny windows over my sofa delineating the space between us. The dark hardwood floors didn't gleam the way the ones in his lake house did. My furniture was shabby. The sofa was now stained with blood. My rugs were cheap imitations, but they were mine. I'd pulled this apartment together to make my own little nest, and now it was being violated. Again.

"You could at least ask me before you high-handedly decide what to do with my life."

He seemed genuinely puzzled. "I didn't think you'd mind. I'm sorry."

And yeah, he was sorry, but he didn't feel or understand the depth of my emotion.

"Maybe I wanted to go through things on my own. Toss some stuff."

"So toss it."

Was it just me, or was he being awfully dense?

"I don't want strangers fondling my underwear!" I shouted.

That got his attention.

"I don't want strangers going through my personal papers!"

He took a step back.

"What part of 'I don't want you controlling my life' don't you understand?" I threw the keys to the SUV at him.

He caught them. Show-off.

"Calm down."

"I've been calm, and you just don't get it when I'm calm."

I went into the kitchen where a slender blonde in blue jeans was wrapping my blue willow plates.

"Stop," I commanded. "You're fired."

I might as well have been a ghost, the way she looked through me to find Tripp and await his instructions. Enough was enough.

"Call them off right now," I said, keeping my voice steady and quiet. "I mean it."

He must have seen my determination and acknowledged, because he nodded to the woman in the kitchen.

"You'll be paid for your time," he assured her.

She shrugged, as if it didn't matter, and went, I assumed, to gather her coworkers and leave.

The apartment was stifling. Uncomfortable. But it didn't matter.

He leaned against my kitchen counter, arms crossed over his chest. "What's wrong with you?"

Wrong with me?

I inhaled deeply but said nothing. I waited until the crew of four (four!) left my tiny apartment, wadding my fists at my side so I wouldn't jump and frisk them as they filed out the door. I waited until the last clump of footfalls on the stairs faded. I waited until I heard a vehicle start and then drive away.

The whole time, I kept trying to tell myself that Tripp was being generous, he loved me, he wanted to give me things, and he didn't want me to have to worry about anything...and that worried the daylights out of me.

"Want to tell me what that tantrum was about?" His tone was cool. At least it wasn't as frigid as the one he used with Maura.

I swallowed. Hard. "Look, I appreciate your generosity."

He arched an eyebrow.

"Spencer started out this way with Caitlin," I blurted. "Nothing was too good for her. It was a control thing. I know it's not a control thing with you." I hoped. "But it feels...creepy."

His mouth thinned into a hard line. Difficult to imagine kissing those lips when they were so...angry.

"Not that you're creepy or anything even close," I hastened to add. "But some of the things you do are sending up warning flags, and I can't ignore them."

There. I'd said it.

He flipped the keys to the SUV back to me. "There you go. Feel free to leave."

"This is my apartment. Unless you're going to tell me it's yours because you paid the rent."

"No, it's yours. So is the car. No strings."

I closed my eyes for a minute, trying to calm the whirling dervish of my thoughts. "I love you," I whispered. "But you have to consult me about me, not just take over."

"I don't appreciate being compared to a wife beater." His tone was still cool and still steady.

I opened my eyes again. "I wasn't comparing you and Spencer."

"It sounded like it to me."

I shook my head.

"I have never hit a woman in my life and have only wanted to maybe once or twice."

"I know that," I said. "My heart knows that."

"Then what the *fuck* is the matter with your head?"

I didn't think my legs were going to support me much longer. My ankle started bothering me again, even though over the past couple of days I barely remembered I'd sprained it.

I'm not good at confrontation. At least I wasn't crying. That helped.

"My head knows it too, but my head also sees something beyond physical abuse."

I couldn't believe I'd just said that out loud.

But it was true. I had vague and probably inaccurate memories of my mother changing to appease the man du jour. I had very clear memories of how Spencer mastered Caitlin, until she was completely helpless.

I wanted better. I wanted more. Maybe I didn't go to college and wasn't book smart and polished, but I was smart enough to support myself. I was smart enough not to need a man to survive.

Maybe that was all my heebie-jeebies were: Grandma Judy's lessons questioning Tripp's actions.

"Okay, that's enough." Tripp sounded furious. "Just stop right there."

I didn't want to walk away from him, but my legs were shaking. My kitchen was so tiny there wasn't room for a seat of any kind, so I turned and walked into the living room. I avoided the sofa and sat instead in Grandma Judy's bentwood rocker.

Tripp didn't follow me, even though I had expected him to.

I wished Foggy was there to curl up in my lap, so I could pet him while I rocked and ruminated.

My home had been violated. Tripp's packers hadn't even started in the dining room, where my books, movies, and CDs still lay strewn across the floor.

Too fast. Everything was happening too quickly. Tripp, marriage, job, and a new life. A new Chelsea, when I'd been mostly content with the old one.

I wanted to crawl into my bed and hide under the covers. I settled for burying my face in my hands.

Okay, maybe I'd just insulted Tripp, which probably wasn't a real great thing to do to someone I professed to love, but weren't his actions toward me an insult too?

I was a capable adult. I'd managed my life just fine since I was sixteen. I would have found a way to deal with the money mess Caitlin made. Somehow.

I hated being dependent. Hated it.

And Tripp didn't seem to be hearing me. I wanted a partner in marriage, not a keeper.

Okay. We both had a learning curve here. We'd jumped into this relationship without knowing a thing about each other. Maybe the whole thing was just sex.

Amazing, soul-shattering, ruin-me-for-anyone-else sex. I really didn't want to believe I was that shallow, but the possibility had to be considered. I had given up everything—every single thing except my cat for him.

And even Foggy had nearly died because I hadn't been home to protect him. Maybe none of this awful stuff that had happened in my apartment would have happened if I'd just been there.

My lap and my hands felt empty without my cat.

And where would I put Grandma Judy's rocking chair in Tripp's designer living room? Not to mention my movie collection. Or was I supposed to shed these things too along with my apartment, my car, and my job in order to be with him?

Or maybe Ali McGraw had it wrong in *Love Story*. Maybe love really means *always* having to say you're sorry.

The rocker creaked. It was comfort music for my soul.

What did I know about relationships, when the only ones I knew about—really knew about—were bad? What did I know about how to be half of a functional couple? Nothing. Absolutely nothing.

But I had to listen to my instincts, and right now they were screaming.

"Are you finished pouting?" Tripp stood in the archway between the living room and the media room. His tone was cool.

"I'm not pouting," I replied. "I'm thinking."

"You could have fooled me," he muttered.

"We haven't even known each other two weeks," I reminded him. "How would you know the difference?"

He heaved a sigh. Finger-combed his hair. "Look. I'm a team player. I have a team mentality. You're on my team now. Everything I do is with what is best for the team in mind."

"I'm an individual," I replied. "What's best for the team isn't always what's best for a wife or a fiancée. Especially when you just barrel ahead and do it without consulting me."

"That doesn't give you the right to call me a wife beater."

"I never called you a wife beater."

"You may as well have. I *saw* what your cousin's husband did to your cousin. I *saw* what Perry Whitlaw did to that woman back in my Double-A days. Do you have any idea how much you pissed me off?"

"I'm not a teammate who needs a pep talk. I'm a woman who feels as if she's lost control of her life."

"What's that supposed to mean?"

I held up a hand and counted my points on my fingers. "Car, phone, and packing my apartment without telling me.

He had the grace to look chagrined. Still, he asked, "Are you going to get pissy every time I try to surprise you with something nice?"

"Flowers are nice," I replied. "Dismantling my life without consulting me is an invasion."

Maybe I should have softened that sentiment, because his jaw started its throbbing thing again. His lips remained a grim line.

"Movies will always be appreciated," I tried again. "Kissing my neck when I'm washing dishes will work too."

It was probably my turn to make a move, but I couldn't quite do it, not yet.

"Are you going to be upset when I tell you I hired a personal shopper to work with you about clothes and such?"

"What's wrong with my clothes?" I asked. *Besides being cheap,* I thought.

"Nothing! As far as I'm concerned, you wear too damn many as it is!"

"Then why do you keep trying to change me?"

He flinched as if I'd struck him. If nothing else, I'd given him something to think about.

I climbed to my feet. It was time to try to meet him halfway. He was trying. I had to do the same. I walked up to him, draped my arms around his neck. "Can we kiss and make up?"

He gazed at me, his normally caramel-colored eyes darker, more like iced tea. No hint of his aw-shucks grin. Not a sign of his dual dimples.

"You dumped some pretty serious stuff on me."

"I'm not going to apologize for letting you know how I feel. Unless I tell you, how will you know?"

He considered this for a moment. "Fair enough. And now I'm letting you know how I feel."

"Fair enough," I echoed.

"Do you want me to have the lawyer change the prenup to include abuse?" he asked.

"Only if it will make you feel better," I replied in a civilized tone that belied the spurt of anger his suggestion generated.

He kissed me, but it wasn't one of his bone-dissolving kisses. It wasn't gentle or loving, or even particularly nice. Then he carefully removed my arms from around his neck.

Whoa. Rejection. I could take a hint.

"Maybe you should go home alone tonight," I said. "I think we need a little time apart."

"You're not staying here tonight."

He was right. I'd be too lonely without Foggy. Maybe I'd go to Caitlin's house. She was in the hospital. I'd just have to get her keys and her alarm code from her.

And what did it say that she'd had full access to my home and my finances, yet I'd been to her house maybe twice a year since she'd been married? The Thanksgiving and Christmas obligation.

And all of a sudden I wanted to cry. Climb in my shower and howl like a banshee.

"We need to see the lawyer to sign the prenup," Tripp reminded me.

Right.

I thought about all the things in my life that I needed to attend to. Little things, like making an appointment with my GYN to discuss birth control, because despite all of Tripp's talk, I really didn't want to start our family right away. I wanted some selfish time with him.

On the other hand, this afternoon hadn't been such a great idea.

Still, he wanted to sign the prenup, so my perceived insult hadn't changed his mind about marriage to me. That was a good sign, wasn't it?

"I have a lot of things I need to do in town tomorrow too," I said. "It doesn't make sense for me to go back to Cooperstown tonight."

"What things?"

I just stared at him.

"I just want to know that you're going to be safe," he said in a soft voice. "Your cousin's husband is still out there. I'm trying to protect you, yet you act as if I'm the one you need protection from. That hurts."

"It's just female stuff," I said.

"A Brazilian wax?" He sounded...hopeful.

I cringed. "No. I have some bills I need to pay now that I have my final paycheck. I want to see my cat. I need to make a doctor's appointment."

"Doctor?"

"I need to see my GYN. Talk about birth control options. I told you. I don't want to start our family right away, and I think if I go on the pill or something, it will make your life easier too."

"Right." His eyes gleamed. "Okay, we'll go back to the hotel."

We'll go back to the hotel. No alone time.

My other option was to beg Caitlin for a house key and her security code.

So we signed the revised prenuptial agreement and then went out dinner before heading back to the hotel, where we kissed and sort of made up enough to have sex.

It wasn't the worst night of my life, but I'd certainly had better.

Chapter Seventeen

"What happened to you?" Dr. DeMarco, my GYN, asked when she saw the bruises decorating my body.

"I fell and sprained my ankle." I stuck out my foot so she could see. "That's made me even clumsier than usual, so I keep bumping into things and falling."

I don't know if she believed me, but did it matter?

I left her office with my first month's worth of birth control pills and assurance that I would have only four periods a year while I was on them. The concept was nice, and I knew Tripp would appreciate it. On the other hand, there was something creepy about that kind of manipulation of my body's natural cycle.

The vet let me pet poor Foggy, who seemed happy to see me. I assured him that I'd be taking him to our new home by the end of the week.

He purred a little then. Of course, he didn't know by that time Tripp would have moved us crate, barrel, and garbage bag out of the familiar apartment to his place in Cooperstown. Cat hair would not do much to enhance the decor there.

I met up with Tripp at the baseball stadium, because I'd promised him I wouldn't go back to my apartment alone. He gave me a legitimate reason, and I'm nothing if not reasonable. Most of the time.

I felt weird walking into the players' entrance, where the offices and the players' family waiting area was located. I wasn't exactly family yet. Nor was Tripp really a player. But everyone on the Saltboiler's staff seemed okay with my presence.

"Why didn't you answer your phone?" Tripp greeted me.

"It's against the law to use a cell phone and drive at the same time in New York," I reminded him.

"That's why I bought you an earpiece," he reminded me. "Use it, okay? So I don't worry."

Hard to argue with that logic.

Tripp introduced me a man he called Vic. "Vic rents furnished apartments to the players while they're in town," Tripp explained. "I figured we should rent a place to stay while we're packing up your stuff. He's offered to show us a couple places he has available."

I didn't know what to say. I smiled and nodded. I was actually getting some sort of input into the plans Tripp was making for our lives.

We held hands as we looked at several apartments. None of them was a place I could ever feel comfortable. They felt temporary, not like home at all. But that was all they were meant to be, so I sucked it up and chose the one trapping the most natural light, a space for Grandma Judy's bentwood rocker, and a separate room where Foggy could hide.

"You're sure this is the one you want?" Tripp asked for about the fifth time.

I had to give him credit for trying.

"Yeah, unless there's another one you like better." I wasn't trying to be a princess or anything. I just wanted a say in my own life.

"Well, that second one had a hot tub," Tripp said. His aw-shucks grin reappeared. A hint of the South colored his words. "Hot tubs are real nice."

Okay, there was that.

"Can we look at it again?" I asked Vic.

Of course he wasn't going to say no. This was his job. Tripp was his customer.

We went back to the second place in trendy Armory Square. Lots of warehouse brick walls. Gloomy. A little on the small side. Vic probably installed the hot tub to make up for all the other shortcomings.

I could tell the place was a converted factory and understood why the workers had unionized. If I sniffed deeply enough, I could probably smell old engine grease.

I hated it. I really, really hated it. The dim light and dark brick would certainly spur my efforts to pack my apartment. "How long will we be here?"

"As long as we need, unless you think we need a regular place in town to stay." Tripp's thumb massaged my palm.

I looked at his golden gaze, shining and hopeful. Because of a hot tub. I looked at the tasteful grime-colored furnishings. All I could think of was the gray-brown gook on a computer keyboard, on the light switches in my apartment, or on a car's steering wheel. Yeah, *that* color. It went really well with the exposed brick.

Temporary, I told myself. I would be spending most of my Syracuse time at my apartment. I'd be here only in the dark.

Maybe Foggy could stay at the old place until it was time to move him to Cooperstown.

"Well," I said, "I like the last place better. It's bigger and seems airier, but if it's only for a couple of weeks...."

So in the end, all my yelling didn't mean anything. Tripp Shaneybrook still got his way.

Tripp signed the short-term lease right then and wrote a check for three months' rent. Vic was willing to let us move in that day.

I loathed the hot tub. The jetting water made my butt itch. Whatever solution was used to clean the jets made me break out in hives. Huge, ugly red welts.

The next day, I started cleaning out my clothes. I had a lot of old stuff—things that no longer fit, moth-eaten sweaters, stained blouses, and skirts and slacks with shiny seats. Even the Salvation Army wouldn't want this stuff. I stuffed black garbage bags while Tripp boxed up my movies and music. He refused to leave me alone in my own apartment because of Spencer.

He looked at the mound of black garbage bags. "I didn't think you had that much closet space," he said.

"I'm creative," I replied.

I wouldn't need work clothes to wear to an office anymore, but I was going to need things for my new job. There were bound to be meetings or conferences. Tripp hadn't been very specific about what he wanted me to do, but since it was his charity, I'd probably have a lot of good-wife stuff expected of me. And I didn't have time to go shopping, not now.

So I summoned my courage and asked, "Is your offer of a personal shopper still good?"

Chloe of Chloe's Closet flew to Syracuse the next morning and then took a cab to the new apartment.

Maybe someday I would understand the inner workings of being wealthy, but since those kinds of numbers were beyond the scope of my imagination, except in abstract, I very much doubted it. If Tripp had this kind of money to waste on me, why did he need to raise funds and apply for grants for Camp Home Safe?

Chloe was a pallid, frail thing with limp, washed-out blonde hair and pale blue eyes. She dressed in an ash-gray pantsuit that hung on her skinny frame. I had second thoughts about letting her buy me clothes. I had a very clear sense of my own style. Anything else would make me uncomfortable.

I wore my long pearl-white satin robe for our meeting. "I don't need a lot of casual clothes right now," I told her. "But I could use some work stuff. A couple of blazers, a skirt, and some slacks. No pleated fronts. I'm a size six."

She put down her phone. "I'm going to measure you," she informed me in a lofty tone. "That's the surest way to make certain we have the correct fit."

She whipped out a tape measure.

"No underwire or foam rubber bras," I said, my voice turning watery. "I'll only rip out the wires."

Chloe rolled her eyes. "Shall we get down to this?"

"Fine." I stood there, awaiting her instructions.

"Lose the robe."

I'd been afraid of that. I wore a bra and matching panties under the robe. They were among my better sets of under things. But I wasn't a pretty sight.

The bruise on my ribs where I'd hit the rock when I fell at the opera was finally starting to fade, but fade in this case merely meant turning the olive drab of an army uniform. And my upper arm, where I'd fallen into the shower door, had only turned more yellow and green in the past week. Sometimes when I caught sight of myself in a mirror, it looked like a botched tattoo. My forearm still bore the stripe of hitting the railing in my dark stairwell. The side of my knee was a lovely shade of deep lavender thanks to the gear stick in Tripp's Jeep.

I was a catalog of clumsy living. If my GYN had been concerned, I couldn't imagine what this stranger might think.

Chloe never even blinked.

Maybe she saw lots worse in her job. Someone in her position would have to be very discreet in order to stay in business.

She measured me in places I didn't realize had dimensions. She held fabric swatches against my face. Told me I needed to do something with my hair color. Handed me the business card of a "miracle worker" in Manhattan. Then she took a cab back to the airport.

Good riddance. She was scary.

I dressed in khaki shorts and a white camp shirt and then called Tripp. He'd planned to take me to Camp Home Safe that afternoon so I could get a feel for the place. Not that I'd be working at the camp itself, but he seemed really proud of it and wanted to show off for me.

And I needed to get out of the apartments.

My old place felt abandoned—which it was, I suppose. And the new one depressed me. But I didn't want to go back to his Cooperstown house, either. It was a nice summer home, I suppose, but I didn't want to live there. I wanted my own house. One I decorated, where I could cook hearty winter stews and bake Christmas cookies with our kids.

God, that sounded so good. Not that I knew what any of that entailed. Grandma Judy wasn't the most domestic of caregivers. But I knew what families in the movies did.

Penn called while I waited for Tripp. "It's not the right time of year to do *Spring Party* for your reception," he told me. "I went online and looked up more of that Fish chick's paintings. I think you should go for *Peaches, Black-eyed Susans, and Teacups.*"

I used my new laptop to see what he was talking about.

Oh.

Penn *got* it.

He understood about the light. The flowers. The color of the pressed glass dishes. "Thank you," I whispered.

"My pleasure," he replied, sounding as if he meant it.

I was hanging up the phone when Tripp arrived. "Your brother is amazing," I said as I looped my arms around Tripp's neck for my kiss.

"I'm glad you're making an effort." Then he kissed me. Soft. Gentle. "Are you about ready to go?"

I nodded. I'd packed a small bag with additional clothes for Cooperstown. I didn't know how long we'd be staying before we came back to Syracuse.

Now that I'd signed the prenuptial agreement, Tripp didn't seem in any hurry to find a justice of the peace and do the deed. I was content to wait until Caitlin felt better.

He looked me over a bit critically. Or maybe it was leftover paranoia from being with Chloe that morning.

Nope. Critical.

"You should probably change into longer pants," he said.

The temperature outside was at least ninety degrees and climbing.

"Deer ticks?" I asked.

"Bruises." He pointed to my mottled thigh and knee. "These kids come from abusive situations. If they see that, it might upset them."

Well, darn. That made sense.

It took me only a minute to shed the shorts and pull on a pair of capri pants. Of course, between the two acts, Tripp decided I'd been ignoring him too long, so we grabbed a quickie on the squeaky bed. It was a wonder I wasn't bowlegged from knowing him.

I tried calling Caitlin from the car as Tripp drove my new SUV to Cooperstown, but as usual, she wasn't answering. I'd been to the hospital to see her every day, and she was sullen, sulky, in pain, and drugged up. I left a message on her voice mail telling her where I'd be and to let me know if she needed anything.

"Stop fretting," Tripp commanded.

"Easy for you to say," I muttered. I adjusted the vent to blow on me. The vehicle still had the new leather car seat smell going for it.

"So where's the camp?" I asked. It behooved me to know at least something about my employer.

"Outside of Cooperstown on one of the smaller lakes," he said. "It made sense to put it there because of the proximity of the Hall of Fame and Museum. Makes them part of the experience."

I nodded. My eyes filled with tears because he cared so much for the campers. I was so lucky to have him in my life.

Camp Home Safe was a fifteen-minute drive from Tripp's lake house. The driveway left the main road and wound down a hill in serpentine curves through thick woods. At the foot of the hill, the forest gave way to a large clearing at the edge of blue water. A raft with a high dive drifted some ways offshore, and white buoys delineated the swimming area.

Two baseball fields like something out of *Field of Dreams* swarmed with players. Their exuberant voices carried even into the closed cab of the SUV.

Five cabins huddled around a central green. A larger building stood off to one side, a burned-wood signed declaring it to be the dining hall. That confused me. For some reason, I had my head filled with visions of ballpark food for the campers: hot dogs, nachos, and popcorn in a helmet.

I waited for Tripp to open the door for me. The heat hit me with a physical force, blowing wisps of hair off my cheeks.

Faboo came out of the dining hall, carrying bottles of water. "Hi, Boss. Chelsea."

I was glad to see his bland, familiar face.

"Tripp, I need to talk to you. Alone." Faboo handed me a bottle. Cold condensation dripped down my arm.

I spied a bench under a tree. "I'll be over there," I said, gesturing with the bottle.

Tripp nodded. "What's up, big guy?"

Faboo waited until I was out of earshot. I hoped it wasn't anything awful.

I really didn't want to sit. I'd been sitting all the way from Syracuse. So I wandered toward one of the cabins.

"God *fucking* damn it!" I heard Tripp say. "Where's Marty?"

Not a good sign.

Speaking of signs, there was another burned-letter sign—so rustic—over the door of the smaller cabin. *Honus Wagner.* As I looked around the green, I noticed each cabin was named: *Christy Mathewson, Babe Ruth, Ty Cobb,* and *Walter Johnson.*

I also noticed Faboo lumbering in my direction.

"Hi," I called. "I was just wondering about the names of the cabins."

I don't think it was my imagination that his normally bland expression looked a little grim.

"Tripp got tied up with something and said to tell you he'll meet you at home."

"He couldn't tell me himself?" Maybe I asked a little too sharply, and it certainly wasn't fair to keep putting poor Faboo in the middle of our spats, but still.

"He's a little upset right now," was all Faboo could say. I started toward the dining hall, but Faboo caught my arm. "It's not a real good time."

I raised my chin. Faboo was even taller than Tripp. "I don't know how to get to the lake house from here," I said. It was true.

I also didn't know if Tripp even meant the lake house when he'd told Faboo he'd see me at home. We didn't have a home yet.

"I'll program your GPS for you," Faboo said.

Yeah, the new SUV came with a built-in GPS, which was kind of creepy. Why would I want any satellite to know where I was at all times?

Faboo showed me how to work the thing. Tripp or someone had already programmed in the lake house address. Faboo stood and watched as I adjusted the seat and the mirrors and then turned the vehicle around. I waved bye-bye with a big smile as I drove up the hill to the main road.

The GPS got me to the lake house without incident. Unfortunately, it couldn't get me *in* to the lake house. I didn't have a key. A fact Tripp seemed to have conveniently forgotten.

I sat in the driveway for a few minutes, debating whether or not to wait on the deck, but it was too hot. I wanted air-conditioning.

I turned around and drove into the village. I knew Tripp usually parked behind the building when we went to Shaneybrook's so I helped myself to his spot. I was hungry, I was thirsty, and I was worried about Tripp.

I walked around the building and went in the front door like any other paying customer.

"Chelsea!" Josh of the curly red hair seemed surprised to see me. "Is Tripp with you?"

"He got tied up." I echoed the excuse Faboo had given me. "I thought I'd grab something to eat. Maybe a cold drink."

"Uh, sure," Josh said. He showed me to a small table in a corner. A single black-eyed Susan graced a turquoise cut-glass bud vase in the center of the table. I ordered a glass of the sauvignon blanc. The wine was as smooth as silk going down.

Then I saw Baird McKechnie sitting at another table for one. I picked up my glass and crossed over to him.

"Hi," I said, smiling as broadly as my mouth allowed. "I just wanted to thank you for abandoning me here a couple of weeks ago. Turned out to be the best thing that ever happened to me."

He smiled at me. A smarmy smile. "Oh, I wouldn't be too sure of that," he murmured.

"Chelsea!" Penn hurried from the kitchen before I had a chance to ask Baird what he was talking about. "Josh just told me you were here."

"Yeah, Tripp got tied up, so I decided to come into town."

"Come back to the kitchen," Penn urged me.

"Josh just showed me to the cutest little table over there." I pointed with my glass.

"I had some more ideas about your party," Penn said.

He seemed...jittery. Nervous. He and Baird kept exchanging meaningful looks that weren't sexual in nature.

"Okay," I said, puzzled by their behavior.

Penn seated me at the same table Tripp had sat me the night I'd first met them. The night Baird abandoned me.

"Did you guys listen to the radio on the way to town?" Penn tried to act casual, but he wasn't doing a very good job.

"No. Why?" Now I was getting worried. Everyone seemed to know something I didn't. "What's going on?"

Penn shook his head. "Tripp should be the one to tell you."

I stood. "My car is right through that door." I pointed to the back door of the kitchen with my half-empty wineglass. "All I have to do is go out there and turn on the radio, or get my laptop and sign on to the net."

"Sit down," Penn said, his tone a gentle one. One I'd never heard from him before.

"I signed a prenup," I told him. It was a non sequitur at that moment, but I wanted to reassure him, because he seemed so...shaken.

"It doesn't matter. Not now." He sat across from me. He took my hands in his. I realized then that Penn had been different toward me since he'd seen *Spring Party*.

"How much do you know about Tripp and Maura St. John?"

I set my wineglass on the table. I was proud that my hands didn't shake at all. Neither did my voice. "More than I want to."

I sounded so calm and so serene.

Distress contorted his features. "She's claiming that she's pregnant and that Tripp is the father."

Okay. I could handle this. The initial shock of this allegation was already in the past.

"Yes. I know," I said.

Penn seemed surprised. "You know?"

I nodded. "She came to the house the other night."

Penn heaved a sigh. "You're taking this pretty calmly."

"Now I am," I admitted. "Things weren't so pretty the other night. But Tripp says he doesn't think she's pregnant, and even if she is, he doubts the baby is his."

Maybe I shouldn't be sharing all this private stuff, but Penn was Tripp's brother. They were close.

"If Tripp says the baby probably isn't his, then I believe him." I mean, I didn't have any choice, did I?

"I wonder if my brother knows how lucky he is," Penn said. He squeezed my hands.

"Probably." I smiled. Anything to keep the imminent tears at bay. "He wants DNA testing, and if the child is his, then he and I are going to raise it." The words caught a bit, but I managed to choke them out.

Penn brought my hands to his mouth and carefully kissed each finger. "Your value is above rubies," he murmured.

"Huh?" I said.

"It's a poem," he explained. "Just so you're aware, Maura has gone public with her allegations."

My smile felt wooden, mostly because my face was completely numb.

"She blogged about her affair with Tripp and claims he threw her over for you once he learned she was pregnant."

I inhaled deeply, trying to center myself as instructed in some long-forgotten yoga class I'd once taken in a spurt of needing self-fulfillment. "No," I said. "She never told him until the other night. After you left. I was there. I heard everything."

"How are you holding up? Do you need more wine?"

"I'm pretty pissed off, actually," I said. "He had no business sending me away. It's not as if I didn't already know."

And I burst into tears.

Penn couldn't have looked more surprised if I'd burst into flames. Chelsea Jubilee.

He drew back, probably in horror. I didn't blame him. I'm not a pretty crier. He'd probably been expecting this, and that was why he'd dragged me out of the public dining room.

He signaled to Josh, who rushed forward to refill my glass of wine.

I tried to rein in my emotions. Penn didn't need to see the ugly side of his sister-in-law-to-be. We'd already started out on the wrong foot, like a gimpy centipede.

A box of tissue appeared in front of me, and I grabbed two fistfuls.

"Why did he send me away?" I tried to ask Penn, but my throat was so tight, making my voice so high-pitched that only the neighborhood dogs could have heard me.

"Because he's trying to protect you." Penn didn't hesitate at all before he answered me. "He's never been like this with anyone else before. He really loves you. Maura St. John? She was convenient because she kept throwing herself in his path."

"He shouldn't have had Faboo send me away," I sobbed. "I didn't send him away with all the stuff with my cousin."

"What stuff with your cousin?"

I didn't want to get into Caitlin, Spencer, or domestic violence. Even if I could have put it in any kind of coherent cohesiveness. Which I couldn't because I was too upset with Tripp.

"Your cell phone is ringing," Penn said, looking at my purse.

I wasn't used to the ring on my new phone, and I hated wearing the earpiece, even though Tripp kept reminding me. I dug through my bag until I found the phone, but by then the call had gone to voice mail.

I tried to figure out who called, but I wasn't at all familiar with the device. I wanted my old flip phone back from the cops.

"Here." Penn took the unit from me and pressed a few buttons. "That was Tripp," he said. Of course he would recognize his brother's number. "You should call him back."

I didn't want to call him back. I didn't want to talk to him at all. My feelings were hurt. I was being childish, I knew, but that didn't stop my aching emotions.

The phone belched.

"You have a new message," Penn said.

"I don't know how to retrieve messages," I said. All of this was part of Tripp's makeover of me. I didn't get any of it.

Penn did something and then held the phone to my ear.

"Jesus H. fucking Christ." Tripp's voice exploded in my ear. *"Where the fuck are you?"*

I mopped my face with another fistful of tissues, took a huge gulp of wine, and then hit the button that would automatically redial the caller.

Tripp answered on the first ring. "Where the fuck are you?"

"At Shaneybrook's," I said, pleased that my tears weren't evident in the tone of my voice.

"What the fuck are you doing there?"

"I don't have a key to the lake house," I reminded him. "And you told me to get lost." The temptation to disconnect the call itched in my fingers, my palm.

"I didn't tell you to get lost." His tone was tight. He sounded as if he were ready to snap.

"You could have told me what was going on," I said. "It's not as if I didn't know about Maura's allegations."

"I wasn't thinking clearly, okay?" Tripp shouted. "Her announcement blindsided me."

"Okay," I said. "You don't need to take it out on me."

"You're not where I told you to be."

"I don't have a key," I repeated. "It's not as if I drove back to Syracuse or something. I'm at your brother's restaurant." It made perfect sense to me.

"Don't move," Tripp said. "I'm coming to get you." He hung up before I could reply.

I dumped the phone into my purse and then drained my glass of wine.

"I hope you're not planning on driving," Penn said.

I shook my head. "Tripp is on his way to meet me here."

"You were great just now," Penn said.

"Of course I was," I replied. "I'm sure I saw it in a movie."

Penn laughed. "I'm not sure my brother deserves you."

"What's that supposed to mean?" Baird stood in the doorway to the kitchen. "She's just my leftovers."

"Oh, bite me, Baird," I said. "I could only be a leftover if you'd ever had me. The only thing you've got going for you is your name."

Penn roared with laughter. I thought I saw a smile twitching at the corners of Josh's mouth.

Baird's face turned a deep and mottled red. I was with friends. He may have known them first, but he'd abandoned me here. They had rallied around me to care for me. And what did that say about him? Not a lot. He might be Penn's lover, but that didn't make him into a likable human being. The only thing he had going for him, really, was his name.

And Tripp was right: it was a stupid name. I couldn't believe I'd ever gone out with him based on something as random as a name.

Baird left the kitchen. Penn rolled his eyes. I hiccupped.

Tripp showed up ten minutes later.

CHAPTER EIGHTEEN

Tripp burst through the back door of the restaurant as if every demon of hell were chasing him, instead of a vindictive former lover. Of course, I didn't know Maura St. John. Maybe her wrath equaled the combined denizens of the underworld.

He stood in the doorway, glaring at me. I lifted my wineglass in a mock salute. I expected him to start yelling.

"I'm sorry," he said. He combed his hair with his fingers. "Maura pissed me off so badly. I wasn't thinking straight."

The last thing I expected from him was an apology. I shouldn't have been surprised. He'd apologized to me before unexpectedly.

He glanced at Penn. "Thanks for taking her in."

Penn shrugged. "She just showed up."

"Thanks anyway."

Josh hurried through the door from the dining room. "I think a reporter just pulled up," he said in a low voice. "And I'm pretty sure McKechnie is the one who called and ratted out Chelsea's whereabouts."

"McKechnie is here?" Tripp sounded dangerous. He started across the kitchen, toward the dining room.

I got up from my chair and put my hand on his arm.

That was all it took to stop him.

"Do you really want to give the press a story?" I asked. "Or do you want to go home and hope they don't find us?"

"She's right," Penn said. "I'll take care of Baird."

Tripp cupped my elbow and steered me through the back door. He'd parked his SUV behind mine.

"Does the press know your vehicle?" I asked.

"Maybe."

"Then let's leave it here and take mine. And you can drive."

"How much wine have you had?"

"Oh, not even a full glass," I lied. "I wasn't trying to get drunk or anything."

"Did you eat anything?"

"You came to my rescue before I could order."

He grinned. Fine lines fanned out from the corners of his eyes. He looked exhausted. "Maybe you should drive. They won't be expecting you."

I probably should have told him how much wine I'd had.

We swapped parking spots and then bumped our way over the broken pavement in the narrow alley separating Shaneybrook's from the baseball card dealer next door. I was barely able to navigate the opening to the street because of the cars gathering in front of the restaurant.

"I've already asked the cops to block off access to the road to the camp." Tripp sounded grim. "Home Safe is private property. But blocking access by water or along the shoreline is going to be tough."

I resisted the urge to one-finger salute a reporter standing next to a satellite truck parked across the street from Shaneybrook's. "Why would the press bother the campers? The kids wouldn't know about you being a notoriously promiscuous professional athlete." My attempt at humor fell flat.

"It's not my baby." His voice shook.

I reached over and took his hand. "I know."

"Why would she do this?" He sounded bewildered. "We were never that serious."

"Maybe you weren't. She obviously thought differently."

I was trying not to let this newest wrinkle upset me. I realized I was marrying someone who had once spent a lot of time in the public eye and who, by virtue of his name alone, could still command publicity, especially when scandal was attached.

Except…unwed pregnancy wasn't really a scandal, not like it had been when I was born. Celebrities gave birth without marriage more often than within marriage. At least according to tabloid media.

"Why is this such a big deal?" I asked as I turned off the highway and onto the road that led to the lake house.

Tripp didn't say anything.

Maybe I hadn't been told the whole story. I reached for the radio, but Tripp's hand closed over mine.

"Later," he said.

Nice to know all my instincts hadn't gone dormant.

"I'll get you a key made tomorrow," Tripp said as he unlocked the door of the lake house. It appeared our privacy hadn't been violated.

"We can hole up here for a few days," he said as he rummaged through the refrigerator. He came up with a bowl of green grapes and blueberries and a bottle of the sauvignon blanc that I liked so much.

I plopped onto the sofa. "So what exactly is going on?"

Tripp placed the grapes, the bottle, and two glasses on the coffee table. "All in good time, honey."

Seemed as if he hadn't called me honey in a long time. I liked hearing it again.

I waited while he made a show of uncorking and then pouring the wine. Outside, the blazing sun started fading toward evening. Long shafts of reddish-orange light pierced the surface of the calm lake. Tripp had turned on the central air as soon as we arrived, and the stuffiness was beginning to evaporate.

"To us," he said, tilting his glass toward mine.

"To us," I echoed as our glasses clinked. I sipped. Savored. Swallowed. "So what is going on?"

All emotion left Tripp's face, as if life itself drained from him. "I gather you've heard that Maura went public with her accusation that I'm the father of her baby."

"Yeah? So? You know it's probably not true, I know it's probably not true, and people have babies every day. What's the big deal?"

His knuckles whitened on the stem of his glass. I saw as he raised it to his mouth.

"The big deal, the *story*... She's accused me of beating her to force her to miscarry because she refused to have an abortion."

The glass slipped from my fingers and shattered on the edge of the table.

Neither of us made a move to clean up the glass or the wine.

"What?" My throat felt as if one or more of the shards were lodged there.

He nodded. Just once. Our gazes never wavered. "And there are pictures."

"You didn't do it."

"I can't prove it."

"Sure you can. You were with me. In Syracuse."

He looked at me, shook his head. "Of course you'd say I was with you."

"Wait a minute," I said. "What's that supposed to mean?"

"We're engaged. You'll say anything to protect me."

"Well then, how about the car dealer, the phone people, the people in the Saltboiler's front office, Vic the apartment guy, or those creepy movers? And then there are all the people at the hotel, the hospital, and at the veterinary hospital. Just when were you supposed to have...hurt her?"

The muscles in his jaw started working out. "The night she came here."

I shook my head. "No. I was here. I saw everything. Heard everything. You never even threatened her except to call the cops. And she came back the next morning. She was fine. It's just her word against ours."

His eyes glittered. He fumbled for my hand, brought it to his mouth. "I love you so much."

"I love you too." I looked at the mess my broken wineglass had created.

"There are pictures all over the Internet and tabloid TV," Tripp warned me.

I felt a little sick to my stomach. "Did she lose the baby?"

Tripp shrugged. "I don't know."

"The press would be making a big deal out of it if she had," I agreed. "Who are your enemies?"

He sighed. "Marty and I have been through all of this while we were at the camp," he said. "That's why I wanted you to come here. You didn't need to hear all that stuff."

"You really have enemies?"

"Not really," he said. "I retired with no real hard feelings from anyone, so I don't think it's another ballplayer. I'm not involved in broadcasting, politics, or anything else that could be construed as controversial. And another woman sure as hell didn't beat on Maura."

I had to smile. Of course he'd left some broken hearts behind. He was too wonderful to not have women falling in love with him from a mere smile.

"Any clue as to who else Maura might have been involved with?"

He shook his head. "I've racked my brain. I don't understand why she's so determined to bring me down. We were never that close. We never had a real relationship. I think I can count on one hand the number of times we fucked."

I didn't think I wanted to know about that.

"And honestly? I don't think I even initiated anything." He sounded...glum.

And I definitely didn't want to know about Maura St. John's seduction tech-niques.

My phone chose that moment to shrill. Caitlin. I glanced at Tripp, who signaled me to answer it.

"Hello?"

"Chelsea, oh my God. Are you all right? I saw the news and the pictures of that poor Maura St. John, and—"

Why did Caitlin only want to discuss gloom and doom with me? When I'd suggested that Tripp and I get married in her hospital room, she'd been barely receptive. Heck, she'd hardly responded to my daily visits. Almost as if she blamed *me* because Spencer beat the crap out of her.

Why all the sudden enthusiasm for my relationship with Tripp?

"Slow down." I interrupted her babble.

Tripp heaved himself off the sofa and grabbed a roll of paper towels.

I should have been the one to clean up the spilled wine and broken glass.

"I'm upset," I said. "Of course I'm upset. Tripp—"

"You sound just like me," Caitlin said. "I know. He didn't *mean* to do it." Her mocking laugh sent chills through me.

"No," I said, my tone icy. "He didn't do it. Period."

"C'mon. This is me, remember?" she said.

"If you or anyone else I know fuels this smear campaign, I will sue you for slander," I said. My voice shook.

Tripp paused, staring at me. I thought he looked a little paler than he had.

"Why," Caitlin demanded, "is my life an open book for your gloating, but yours is freaking holy ground?"

I closed my eyes. My voice wasn't the only thing that shook. My hands looked as if they were palsied.

"My relationship with Tripp has nothing to do with the lies Maura St. John is telling about him," I said. "Tripp would never lift a finger to hurt a woman or a child. In fact, we'd already agreed that if the baby was his, we'll raise it together."

"You knew she was pregnant?"

"Yes. She came here and told Tripp. Then she came back to make sure I knew. It was about as civilized as something like that can be. No catfight. No hair pulling, scratching, or screeching."

"Well, this doesn't make your golden boy look very golden anymore." Caitlin sounded almost gleeful. "What with his camp and all that."

I hadn't even considered what this kind of publicity could do to Camp Home Safe. This had to be a public relations nightmare. And grants. Oh. Dear. God. This kind of notoriety would kill any chance of the camp receiving any grants ever. Forever.

If Maura was seeking revenge, she couldn't have chosen a better way to completely undermine everything Tripp Shaneybrook stood for.

"If you only called to gossip, then I have to go," I told her. "If you called to see how I'm doing, I'm very concerned about Tripp. Thanks for asking. He needs me right now, okay? I'll talk to you tomorrow." And I disconnected the call.

My vision blurred as tears filled my eyes. I got up and went to Tripp, who was standing at the breakfast bar. I wrapped my arms around his waist and rested my cheek against the broad expanse of his back.

"I'm so sorry," I whispered. "This just keeps getting worse, doesn't it?"

"I need to clean up the glass," he said.

Okay. Avoidance. I understood that strategy all too well. Heck, compared to me, Tripp was an amateur.

I let go of him. He fetched a vacuum from the entry closet. The man who didn't even have to buy his own underwear did a nice job vacuuming the bits of glass from the floor. A man of many talents, not all of them on the diamond or in the bedroom. He didn't deserve what Maura had done to him.

He poured me another glass of wine. I took it, even though I wasn't sure I wanted another glass. What I wanted to do was think, and that required the edges of my brain not be fuzzed by alcohol.

Something about Caitlin's phone call was off. I got the gloating thing, but my instincts insisted there was something more. Something I probably wouldn't like. I tried to shake off the feeling, telling myself the sense was based only in that I knew Caitlin so very well. The gloat factor was high, especially after I'd cut myself off from any more involvement in her marital woes.

Tripp and I tried watching a baseball game, but no matter which game he tried—he had satellite, so there were a lot from which to choose—the announcers just had to commentate on the baseball news of the day. Which, unfortunately, was Tripp and Maura. We tried turning down the sound and listening to the play-by-play on the radio, but the great thing about baseball worked against us that night. Yeah, we could have a conversation at the same time we watched the game without being distracted, but what if we didn't like the topic of conversation? Watching in silence didn't work either, although I offered to pop some corn to lessen the sensory deprivation.

We ended up going upstairs to bed, the topic heavy on our minds—on mine, at least—but no longer under discussion.

And when Tripp was done and had rolled off me, he said, "Don't ever fake it with me again."

Chapter Nineteen

We didn't leave the house. Penn delivered meals for us, acting like a church lady confronted with death, except there was no ham, no scalloped potatoes, and no green gelatin salad.

Penn wanted to talk about the reception, ideas he'd had since seeing the posters and actually watching *Mamma Mia,* but I wasn't in the mood. How could I talk about a party when Tripp was hurting so badly? Besides, who was I kidding? I didn't have anyone to invite to a party. Any wedding reception, delayed or not, would be for Tripp's people. He should have what he wanted.

The vet called to tell me Foggy was holding his own. I shuddered to think of the bill, but after what he'd been through, my poor cat deserved every penny.

Tripp's agent showed up on Friday. Marty Fiscoe. Young. Energetic. Exhausting to watch and listen to for long.

"Jesus, Tripp," he said when he saw me. I was in shorts and a tank top, so the bruises on my legs and arms were visible. I went upstairs to change.

Hadn't I listened to Caitlin's tales of falling down stairs for years? I knew the drill. Only in my case, it was true.

I wondered if I could find the elderly gentleman who'd helped me to my feet the day I'd fallen down the hill at the opera. Even if Baird cooperated, and I doubted very much that he would, he would be no more believed than I, because of his involvement with Tripp's brother.

I came downstairs in my white jeans and one of Tripp's fruit-colored T-shirts.

He smiled when he recognized it.

There is something so comforting about wearing your lover's shirt.

"Anybody gotten a gander at her?" Marty jerked his head toward me.

We exchanged a look. I shook my head. I'd been really careful in public. Tripp had even made me change before we went to the camp, because he didn't want the kids to associate me with their mothers.

Oh. Wait. Two people had seen me. "My doctor," I said. "She commented on the bruises. And Chloe."

Tripp swore.

Yeah, Chloe. The personal shopper. Who'd been his idea. We had to trust my GYN with doctor-patient confidentiality, but Chloe...

"Chloe can't say anything," I said. "Not if she wants to stay in business."

"You'd better hope she keeps her mouth shut," Marty muttered. "Whoever the fuck she is."

"Too late." Faboo came into the house through the deck door. "Turn on the television." He named one of the sleazier tabloid channels.

Tripp reached for the remote.

There, in living color as vivid as a peacock's feathers, were my bare and bruised legs, the fist-size contusion on my ribs, and every black-and-blue mark on my body exposed by my skimpy two-piece swimsuit.

"Where did that picture come from?" Tripp asked.

I didn't have an answer. The background was indistinct, so I couldn't even tell where the photos were taken. But I couldn't recall wearing that swimsuit except at Tripp's house.

"Interview with Caitlin Madison from her hospital bed," the TV announcer intoned.

"Who the fuck is Caitlin Madison?" Marty asked.

It felt as if all the blood cushioning my brain evaporated from the heat in my face. I was dizzy. Nauseated. Furious. Tripp stared at me with his honey-toned eyes, waiting for me to admit the relationship.

"My cousin," I managed to squeak.

"What's this hospital bed shit?" Marty asked.

"She's is in the hospital."

"And is she alleging Tripp put her there?"

"How should I know? Shut up and listen."

I found my gumption. I was not responsible for Caitlin. No more. Even Tripp agreed. I'd drawn the line.

"This is so embarrassing," I heard Caitlin say, her voice weaker than it had been when she'd called last night. Her face was still swollen. Her bruises were still vivid.

"I mean, Chelsea and I are cousins, but we're very close. She's always been there for me. She even moved from our home town to Syracuse when I got married just to be with me."

Because she'd begged, pleaded, and nagged until I caved.

But Caitlin wasn't finished. "Until she hooked up with this baseball player."

The room went so quiet you could have heard a mosquito sucking blood. "She told me he didn't want her hanging around with me anymore. I think it's because I would recognize what he's doing to her."

"What?" My gasp shattered the stillness.

"She showed me this huge bruise on her arm, said it was his fault," Caitlin continued.

My head swiveled to Tripp, who was staring at the screen as if it contained the secrets of the universe.

"Tripp, I swear—"

"Shh," he said.

"It was huge. On her upper left arm."

I *did* have an enormous bruise exactly where she said, but I never, ever attributed it to Tripp. I'd gotten it when I hit my arm on the shower door.

Marty grabbed my arm and rolled up my sleeve. Yep. There was the bruise.

"Someone want to tell me what's going on here?" he asked.

Tripp's jaw muscle began throbbing. I wanted to run my fingers over that pulsing bulge, erase the anger that fueled it.

"How'd you get this?" Marty asked.

"I fell." I lifted my chin and dared him to contradict me.

"So why did you tell your cousin Tripp hit you?"

"I didn't."

"Are you sure you didn't tell her I'm *abusive*?" Tripp asked.

He sounded as if he spoke through clenched teeth.

I flinched. "What?"

"You heard me."

My insides froze. "Why would I tell Caitlin something like that?"

"The same reason you told me?"

I couldn't breathe. I couldn't move at all, except for the shaking inside me.

"Whatever I said to you was between you and me, and I never, ever, even hinted that you would even consider..."

I stopped. There was too much of an audience, and what I'd said to Tripp was between him and me. He shouldn't have brought it up in front of his agent or Faboo.

"Everything I have worked for since I retired from baseball is *gone*," he said. "Everything I've tried to do for those kids... Poof."

The contempt in his gaze was diamond bright, diamond hard, and diamond sharp, slashing my insides, my heart, and my soul.

Well, I wasn't going to beg him to believe me, forgive me, or second chance me. I hadn't ever said any such thing to Caitlin, but this was such typical Caitlin. I shouldn't have been so...devastated.

I bit my lips to keep from saying anything else. I refused to grovel. Either Tripp believed me, or he didn't.

"How could you do this to me?" he asked.

"I didn't." I grabbed my purse from the kitchen counter and walked out. I didn't need to stick around and play scapegoat for Tripp and his entourage.

I thought I heard Tripp say my name, but I was too angry to care. The white noise of self-defense roared in my ears. I drove the SUV to Shaneybrook's, where I parked it behind Tripp's vehicle. Mama would have kept the fuel fiend, but I put the key under the driver's mat and locked the doors.

Fortunately, the shopkeepers in Cooperstown were used to tourists and questions, like "Where's the Hall of Fame?" and "Where's the bus station?" Some of them might have recognized me, but I'd kept a low profile.

I learned Tripp hadn't lied when he told me there was no bus station, just a stop in front of the auto club.

I missed the westbound bus to Syracuse by ten minutes. The next one wouldn't be until Monday. Tripp hadn't lied about that either.

I should have pulled a Mama and kept the SUV.

I trudged back to the little information park at the corner of Pioneer and Main, my flip-flops sticking to the melting blacktop. Heat shimmered up my legs, already sweltering in the heavy denim of my jeans. I found a bench in the shade and hunkered down to regroup. I tried not to think about Tripp and what he'd said to me. How he'd looked at me.

I kept my sunglasses on. At least Tripp's T-shirt and my jeans covered all the damning evidence, circumstantial as it was. I'd mail him his T-shirt once I got myself resettled.

I found a notebook and roller ball pen in my purse. Lists. I could start making lists of everything I needed to do to get my life back. Job. Apartment. Maybe I could convince Tanner to let me stay on in the place over the clock shop. I stared at the ring on my finger. Maybe I could pawn it.

I'd rather mail it back to Tripp with his T-shirt.

I probably should have left them both in the SUV.

Maybe I was overreacting, but I probably wasn't. If there was no trust—and he'd made it diamond clear that he didn't trust me—then everything else fell apart.

Tears splatted on the paper, smearing my notes.

Instead of looking at the obvious, which would be me, Tripp needed to figure out who had the most to gain by discrediting him. He needed to look for motive instead of lashing out, looking for a scapegoat.

The more I thought about it, the angrier I became.

Someone sat next to me.

Tripp!

Nope. It was Penn. Probably there to do his brother's dirty work.

"I saw you park behind the restaurant," he said.

I tugged the engagement ring off my finger and held it out to him.

Penn shook his head. "Tripp is going to meet you at my apartment."

"I don't have anything to say to him." My voice sounded old to my ears. Decrepit.

"Tough." Penn narrowed his gaze at me. Yeah, there was a family resemblance, but he didn't glow like Tripp did. Penn lacked the aura of success that shone around Tripp like a body-wide halo.

"Since when do you run away?" he asked me in a low voice.

"You don't even like me," I reminded him. "Why do you care?"

"I'm starting to like you," he said. "And I care about my brother."

"Your brother thinks I started those rumors." My voice shook. "Your brother doesn't *trust* me. He doesn't *believe* me when I say I didn't tell my cousin anything at all like what's she's saying. I can't be with someone who doesn't trust me and doesn't believe me."

"Well, he's pretty upset you walked out."

"He hasn't gotten his pound of flesh yet," I snapped. "I don't need to stick around and let him try to make me feel repentant about something I didn't do." I held the ring out to Penn again. "Give it back to him, will you?"

"Look." Penn's fingers combed through his hair in a gesture so similar to Tripp's that my heart clenched. "My brother loves you. Giving him back your ring isn't something I'm going to do. And I'm not going to sit here arguing with you."

"Then leave," I said. I spoke as softly and as gently as I could. It wasn't Penn's fault Tripp had tried to use him as an intermediary.

I pocketed the ring and climbed to my feet. Tripp Shaneybrook had infuriated me. I longed to teach him a lesson he wouldn't forget.

Penn fell into step beside me, as if he were escorting me back to Shaneybrook's.

I checked my phone and found twenty missed calls, mostly from Tripp, a few from Caitlin, and one from Tanner. I didn't want to talk to any of them.

I found myself outside the restaurant. Tripp's luxury sedan was parked at the curb, near the pink and white petunias. I should have kept the SUV keys.

I was going to have to talk to Tripp.

Or not.

Maybe he was inside, waiting for me. I had a spare key to the sedan in my purse. I'd forgotten about that. If there were only some way to keep Penn from warning Tripp.

Oh. There was.

I pulled out my phone again and texted Tripp: *meet me in the apartment.*

I waited a moment, hoping he'd assume Penn's apartment. Then I ran down the street, ignoring the humidity and the new pain in my bad ankle. Key in hand, I let myself into Tripp's car. It started first try. I pulled into the street after checking the mirrors.

I didn't see either Penn or Tripp.

I'd made a clean getaway.

CHAPTER TWENTY

I drove straight to the hospital in Syracuse. No one stopped me. Tripp hadn't reported his car stolen. I would have in his place.

I knew I looked like crap: no makeup, worn jeans, oversize T-shirt, and rubber flip-flops, but I didn't need to impress my cousin with fancy ha-ha-better-than-you adornment.

I walked right into Caitlin's room. "How much did they pay you to lie?"

She looked as if she might be sleeping, but I really didn't care. I grabbed her shoulder and jostled her.

"Wha—" She started awake, terror in her eyes. Then she saw it was only me, and wariness replaced the fear.

"Who got to you, and how much did they pay you to lie?"

"I don't know what you're talking about." Her tone was sullen, and her gaze wouldn't meet mine.

"Oh, yes, you do," I said as softly as I could, despite the fury shrieking inside me. "I can find out who visited you. All I have to do is ask the nurses."

"Only you and my Vera House counselor."

"Your mother-in-law hasn't been by?"

Caitlin shook her head.

At least Caitlin was speaking with a Vera House counselor.

"Tripp is pretty pissed off you talked to the media. You *lied* to the media."

Caitlin swallowed hard. Her eyes met my gaze, then skittered away. "They came to me. I didn't go to them."

"It doesn't matter. You lied to them. So they must have paid you. Good. Now you can pay me back the money you stole from me."

Her head jerked. "I never stole anything from you. My name is on your credit cards and your bank accounts."

She didn't get it. She never would.

"And how did the press find out about you?" I asked. "Did you volunteer something?"

"Maybe they were investigating your famous, rich fiancé after his ex-girl-friend went public, and your name popped up. And where your name pops up, mine isn't far behind."

Okay. I hadn't thought about that. My past was so spectacularly boring that I didn't understand why anyone would even bother investigating me.

"He proposed to you very publicly at a baseball game. And didn't he take you to some health center in Cooperstown for X-rays a couple of weeks ago?"

My insides flash froze to subzero. "There are HIPAA laws," I said. "And besides, I fell."

Caitlin shrugged.

"I will never forgive you for talking to the media. For lying about me and Tripp to the whole world," I said. "Ever, Caitlin. Have a wonderful life with Spencer's family, because you're no longer part of mine."

I left her room.

I forced a smile to my face as I approached the nurses' station. I tried to act as if nothing was wrong, that my world was intact instead of in shards of hurt and betrayal.

"Is there any way to find out who's been in to visit my cousin? Her husband has a lot of...contacts, and I'm worried."

The two nurses exchanged a look. "A news crew from one of the local stations was here," the younger nurse volunteered.

Terrific.

"Besides the media." My face hurt from smiling.

"We don't keep track of things like that," the older woman said. Her tone was brusque. "And even if we did, that would be confidential information."

I nodded. "Well, thanks anyway. And thanks for taking care of my cousin."

I felt their gazes on my back as I left. I slipped on my sunglasses before I got into the elevator.

I tried to think beyond the obvious culprits—Maura St. John and Caitlin. Maura was Tripp's problem. I would never get past Caitlin's twisted definitions of right and wrong or of honor versus survival.

I wasn't close to anyone. I didn't associate with the people with whom I'd grown up. We had nothing in common. I didn't get pregnant, married, pregnant, divorced, pregnant, pregnant, and pregnant starting at sixteen. Plus I'd moved away. And I've never been a joiner, so I didn't have associates. Maybe I should have joined a church when I first moved from Akron, gone to their singles clubs, or become a Friend of the Symphony or something—not that I had the kind of money that type of friendship required—but I didn't have the social skills. I wasn't a joiner. I watched movies.

I had no support systems. I had Caitlin, my coworkers, and my movies. That made me pretty damned pathetic. No wonder Baird McKechnie had seen me as easy pickings for his stupid games with Penn Shaneybrook. It was a wonder someone hadn't come along to mess with my head sooner.

Maybe it was time to visit the Genevieve Hart-Darling Foundation, although I couldn't picture Jeanie pulling a stunt like this.

I glanced down at my white jeans. Completely inappropriate dress for the Foundation, especially if I wanted my former job back. And I probably would.

I'd transferred my work clothes from my apartment to Armory Square. I'd have to go there to change. I didn't like that, but I also didn't have a choice. I couldn't drop in to the Foundation looking like a refugee. Even if I was one.

"Where the fuck have you been?" Tripp greeted me as I let myself into the Armory Square apartment.

I should have known he'd follow me. I should have known he'd either be here or at the animal hospital. Obviously he hadn't hurt me enough today. Maybe he'd kill my cat too.

I ignored him, pushing past him so I could get to the bedroom and the closet containing my work clothes.

"I thought I told you to wear your earpiece when you're out driving. I have been going out of my mind," he said, as he followed me. "Spencer Madison is still at large."

"You are out of your mind," I said. I opened the closet door and pulled out an ankle-length aqua dress with matching jacket.

I needed a shower. Not that I wanted to take one with Tripp in the apartment, but I didn't have a choice. I gathered clean underwear along with my dress and locked myself in the bathroom.

I half expected Tripp to pound on the door, pick the lock, or something. But he surprised me by being smart enough to leave me alone.

Tripp was waiting for me in the living room. The television was on, although the audio was muted. He perched on the edge of the grime-colored sofa and flipped through the channels.

He patted the cushion next to him when I entered the room.

I ignored him and grabbed my purse from where I'd dropped it.

"I confiscated all your vehicle keys," he said.

It didn't matter. I planned to walk from Armory Square to the foundation's offices in traditional downtown, so I wouldn't have to look for parking.

I said nothing but slung the straw bag over my shoulder and opened the door.

"I'm sorry!" he shouted as he leaped from the couch and slammed the door shut. "I was an asshole, and I was lashing out. I didn't mean it. I know you didn't say those things."

He leaned against the door so I couldn't get past him.

"I love you, and you didn't deserve that."

I didn't deserve a lot of things that had happened to me in life, but that didn't change the fact that they had happened.

I set my jaw and glared at him.

His gaze flickered to my left hand, where his ring winked back at him. Yeah, I'd rescued it from the pocket of my jeans.

"We'll figure out what to do. How to spin damage control. That's what I pay Marty to do." He raked his fingers through his unruly half curls.

Something must have happened to change his mind about my involvement. He couldn't have come to his senses without a major kick in the backside.

He reached for me. I took a step back. I was afraid of him. Afraid that if he touched me, I would melt, I would forgive him, and we would end up naked and in bed, and that wouldn't solve a thing.

I believed in him. I believed him when he told me he wasn't the father of Maura's baby and when he claimed he hadn't beaten her. I believed him, and he hadn't returned the trust.

That hurt.

That was going to take some time to get over. If it could be gotten over.

I wasn't a movie heroine, with a scriptwriter ensuring happily ever after. I was just Chelsea Lyndon, a girl who'd fallen in love with a baseball star and who couldn't handle the pressure of the spotlight.

He couldn't pay Marty to turn back the clock to the moment before he'd uttered those hateful, soul-destroying words.

Okay, so he thought he wasn't going to let me leave the apartment.

"You're doing it again," I said. My voice felt rusty from disuse. "You can't control me. You can't force me to stay here."

His shoulders slumped. "I know. But I need you to listen to me. Please. I want you to hear me out."

"Step away from the door. I need to do something before I can listen to you, okay? I'll come back here."

As if I had anywhere else to go.

"Can I go with you?"

I shrugged. I guessed it didn't matter if I dropped in on Jeanie and Haley alone or with him.

He still wore his khaki cargo shorts and melon-colored golf shirt from earlier.

"You'll have to change," I told him.

The look in his eye turned wary.

"I'll wait," I said.

"In the bedroom," he countered.

I shook my head. "Right here. Leave the door open if you want."

I wanted to see if he'd trust me at all.

He finally seemed to realize what I was asking. He nodded just once before hurrying to the bedroom. And he closed the door.

I released breath I hadn't known I'd been holding. I plopped onto the sofa. The television was still on. It was on one of those full-time allegedly all-news networks that blew life out of proportion to fill their twenty-four sevens.

And there was a younger Tripp, looking sharp in his baseball uniform. I don't think I'd ever seen him in it before. And there was Maura St. John strutting across the cover of one of those glossy magazines. That shot was followed by the photo of Maura's bruised and battered face, then one of me, wearing nothing but one of

Tripp's T-shirts and the tops of my legs looking like a pinto pony. Some computer geek zeroed in on the bruises. Then Caitlin appeared on the screen.

How could he stand to watch this...garbage?

Except Baird was on after the piece on Caitlin. I found the remote and unmuted the sound.

"Chelsea Lyndon met Tripp Shaneybrook through me," he said.

Of course he would snatch the spotlight.

"Actually, Chelsea was with me when she fell. There were plenty of witnesses. She had on these silly shoes with six-inch soles—"

"Four-inch," I muttered.

"And we were walking through a meadow when she fell out of her shoes. Sprained her ankle. Tripp was the one who insisted on taking her to the Health Center to have it looked at."

The bedroom door opened.

Tripp stood there, watching me. I turned off the television. "I guess we can cross him off the list."

"Yeah. Surprised the heck out of me and Penn too." He swallowed hard. "Where are we going?"

"I'm going to pay my old boss a visit," I said. I didn't include him either way. He'd followed me from Cooperstown. I couldn't stop him from following me downtown.

The day was brutally hot and steamy, and I missed the coolness of Tripp's house on Otsego Lake. Heat shimmered up from the sidewalks. Every kind of bad smell imaginable wafted around us in putrid waves. I thought I could even smell the strong onion-unwashed-human-horde stench of nearby Onondaga Lake.

By the time I'd walked four blocks, my dress was sticking to my perspiration-slicked legs. Tripp strolled at my side, but he was smart enough not to reach for my hand. I could feel my makeup melting in tiny rivulets down the sides of my face.

I hadn't eaten all day, nor had I had much to drink, which I knew was bad in the heat. I stopped at a street vendor and bought a lemonade. I even let Tripp pay for it. The lemonade was cold, tart, and just what I needed to keep walking.

The lobby of the building where the Genevieve Hart-Darling Foundation was housed was frigidly cold. My nipples responded immediately. I looked down to make sure my jacket covered them.

Tripp never said a word the entire time we walked or in the elevator up to the sixth floor to the foundation offices.

I entered the suite with my head held high. Jeanie was in the outer office, going over something with Haley, who looked stressed.

Haley's gaze went past me and fixed on Tripp. She smiled, frazzled replaced by dazzled.

"Chelsea," Jeanie greeted me. Her gray-and-brown-streaked hair fell just below her in chin in a simple, basic bob. Classic. That was Jeanie. Class.

"I take it you're Tripp Shaneybrook," she greeted my companion.

He jerked his chin in a semblance of a nod.

"Did anyone contact the foundation asking about me?" I asked.

A deep vee formed between Jeanie's eyebrows. "We don't give out information about employees. You know that."

Yeah, *I* knew that.

I looked past Jeanie to Haley. "Does Haley know that?"

She'd been told. I'd told her myself on several occasions. But her fair cheeks turned an unbecoming shade of mottled pink.

Jeanie's frown deepened. "Haley? Did anyone contact the foundation about Chelsea?"

Haley bit her lip, lowered her gaze from Tripp, and nodded.

My hands curled into fists at my side. "Who did you speak to, Haley?" I asked, my tone surprisingly calm.

"I'll handle this," Jeanie interjected. "Well?"

"Maura St. John came in," Haley replied in a small voice. Then her tone went defensive. "It's not as if Chelsea works here anymore. You asked her to resign."

"We don't discuss personnel of the Genevieve Hart-Darling Foundation at all." Jeanie's tone was frosty. "I hope you told that to Ms. St. John."

"Do you have any idea what you've done?" I asked Haley.

"Well, it's not my fault your cousin was always calling here," Haley snapped at me. "Kind of hard to miss what was going on there."

"Haley," Jeanie said in a sad, chiding tone.

"And I saw you when you came back from Cooperstown after your opera date. Your ankle was a mess."

I could feel Tripp go tense behind me.

"What did you tell Maura about that?" I asked.

"That you came back from Cooperstown a mess."

Great.

"And I might have mentioned that you threatened to kill your cousin." She glared at me. "You did."

If Haley had slapped me across the face, she couldn't have surprised me more. Granted, Caitlin had infuriated me over the past couple of weeks, and I very well could have spouted off an empty threat. Caitlin would know it was empty. Haley would not.

"Chelsea, I'm so sorry," Jeanie said. She was sincere. She never said anything she didn't mean. "I'll deal with this."

Discretion was one trait Jeanie demanded from everyone. Haley wasn't long for the Genevieve Hart-Darling Foundation.

Tripp's hand was warm on the small of my back, a mute signal that it was time for us to leave.

"Thanks, Jeanie," I said. I didn't even look at Haley.

Tripp guided me to the elevator like a helium-filled balloon, with a gentle, barely there pressure on the small of my back.

I held myself stiff, and once we were in the elevator, I stepped away from his touch.

It was tougher walking back to Armory Square than it had been walking to the foundation. I thought about all the things I needed to say to Tripp. Things I couldn't discuss on the street.

When we arrived at the apartment, Tripp returned the keys to all the vehicles. His phone vibrated. He glanced at the screen.

"Have you talked to Caitlin?" he asked.

"I went directly there from Cooperstown. She lied to me. But I knew she would. She always has."

"I'm sorry."

"I disowned her. I told her today that I hope she enjoys being in Spencer's family."

A tear fell onto my hand.

I shouldn't have been crying over Caitlin. Still, disowning her left me completely alone in the world. Tripp rubbed the tear into the back of my hand.

"You still have me. And Penn if you need a brother."

Penn. Defending me. The lonely world was all awry.

"Do I?" I asked. The ugly apartment shimmered through the tears that refused to behave.

"You're still wearing my ring."

"You said some pretty awful things to me."

"Yes I did, and even if I apologize to you every day for the rest of our lives, I will never be able to make up saying those words. If I could take them back, I would." He inhaled deeply. "I know you never told Caitlin that I hit you. I know you never told Caitlin that I'm abusive to you. And I should have thought before I spoke."

"You didn't trust me," I whispered. "You didn't believe me."

"I should have, and about twenty seconds after you left, I knew that."

Which was about a minute after the damage was done.

And yet, as he had pointed out, I still wore his ring. Hurt didn't mean stop loving.

"You took away my car keys while I was in the shower. More controlling maneuvers. I won't live like that."

"I couldn't let you walk away from me again." His voice broke. "I couldn't risk you leaving me again. So if I have to play dirty with you like that, then I will."

I blinked.

"Look." He raked his fingers through his hair. "You want to go out for Thai? There's a great Thai restaurant around the corner."

I shook my head. "I want an explanation of why you were so quick to believe the worst of me. Distrust and disbelief *are* the worst, and I didn't deserve that."

He leaned back on the sofa and stared at the dingy industrial-gray ceiling with its exposed ductwork and other features of alleged architectural interest. "Abuse is a touchy subject with me."

No! Really?

"Did your father hit your mother?" The idea scared me. I knew the statistics. Abuse is practically hereditary.

"I don't think so. He left when Penn and I were real little. I have vague memories. One, actually. It must have been the day he left. 'You're the man of the family now,' he told me. 'A man takes care of his own.' So I took care of Penn when he was tormented in school and by the stepfather. I tried to take care of my mom. Her second husband had a nasty tongue and a nasty temper, especially when he'd been drinking. He was a stereotype, you know?"

Tripp looked at me. "You accused me of being controlling, of being like your cousin's husband, and I am not like him."

"You are controlling."

"You're confusing controlling with taking care of you."

"I think you're the one who has them confused. And I have never thought you abusive, even when you've had provocation."

"Why won't you let me take care of you?"

I blew a wayward hank of hair off my forehead. "I let you take care of me." Even I heard the evasive tone in my voice.

"I told you about the stepfather," he reminded me.

Interesting that he didn't say *my* stepfather. That was some denial.

"At least he married your mother," I retorted. Then I bit my lip. I hadn't meant to say that.

Tripp waited.

I squeezed my eyes shut. *Damn.*

"A lot of men promised to take care of Mama," I finally admitted in a low voice. "She died waiting for one of them to keep that promise."

Tripp didn't say anything for a long time, and I couldn't look at him. I opened my eyes but found the ceiling as fascinating as he had. I'd just told him more about my life than I'd ever told anyone.

"My grandmother raised me and Caitlin. She wasn't happy about it. She wanted someone to take care of her, not two more kids to raise. The thing is, Grandma Judy, Mama, and Caitlin's mother weren't very good at taking care of themselves, much less being responsible for anyone else. That's not going to happen to me."

"Needing someone's help doesn't make you weak," Tripp finally said. "Letting me do things for you won't make you vulnerable."

"You're not responsible for me."

"I'm not responsible for you," he agreed. "I'm not trying to control you either. I'm not even trying to change you. I'm just trying to do nice things for you. You deserve nice things. One of the things that first drew me to you was your strength. Your independence."

"I need to work."

"I thought we settled this. You can work for Camp Home Safe. We need someone with grant-writing expertise."

"It's not just a make-work job?" My suspicions remained, especially since Maura had voiced them first.

Tripp shook his head. "We're a charity, but not to our employees. We depend on volunteers. Our paid staff isn't highly paid like other not-for-profits. People who work for Camp Home Safe *believe* in what we do."

Okay. I could get behind that.

"So what happened with your mother?" I asked.

His mouth thinned. The muscle in his jaw did its pulsing thing. "She eventually chose her husband. He could take care of her, whereas Penn and I, especially Penn, were too needy."

Amazing how similar our backgrounds sounded. No wonder he wasn't shocked when I told him about Mama.

"Of course, after I'd made a bit of a name for myself, she showed up. The husband had left her. Her existence was...precarious, so she figured I'd support her. Except I kept seeing and kept remembering how she turned her back and looked the other way with the husband tried to beat the perversion out of Penn."

His short laugh contained no mirth. "She reminded me of what my father used to say—a man takes care of what's his. So I did. I took care of my brother after our mom abandoned us. Emotionally at first. Then in reality."

"Did...did your stepfather ever hit you?" I choked on the question.

He shook his head. "I was already a baseball star in our town. There were times I used to think he married Mom just so he could brag on me."

"What about your father? Your real father. What happened to him?"

Tripp's mouth twisted. "He was killed in one of the embassy bombings in the Middle East."

"He was a diplomat?"

"A soldier."

CHAPTER TWENTY-ONE

"Let's go to a baseball game."

I stared at Tripp, who seemed antsy. Then I realized he was reaching for normalcy. His cocoon.

I had a lot of thinking to do, and doing it at Saltboiler Stadium would be easier than in the apartment, if for no other reason than Tripp wouldn't be trying to get me out of my clothes.

It was a beautiful night for a ball game. We sat behind the visitor's dugout with our feet propped up on the concrete roof. A huge Moonsinger beer logo marked our spot.

"How can you still be with him, honey?" one woman asked me when we were on line to buy hot dogs.

"Because I don't listen to lies," I replied.

Tripp hushed me.

For the first time, no fans approached him for autographs. He turned off his phone and just sat there. He didn't even react to the shouts of "Heads up!" when foul balls flew our way.

Definitely cocoon.

Me? I discovered a calm while sitting there. A weird peace. A way to transcend the minutiae of my life. I liked that there was no clock imposing a deadline. The game would be over when it was over. The players simply did what they had to do without racing against time. I liked the dimension real time added to the experience.

We got back to the apartment around eleven.

"I hate this place," I said as he opened the door for me.

"You do?" He seemed surprised.

"Yeah. It's gloomy. There's nothing cheerful here. No light. No color."

He looked around the grim living room.

"It even smells like old engine oil." I made a mental note to invest in heavily scented candles if we were going to keep the place.

We. Keep.

Apparently I'd made a decision without realizing it.

"It seems cozy to me," Tripp said.

"Like a sweatshop is cozy," I countered.

"It's just a short-term lease. And it has a hot tub."

"That gives me the hives," I reminded him.

He reached for me, but I evaded him. "You told me not to fake it with you, so I'm telling you right up front, I'm not in the mood for sex tonight."

He closed his eyes. "How long am I going to be in the doghouse?" he asked.

"I don't know," I admitted. "But I'm still here."

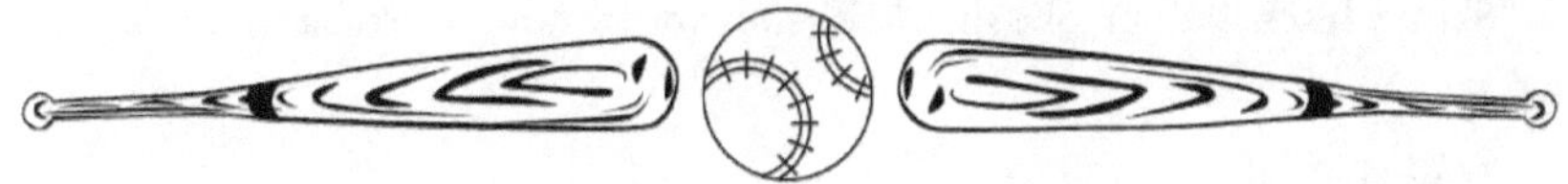

He woke me up in the middle of the night to make love. I clung to him with a desperation that shocked me. No faking. I climaxed almost as soon as he thrust into me.

But I knew now that it was more than sex that connected us. If we could hurt each other as deeply as we'd been hurt, then our hearts were definitely involved. I no longer questioned the brevity of our courtship.

I was committed for the long haul.

Marty Fiscoe showed up at the apartment before we were out of bed the next morning.

"You two patch things up?" he asked Tripp.

"Mostly," Tripp replied.

I ignored Marty. Tripp might like him as an agent, but I didn't have much use for him as a human being.

"So I was thinking," Marty said as he knocked around the kitchen, making himself at home and brewing a pot of coffee. "We can sue the bitch for slander. You can demand a DNA test on the baby."

"I already told Maura I wanted a DNA test. If that kid is mine, she's at least six months pregnant."

"Skinny bitch like her. She should be showing by now, don'tcha think?" Marty asked.

"How the hell would I know?" Tripp snapped.

"Maybe not if it's her first," I said. "I had a friend in high school who went seven months before anybody noticed her baby bump."

Marty ignored me.

"I tried to talk to my cousin yesterday," I told him. "I'm pretty sure Maura visited her in the hospital. I've confirmed she went to my former employer looking for dirt on me."

That got Marty's attention. "Keep talking."

"I was with her," Tripp confirmed. "Maura is definitely part of the conspiracy."

Conspiracy? I didn't know if I'd go that far...

"We'll subpoena your cousin," Marty said, punching something into his phone.

"She's still in the hospital," I reminded him.

"So the question is who knocked the bitch up," Marty mused. "We figure that out, we know who's behind this smear campaign."

I hoped Tripp wasn't paying Marty for his logic.

I poured myself a cup of coffee and sat at the tiny round table in the minuscule kitchen. Thank goodness Tripp had signed only a short-term lease on the horrid little place.

"Maybe someone wants to shut down Camp Home Safe," Marty said.

Tripp poured himself a cup of coffee, tasted it, and grimaced. "I have no idea. No enemies unless Chelsea has a jilted lover somewhere."

He smiled at me so tenderly and so lovingly, I couldn't help but smile back.

"There has to be someone besides the St. John woman," Marty insisted. "Someone who's using her to get to you."

Tripp looked bewildered. "I'm a nice guy. I don't go around making enemies like some guys do. I was an honest ballplayer. I treat women well. I never took steroids in my life, and I never ratted on anyone I thought did."

"What about the guy who tried to kill his girlfriend?" I asked. "The reason you started Camp Home Safe."

Tripp stared at me. "Perry Whitlaw? He isn't the sort of guy Maura would get involved with."

I had to trust him on that.

"I contacted the local TV station to find out where they got their tip about Kelsey," Marty said. "Dead end. They spouted first amendment bullshit, protecting their sources bullshit, and then they asked me if I wanted to give them a statement. Told 'em their fucking story was bullshit."

"Wow," I murmured. "I'll bet that convinced them."

"They got pictures of you, Kelsey."

"Chelsea," Tripp said.

"How'd they get pictures of her?" Marty asked Tripp.

And so the conversation went.

The vet's office called to tell me I could pick up Foggy.

Marty rolled his eyes. He had more important things to think about than my cat, but I'd missed all twenty cranky pounds of gray fur.

"I'm going to pick him up now," I told Tripp. I had to get away from Marty and his Eeyore-like attitude.

"You need help?" Tripp sat at the table with Marty to strategize our predicament.

"Foggy and I have been together a long time. We're cool."

"Wear your earpiece in case I need to get hold of you," Tripp reminded me.

Foggy wasn't good in cars, and I didn't want his claws shredding the lovely bone-colored leather of my new SUV. His carrier, litter box, and personalized food bowls were still at my old apartment. I needed to swing by there en route to the animal hospital. I wouldn't be there long. Just a couple of minutes. It would be fine.

Tanner still hadn't replaced the front door. He'd repaired it enough to give an appearance of being secure. It looked as if he'd slapped on a coat of paint. I knew better.

I parked the SUV where my little rust bucket had once hunkered. The lock on the door was still wonky, and the stairwell light was still out. I would not be sorry to leave this place.

I emptied the used litter from the box into the garbage and then rinsed the box in the tub. I'd have Tripp pay someone to scour the apartment before I turned over my keys to Tanner. If he wanted to spend money on me, he could spend it something truly worthwhile.

I washed out Foggy's food dishes too, and placed them with the car carrier and the litter box near the front door. There was an unopened twenty-pound bag of litter in the side stairwell, the landing of which I used as a pantry. That was also where I kept Foggy's food. I went into my kitchen and unlocked the door.

And screamed.

Tanner stood there. On the landing. Holding a baseball bat.

"Hi, Chelsea," he said.

I backed up, and he walked into the apartment as if he owned it. Well, he did own it, but...

"Sheesh, Tanner," I said, pressing my hands against my breasts in a futile attempt to calm my racing heart.

"I saw the car outside and was wondering if Shaneybrook was around." He hefted the bat. "I thought maybe I could get an autographed bat to go with my ball."

All the tiny hairs on my body stood on end.

I'd never liked Tanner, but I'd never been afraid of him.

I backed from the kitchen to the dining room, where I stumbled over a pile of VHS movies that hadn't been packed.

Tanner followed me. With the bat.

"Tripp's not here," I said. "But let me call him. I'm sure he'd be happy to sign the bat for you." I lunged for my purse, which I'd left in its usual spot on the small table next to the front door.

Spencer opened the front door. "Hello, Chelsea. I hear you're trying to convince my wife to leave me."

Caught between two angry men.

I'd never been so scared in my life.

I kept a smile pasted on my face, hoping my fear didn't show. I didn't quip, *I think you did a good job of convincing her yourself.* "Well," I said as pertly as I could manage. "The vet's expecting me, so I guess I'll get going."

Tanner smacked the bat against the palm of his hand. Spencer leaned against the closed door.

My phone squealed from my purse. I gestured toward it, but Spencer wasn't budging. "Tripp worries if I don't stay in touch," I said. "You understand how it is."

Spencer looked as if he couldn't care less.

"I don't think Shaneybrook is going to put up with you for much longer," Tanner said. "I was on the back stairs the afternoon you two got into that fight because he had the packers here."

I felt a little nauseated. "You spied on me?"

His smile widened. *Smack.* The bat hit his palm again. "Oh, I watch you a lot. You're a pretty girl."

I was going to throw up. It usually took a lot to make me vomit, but a little Tanner goes a long way.

My phone went off again.

Tanner ignored it. "And I must say, those pictures of you and all those bruises fetched a pretty penny from *Sportsworld Insider.*"

"You took the pictures?" I could barely force the words from my throat.

"Some of them. *Sportsworld* liked having independent corroboration of the other photos they had. Gave authenticity to Maura St. John's story." He took a step toward me. *Smack.* Wood against the flesh of his palm. In syncopation with my pulse.

Then I remembered I was wearing my earpiece.

The phone went off again, and this time I was ready. I tilted the left side of my head away from both Tanner and Spencer and clicked the Answer button while praying the blue light wouldn't betray me through my hair.

"Where are you?" Tripp sounded irked. "Why didn't you answer before? The vet's office called. They need me to sign off on the bill. I'm on my way now."

"Tanner," I said, "I don't understand what the problem is. Tripp will be more than happy to sign that bat for you. I'll take it with me."

"Fuck!" Tripp screamed in my ear.

"But really, the vet's office is expecting me to pick up Foggy, so I need to get going. I only stopped by the apartment to get his carrier, so, Spencer, if you'll just step aside from the front door..."

"You went to your apartment? I told you not to go there alone until the door is fixed!"

I tried not to wince and hoped Tripp's voice didn't carry.

Spencer spread his legs and crossed his arms. "I don't like you in my business. Caitlin will do as she's told. Maybe you need to be taught a lesson too."

"I believe I lent Caitlin the money to pay your bail." I just couldn't keep my mouth shut.

Spencer smirked.

"Chelsea, Chelsea, Chelsea," Tanner said at the same time I heard Tripp tell someone, possibly Marty, to call the cops.

"Look," I babbled. "I'm really thirsty. This heat is really getting to me. You want a bottle of cold water? Spencer? How about you?"

I started edging toward the kitchen. Toward the only other door to the outside.

But I didn't turn my back on either man. I'd seen what a baseball bat had done to Caitlin.

"I'm not thirsty." Tanner said. "But we could go into your bedroom and get out of those clothes."

My gorge rose. "No, I think a bottle of water will do me just fine. From the fridge. That's where I keep it. So it stays cold."

"Actually, I'm late for an appointment." Spencer snickered. "You have things under control here?"

Tanner nodded.

"Keep him talking," Tripp said in my ear. "I'll be there in five."

As if I wanted Spencer or Tanner to start swinging. "So which one of you really hit Caitlin the last time?" I asked. "She says she didn't see who attacked her."

Spencer smiled. "Bye, Chelsea. See you later."

My terror generated points of white light that danced before my eyes as Spencer slunk out of my apartment.

"You and your lover probably thought it was pretty funny to write your rent check on that baseball," Tanner said as we listened to Spencer's footsteps on the stairs.

"Is that what this is about?" I tried to act surprised as I slowly, carefully inched my way through the stucco arch into the dining room. "I thought this was about Caitlin and Spencer and an assault charge."

"Who the fuck does Shaneybrook think he is?" Tanner continued as if I hadn't spoken. "Look at the way he tries to push you around. I was glad to hear you finally stick up for yourself."

I tried to keep my breathing even, not to give in to my panic.

"Then he pulled the shit with the rent check."

"Hold on, honey," Tripp said. "The cops are on their way, and I'm almost there. Does he have another weapon besides the bat?"

I strained my ears for sirens, but the static of my terror drowned out all but the immediate. What did Tripp expect me to do? Ask Tanner if he was armed?

"I'm an honest businessman," Tanner continued. "You're living in my building. I want my rent."

"The baseball is a legal check," I said. "How did you get those pictures of me to sell to the tabloids?"

"Do you see a gun?" Tripp asked.

Tanner's smile turned sly, even creepier than it had been. "I have my ways."

"You probably made back ten times your rent money from those photos," I said.

"Probably," he agreed. The he said, "You'd better stop right there."

"I'm downstairs," Tripp crooned in my ear. "And it looks as if the cops have Spencer."

"Do you think I haven't figured out you're trying to get out the back door?" Tanner asked.

"You mean the side door? The one that comes into the kitchen from the driveway?" I asked. I came to a dead stop.

"Good girl," Tripp said.

I was halfway between the living room and the kitchen. No way could I make a dash for either door without Tanner reaching me with that bat.

Then some of what he said to me sank in. "Wait a minute." My fear evaporated in the heat of my fury. "Do you have a hidden camera set up in this apartment?"

His grin widened.

"You pervert!" Rage exploded in my brain. Rational thought fled. "I am going to sue you twelve ways to Sunday. And every media outlet that used those photos!"

I thought I heard someone on the front stairs, and I thought I saw the kitchen door move ever so slightly. So I kept yelling. "You've been taking pictures of me all along, haven't you?"

The front and side doors burst open. "Freeze! Police!"

Tanner grabbed me as a shield. His cloying aftershave choked me almost as much as his arm around my throat did.

Of course, being that close to me, he saw the blue glow of the earpiece.

"You goddamn bitch." He probably would have hit me if the cops weren't there with weapons pointed right at both of us. Big weapons. Guns. Probably loaded.

I was scared again. I didn't see how I was going to get out of this unscathed. At least Tanner couldn't beat me with the bat while he had me in a chokehold.

He started to drag me deeper into the apartment. Except I wasn't going to let him isolate me in a corner with no way out. I balked. His only weapon was the bat, and he couldn't use it on me and hold me at the same time.

I noticed movement behind the cop in the kitchen.

Tripp.

I hoped like crazy that Tanner didn't see him.

"Heads up!" Tripp shouted, and I instinctively ducked, just the way he'd taught me to do at the ballpark.

Something flew through the air and hit Tanner.

He fell to the floor, dragging me with him. On top of me. Unmoving. I could hear Tripp shouting my name.

I screamed for him. Blood, warm and sticky, dripped on me.

Someone pulled Tanner off me. Tripp pulled me to my feet and pulled me into his arms. I buried my face against his chest, trembling so badly I could barely stand.

He held me close, rocking me ever so slightly.

"What happened?" I finally managed to ask.

"I threw a can of cat food at him," Tripp said.

"Cat food?"

"You keep the cat food in the back hall."

I knew that. "But a can of cat food weighs what? Four ounces?"

"I throw hard." He sounded grimly pleased with himself. "I thought about pitching once."

CHAPTER TWENTY-TWO

Tripp and I pressed charges against both Tanner and Maura St. John.

Tanner had decided to jump on the bandwagon Maura had created and had Spencer threaten Caitlin with additional violence if she didn't play along.

Maura finally admitted Tripp wasn't her baby's father but had felt he'd make a better father than the guy who was. She'd been right about that. When the real father found out she'd tried to get Tripp to take responsibility, he got a little violent with her, which she didn't hesitate to blame on Tripp.

Foggy hated the Armory Square apartment as much as I did. So we moved my stuff into storage, and Foggy and I moved into the lake house with Tripp. We decided to use the lake house as our summer home and find a place together in the village of Cooperstown. We eventually bought a big yellow Queen Anne house with wraparound porches. I was thrilled at finally being able to decorate my own home.

Caitlin and I worked toward a reconciliation. Her interview with one of the big sports networks admitting her husband had threatened her if she didn't lie about Tripp was the first step. One she took without me prodding her. Spencer had convinced her there was so much in the news about athletes beating on their women that no one would doubt her. Tanner had come up with the idea the afternoon he eavesdropped on our argument over the people packing my belongings. The interview from her hospital bed, revealing a rainbow of abuse, added credibility to her confession. Once she realized I wasn't saying she had to choose between me and Spencer but between Spencer and herself, she got herself into a program for survivors.

Spencer stayed in jail long enough for Caitlin to accept that maybe marriage to him wasn't negating the family heritage of crappy relationships. Maybe Tripp and I were setting a better example.

Yeah, I saved the best for last.

One sunny Saturday in mid-August, Tripp told me to get dolled up because he had a surprise for me. So I put on a white eyelet dress with bright blue flowers embroidered at the calf-length hem, a pair of bright blue sandals, and a white straw hat with blue flowers circling the crown.

"How's this?" I asked as I came down the stairs.

He wore a white linen suit and looked so handsome it hurt my eyes to look at him. "You're perfect," he said. He took my hand and planted a kiss in the center of my palm.

We took the sedan.

The road looked familiar. Then we left the tunnel of trees and entered a clearing. The Glimmerglass Opera House was on the right. The parking lot and hillside picnic grounds were on the left. Tripp turned into the lot and spoke to one of the young attendants. He drove the car up a steep trail along the side of the parking lot. There were several vehicles parked in the meadow near the picnic tables.

I felt all warm and fuzzy inside. I waited for him to walk around and open my door for me. He took my hand and helped me out of the car.

Then I saw Penn, Josh, Marty, and Faboo. They'd appropriated one of the picnic tables. Multicolored embroidered flowers scattered across the white linen tablecloth. A deep aqua pressed-glass vase held a spray of black-eyed Susans, and pressed-glass dishes in an array of pinks, greens, and yellows awaited the contents of a large wicker hamper at one end of the table. A silver ice bucket chilled a bottle of sparkling rosé.

I miss Caitlin, I thought. *She should be here.*

Then I saw Jeanie, my former boss from the Genevieve Hart-Darling Foundation, sitting at one of the other tables with her husband. All the tables had been done up with the linens and the colored glass dishes. It was my *Spring Party* poster combined with *Mamma Mia*.

Everything shimmered due to the tears in my eyes.

"Faboo is an ordained minister," Tripp told me. "The Church of Baseball."

I just nodded. I couldn't speak.

"Ready?" He knew I'd figured it out.

I nodded again.

As Tripp and I stood in front of Faboo, Penn moved to Tripp's side, and Jeanie moved to mine.

"Dearly beloved," Faboo began.

Then it was over. Tripp and I were married. Penn catered a wonderful picnic reception without a dab of mayo or a sliver of pink processed meat.

Then after our meal, Tripp and I left the others to clean up, while we went across the road for my very first opera: *The Marriage of Figaro*.

And we all lived happily ever after.

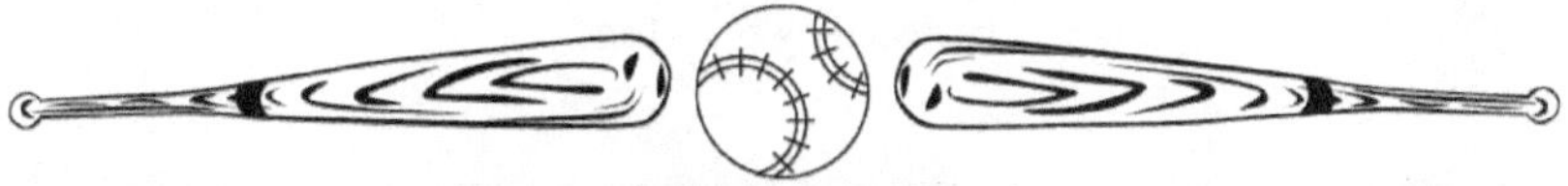

Thank you for reading HIT BY HIS PITCH.

Please sign up for my newsletter for all the news about future releases.

Also By

PARANORMAL SHIFTER ROMANCE

TOKE LOBO & THE PACK
Moonlight Serendade
And Jericho Burned
Omega Moon Rising

SERVICE FOR SANCTUARY
Betrayed by the Moon
Beware of the Moon
Besieged by the Moon

SHIFTER-BASEBALL MASH-UP NOVELLA
Shifting Home
CONTEMPORARY SPORTS ROMANCE

COLUMBIA GEMS BASEBALL

Missing The Signs

Hit By His Pitch

Catcher Interference-Tag & Skye Book 1 (September 2023)

No Doubles Defense-Tag & Skye Book 2 (October 2023)

Batting Cleanup-Tag & Skye Book 3 (November 2023)

HIT BY HIS PITCH

Acknowledgements

The Purple Hazers: Carol Lombardo, Christine Wenger, Kris Fletcher, and Gayle Callen. Your friendship and support continue to bolster me.

Renee Kloecker, who offers her country house as a retreat for a bunch of writers.

Dave "The Maven" Okun, whose insight and generous sharing of knowledge contributed so much to this book.

My niece, Micaela Compton, chef extraordinaire, who patiently answered questions about restaurants.

The Syracuse Chiefs* baseball organization for continuing to provide wonderful entertainment on a summer night.

*Since this book was originally released, the Syracuse Chiefs were sold to the New York Mets and are now known as the Syracuse Mets.

Dedication

This book is dedicated to my husband, Steve, who left work early so we could go to baseball games together and never once complained. Who patiently answers baseball-related questions for me. Who doesn't mind if I sit on a bench outside the stores in Cooperstown in order to absorb the atmosphere while he checks out the merchandise.

Love you so much!

About the Author

MJ Compton grew up near Cardiff, New York, a place best known for its giant—a hoax so successful, P.T. Barnum duplicated it. The tale of the "petrified man" convinced MJ that inventing stories could be a career.

Although her 30 years working in local television included such highlights as being bitten by a lion, preempting a US President for a college basketball game, giving a three-time world champion boxer a few black eyes, and meeting her husband, MJ never lost her dream of creating her own stories.

MJ still lives in upstate New York with her husband. Music and cooking are two of her passions, and she enjoys baseball, college basketball, and sitting on her patio on summer nights to count lightning bugs, but she's primarily focused on writing.